DEARBORN

JENNI MOEN

DEARBORN
Copyright © 2015 Jenni Moen
All rights reserved.

Published by: Jenni Moen
jennimoen@yahoo.com

Editing: Editing4Indies
Proofreading: Prima Editing and Proofreading
Cover Design: JM Rising Horse Creations
Image Design: Staci Brillhart
Main Photo: iStock Photos ®
Background Photo: Dollar Photo Club
ISBN-13: 978-0-9908519-4-3

Prologue

A THIN LAYER OF ICE covered the snow and crunched with every footfall. The air still hung heavy over Woodland Creek. This marked the beginning of months and months and inches upon inches of dismal cold. More would fall overnight. I welcomed it though I couldn't tell you exactly why.

Always on a mission, my feet traveled fast over the frozen surface. They'd run on more treacherous terrain than this. The mountains of Afghanistan had prepared me well for my current task. And this time, no heavy boots. No weapons. No packs. I'd never felt lighter on my feet. A branch slapped me in the face, and I barely felt it.

I am free.

I ran to quiet the noise following me day after dreaded day. It was a sweet relief after enduring the awful, clanging, never-ending racket that came with the memories. They wouldn't let me go. I was bound to them as I was bound to the people in them. It was only recently I'd found a better therapy.

I leaped over a stream and found my footing. It would be a skating rink soon, making it harder to find water. Something instinctual told me it should concern me, but it didn't tonight. Nothing concerned me as I neared the spot where I'd seen her last.

She is here.

Somehow, I could feel her presence ahead of me. I burst through the last line of trees and into the clearing with more gusto than warranted. My feet pounded across the ground until I slid to a stop by the big cedar tree.

Big brown eyes peered at me curiously from across the way. Her hide, a rich coppery color, hadn't turned gray for the winter. She looked out of place against the snowy backdrop and perfectly at home all at the same time.

Just as I had remembered, she was the most beautiful creature I'd ever seen. Dainty but still somehow powerful. Graceful and lithe. Long, thin legs looked as if they could snap under the weight of her, but I knew they were stronger than they appeared. They were made for running and leaping. I longed to watch *her* run.

Large, pert ears stood tall on her head, not missing a thing. She blinked at me and then cocked her head as if to size me up. *I knew you'd come back,* she seemed to say.

'Of course,' I wanted to tell her. 'I came to thank you.'

I wondered how close she would let me get today. I took a tentative step, and she watched me.

She seemed to blink her submission. *Go ahead. Come closer.*

It was delusional to think she was actually speaking to me. Obviously, no audible words were exchanged, but in my head, I could hear her as clearly as if her thoughts were my own. It was almost as if there was a direct line between her soul and mine. Some thread tethered our hearts and gave me access to her thoughts. *Is it okay?*

We can't stay. It's not safe.

I took a few slow steps in her direction and waited. She followed my lead and then stopped. We repeated the dance until less than a few feet separated us. As she circled around me, she suddenly seemed unsure. She craned her long neck as if listening to something behind me.

Shhhhh. Her fear was tangible. Yet, even as it struck, I didn't comprehend the danger. The arrow pierced her flesh with a thud. It shouldn't have sounded so hollow for the damage it was causing. It sliced easily through her chest and protruded awkwardly. Instantly, she was gone, bolting away from her attacker and away from me.

Until that moment, she had been my peaceful place. If there was no peace with her, then there was none anywhere, and I would surely lose the last remaining shreds of my sanity. I followed because I had no other choice. The invisible line tethering us pulled me along behind her as she ran, her previous words echoing in my head. *Come closer. Come closer.*

'I am coming,' I wanted to call to her. 'I will take care of you. I will help you somehow.'

She jumped the fence line, and I winced at the pain in my chest as she landed. She ran north through the western part of the cemetery. I followed, losing sight of her from time to time as she wove in and out of the trees. She crossed the road near where my truck was parked, and I followed.

Flashing lights marked the scene of an accident to the west, but she didn't get close to it. We ran for what felt like miles, parallel to the major roads but far enough away from them to remain unseen. Even when I couldn't see her, the pain in my chest never abated, letting me know instinctually she was there.

The same instinct caused me to stop suddenly just before I got to the creek. She stood on its banks, unable to make the final leap over it. An all-too-familiar house loomed dark and empty behind her.

Not like this.

Before I could get to her, her knees buckled. She wobbled for only a second and then fell to the ground, rolling on her side so the arrow pointed up at the milky gray sky. Her chest rose and fell with every labored breath. Those beautiful, soul-searching eyes blinked at me. I listened for her voice but heard nothing. Maybe it had only been in my head all along. Maybe she didn't exist at all and was the creation of my fragmented mind.

A familiar whomp, whomp, whomp intruded on our moment. I closed my eyes and wished it away. It grew louder, and I imagined it was the sound of her heartbeat, assuring me she was going to be okay. I had myself nearly convinced when it became harsher, turning into something that didn't belong here.

As I had so many times before, I looked up to find the bird in the sky. It flew low, and within seconds, it disappeared over the treetops. The sound of the rotating blades faded but left in its wake the debris of my life. All of the noise I'd successfully evaded had found me again.

I pushed and shoved against it, trying to rid my head of it all. I had to keep it together. She needed me. Our roles had reversed, and I was her only hope. I stared at her, trying to come back to the here and now, all the while knowing the better parts of me were still lost on a continent thousands of miles away.

The doe in front of me let out a bleat that sounded like a plea. It triggered something in me—a survival instinct I thought I'd lost forever—and lifted the fog the helicopter had dropped over me. In its place, the brittle evening air reflected the glitter of the snow.

She shimmered and shook in front of me, and I dropped to the ground beside her. My heart thumped out a beat of shock even louder than the blades of the helicopter.

It was incomprehensible. A complete annihilation of what I thought to be true.

I was naked and bleeding, and my beautiful doe was gone.

One

Willow

"MARRY ME, WILLOW?"

Ryan slid table number four's plate and ticket through the window toward me. He rang the bell—a move intended to annoy me since I was standing right in front of him—and then tapped on the piece of paper with his index finger. I knew without looking what it said, but I peeked anyway.

Thank You!

Marry me?
☐ *yes*
☐ *no*
☐ *maybe*

I grinned at him. His notes never got old even as ludicrous as they sometimes were.

It was a game we'd played our entire lives. One that began in second grade when a gangly boy had abruptly turned around in his seat during a lesson on double-digit addition and slid a note across my desk. *Will you go with me?* it had said. The options had been the same.

At the time, I'd been unsure about him. He'd sat in the desk in front of mine for almost two years without uttering a single word to me. I didn't understand where he wanted to go.

Where? I'd finally written below the answers before shoving the note back at him.

Be my girlfriend, he'd written in response.

I'd started to circle the big blocky *NO*, but he'd ripped the note away from me. In a huff, he'd turned back to his desk. He didn't look at or speak to me again until the next day when he slid a new note across my desk.

Will you go swimming in the creek tomorrow? YES, NO, MAYBE.

I'd chewed my lip and considered his offer. I was spending the weekend with my grandparents while my parents celebrated their tenth anniversary in nearby Louisville. I loved my grandma more than moon pies, but there wasn't a lot to do at her house. Watching her knit blankets for her church prayer group was a little like watching paint dry.

"Come on," he'd whispered when I didn't answer fast enough. "I know you don't have plans."

I'd wondered how he could possibly know that, but I circled *YES* anyway. The fact that I was severely lacking in friends had won out over any hesitation I had about hanging out with a liar.

Since that day, I'd answered affirmatively to almost every harebrained idea Ryan Balere threw at me. For nearly two decades, we'd spent every day together, and I'd watched the skinny boy turn into a beast of a man. He knew me better than I knew myself and usually knew what I wanted before I did. But we were not a couple, and my answer to his farce marriage proposals would always be a definite and resounding, *NO*.

As much as his warm chocolate eyes should have made me all gooey inside, they didn't. It would have been the most convenient and natural thing in the world, but love didn't work like that. My best friend filled my heart to the brim, but he couldn't make it skip a beat. And *that* was what I was holding out for. I wasn't settling for anything less than sudden and chronic arrhythmia.

I didn't want anything less for him either.

"Awww, I love you too, Will." He slapped his chest with his hand. "Can you feel it?"

I rolled my eyes at him in answer and slapped my hand down on the order ticket, pulling it to me. "Get back to work, Balere. You don't want to get caught slacking on the job again. It's bad enough you were sixteen minutes late this morning."

He groaned. "My boss is such a bear."

"Don't you wish," I teased him.

"I *do* wish. It would certainly make my problems go away."

Ahhhhh. My bear-shifting friend was having girl problems. Again. *That* was why he was handing out marriage proposals he had no intention of honoring.

"No, it wouldn't, and you know it, but hold that thought. I need to deliver this before it gets cold or there'll be hell to pay." I nodded at the plate still sitting under the warmer.

"Is that for Old Man Hansen?" He turned back toward the fryer before I could answer. I grinned at his back, knowing he didn't need one anyway. Most of the people who came into Creek Café were regulars. Ryan knew their orders before I even took them.

Clive Hansen was our best customer and a creature of habit. He shuffled up to the restaurant at the exact same time every morning. He tied his dog, Aristotle, to the exact same tree. He always sat at one of the only three tables that provided a good view of what I suspected was his only friend.

Even our conversations were ritualistic.

"This morning's special is blueberry pancakes," I'd say before he cut me off and bark his order at me. During my thirteen years in the diner, his breakfast had never varied, and I suspected his streak went back further than that.

There was only one exception to the rule. Once a year, he ordered a side of birthday hash browns for the mutt outside. It was the only sign of softness I'd seen in Clive. He was a grouch who wanted his breakfast the way he wanted it, when he wanted it, and with as little conversation as possible. We accommodated him, not only because he was a loyal customer, but also because he was different. Neither Ryan nor I could get a read on why that was or even *what* he was. There was no way of knowing what the old codger was capable of, so we fed him.

It didn't matter anyway. There was a lot of *different* in Woodland Creek. I was different. Ryan was different. Janice, who'd owned the diner before me, had been different. Our diner catered to the different because different was not necessarily a bad thing.

Until it was, of course.

Ryan slid a foam to-go container through the window, and I looked at him curiously. "It's not Aristotle's birthday yet."

He nodded and pushed it a little closer. "They both need a little extra love today. Seems that Aristotle may not make it to his next one."

It explained the tremendous sadness I'd felt while going through the perfunctory but necessary task of taking Clive's order. "So I should sit down and see if Clive wants to chat?"

Ryan barked out a laugh. There wasn't a chance in hell the old man was going to spill his guts to me. He wasn't a talker, but we didn't need him to be today. Ryan obviously already had Clive's number.

Ryan's 'intuition' was one of the reasons I could never *be* with him. His 'special gift' was more than I could handle. Not that mine was much better. Between his ability to read minds and my ability to feel others' emotions, the fact we weren't attracted to each other was actually a sweet miracle. Any kind of normal relationship would have been impossible.

I slid Ryan's note into the front pocket of my apron with the intention of discussing it some more after we closed for the day. With a heavy heart and both hands full, I worked my way through the small dining room. It was a classic 1950's diner. The décor was legit, dating back to when Janice Crabtree and her husband had opened the diner in 1952. Black, white, red, and perfect all over. My sneakered feet made no noise on the checkered tile floor as I slipped between the red pleather-covered stools lining the counter and the row of two-seater booths opposite it. A half wall provided the façade of privacy between them and the larger booths on the other side. Four top tables bellied up to the plate glass windows overlooking our small but quaint parking lot. Filled to the max, we could seat fifty people. On mornings like this one, we usually got close.

When I reached Clive's table, I slid his breakfast in front of him and set the to-go box to the side. As expected, he immediately wrinkled his exceptionally long and bony nose at me. "What's this?" he wheezed, pointing at the foam container. "I didn't order that."

"Hash browns. Ryan's idea."

"Well, I'm not paying for it. I didn't order it, and I don't want it."

I countered his grumpy with a smile. "It's a gift, Mr. Hansen. For Aristotle."

The shift in his mood was definite and immediate. Surprise. Understanding. Appreciation. With softer but still narrowed eyes, Clive nodded at me. "Very well. Thank you. Tell him I said thank you."

I nodded and spun on my heel. Table twelve was getting agitated. I returned to the counter and grabbed the coffee pot so I could refill their cups and restore peace and order to my tiny kingdom.

Like Clive, the camouflage-covered men were regulars. They didn't come in daily like he did, but I could usually count on them to show up at least once every weekend and more than that during hunting season. Creek Café was their weekend meeting spot for swapping stories about the big game they'd shot and, more recently, the mythical monster that kept eluding them.

I'd known the men since high school but couldn't call them friends. A few years older than I was, they ran in a different crowd. Even as small as it was, Woodland Creek was like that. The invisible ley lines running through it were an invisible barrier, segregating kids of the same age. The population split evenly between those ensconced in the magic of Woodland Creek and those who had no idea it even existed. Always one to want what I shouldn't have, I'd dabbled with the boys from the normal side of town. I learned the hard way—from one of the men at table twelve, actually—that it was better to stick to your own kind.

The diner didn't operate under the same policy, though. Located directly between Old Town and New Town, it was an equal opportunity dining establishment, catering quite literally to all walks of life.

As I approached the table, I pulled up my wall. Brick by brick it rose, shielding me from anything Tim Reyburn might throw at me. He knew what I was though he proclaimed not to believe it. The wall was a necessary protection mechanism I'd been perfecting my whole life. If I focused on the bricks, the wall was generally strong enough to keep out all but the loudest projectors. I'd have no problem keeping out Tim.

"Fellas." I began working my way around the table, filling each mug as I went. "Did you have a good morning?" It was a benign question though I knew their answers would be repugnant to me.

Tim shook his head. "Nah. It was so foggy this morning that no one could get a clear shot."

I applauded Mother Nature for her plan-thwarting ways. "Oh well, it's only the first week of the season," I said, my voice lacking any real sympathy. "You still have lots of time yet to get your twelve point."

"Twelve point nothing. There have been sightings of an eighteen point roaming around over in Running Deer Forest. It's been a long time since anyone's seen one that big in these parts."

"Not since The Legend back in the early eighties, I think," John Pierce chimed in.

"If and when he wanders onto Reyburn land, he doesn't stand a chance. The Legend put the slip on a Reyburn. It won't happen again."

I smiled on the outside but shuddered internally. "Well, hopefully, he'll make you work for it."

"He better not make me work too hard. I don't have the patience for it anymore."

Of course you don't. "But if you got him now, the fun would all be over, wouldn't it?" I chided him.

John nodded his head in agreement. "The lady makes a fine point. There's no sport in it coming easily."

Sport. I bit my tongue as I filled his mug, resisting the temptation to dump the hot coffee all over his lap. I didn't believe what they were doing was a sport, but I was biased. I had friends and loved ones in those woods, though during hunting season, the shifting community stayed pretty close to the national park where it was safer.

I smiled and poured another cup of coffee before stopping behind the only empty chair at the table. The mug sitting there was still full though it had long grown cold. "Are you fellas ready for me to adios this menu?" I asked.

As usual, Tim was the one to speak up first. The man loved to hear himself talk. "Yeah. It looks like Dearborn is a no-show. Again." He sounded more annoyed than anything else. "What's he hiding for anyway?"

If anyone wanted Quinn Dearborn to come out of hiding, I did. Fifteen years ago, he'd been the shining star in our small town. A first-class athlete who'd led the Craft County Bucks to the state finals both his junior and senior years. Like all high schools, the football players roamed the halls as if they owned the place, but everyone knew Quinn was the biggest buck of them all. He wore a new pair of shoes, and five other guys had them the next day. He smiled at the girls as he walked to his next class, and panties dropped all around him.

He'd ruled the school, but it was here, in the diner, where he'd stolen my heart.

His mother worked at the *Woodland Creek Chronicle* and had to be there early. To ensure her only child went to school with a full stomach every morning, she'd worked out a deal with Janice. Quinn got breakfast every morning, and Janice got a discount on any ads she ran in the paper.

It hadn't taken Janice long to figure out I had a king-size crush on the boy. Janice loved love, so she always made sure his table was in my section and never gave me a hard time when I lingered too long.

We talked about school. We talked about classmates who were in trouble. We talked about sports, books, and music—all normal teenager stuff. Behavior commonplace to anyone else—and probably Quinn, too—was an entirely new experience for me.

It's human nature to focus on the misery of life, and most of the folks eating in the diner reflected that. The negative energy could be hard for me to take at times but Quinn was different. Positive energy practically poured out of him. He was just happy. A completely contented person. He was a beacon of light in the darkness, and I was drawn to him. Even when we weren't talking, I would find myself near his table so I could let his positive energy wash over me.

When he'd left town after graduation, he'd taken all of the positive energy with him, leaving Woodland Creek a little more drab for me. As far as I knew, Quinn hadn't visited once during the last fifteen years. While he'd been away, his friends had flipped an empty coffee cup upside down to reserve his place at their table. It was a tribute to the boy they'd fought for state titles with and a salute to the friend who was now fighting bigger battles without them. I had to admit I found the gesture endearing. Those flipped over mugs even won back a few bonus points for Tim.

Now that he was back in town, they asked me to fill it every week even though Quinn had yet to show his face. It was a standing invitation for him to join them again. Counting today as another no-show, I picked up the unused menu next to the untouched coffee and turned away.

"Have you seen him at all?" Tim asked in his typical share-it-with-the-whole-room voice.

"Not recently," Bryson Rafferty said in a voice much more subdued than Tim's was. "We texted a few times last night, and he said he would try to come. But I guess I didn't really expect him to." Bryson was the one I least wanted to see maimed in an unfortunate hunting accident.

I knew better than to eavesdrop—it was rude—but I couldn't help myself. I began wiping the counter, so I could consider myself a productive eavesdropper.

"I just don't understand. It's been three months, man."

"He made it through alive, and it's time to get back to living."

"It's almost like he's hiding from us." There was an accusation in Tim's voice; a complete lack of sympathy for a man who'd been through God knows what. His attitude certainly belied all of those full cups of coffee I'd poured and dumped down the drain, and I wondered whose idea they'd been. Certainly not his.

"Cut the guy some slack. He'll come around when he's ready." Bryson continued to be the voice of reason in the bunch.

"He's going to miss all of deer season if he's not careful."

"He's missed the last fourteen deer seasons. I don't think he's worried about missing one more. Maybe he's not ready to pick up a gun again or something."

I nodded my head in agreement before catching myself. It was one less beating heart for me to worry about.

"It's bow season, man. That's primal. Man against beast. Nothing like war."

I rolled my eyes, ashamed that I'd dated such an idiot.

As my hands went through the motions of refilling the sugar shakers for the lunch crowd that would start trickling in soon, I got lost in my own thoughts. All I knew about Quinn Dearborn's return was what the paper had printed. The article didn't include many details about the accident that had sent him home. Maybe it was classified. Maybe the *Woodland Creek Chronicle* thought we didn't need all of the gory details. Or maybe his mother, who still worked there, had pulled some strings to guard her son's privacy. Whatever the reason was, all the paper reported was that Quinn had saved two members of his platoon after a vehicle in their convoy detonated a land mine. Four American soldiers died that day, but two of the survivors, one a general, had Quinn to thank for it.

Like everyone in town, I'd read the story. Hell, I'd cut it out and pinned it on the wall in the diner. Mostly, people used the bulletin board to post ads for get-skinny-quick products and lost dogs, but when a townie made the paper for doing something notable, I posted it. The articles instilled a little town pride and helped customers pass the time while they hovered in the hall waiting to use the one-seater bathroom.

Wiping my hands on my apron, I stepped around the corner and came to a stop in front of Quinn's article. "Town Hero Comes Home a National Hero."

It was old news now and partially covered by a cleaning service business card and a handwritten note looking for someone to sublease an apartment over by the college. I took the pins out of those items and moved them to an open spot on the bulletin board so his article was completely visible again.

It was more pictures than text, more focused on his glory days as a footballer than his days as a soldier. I wasn't surprised. Ask anyone in Woodland Creek who Quinn Dearborn was, and they'd tell you, "the best quarterback in the state for two years running." They wouldn't tell you that was fifteen years ago because, in the mind of Woodland Creek, Quinn was still *that* kid.

I ran my finger over the photo taking up the better part of the article. It was his senior picture, and he wore his football uniform. A ball was tucked under his arm, his smile was wide, and his eyes full of anticipation. Everyone expected that year to be a great one for Quinn, and it had delivered. He had a state title in the bag, the prettiest girl in school on his arm, and college recruits fast on his trail. All he had to do was keep his grades above passing and pick a college that would let him keep up his winning streak.

The town invested in him. So much so that when it looked like he might fail a math test and land himself on the ineligible list, someone had anonymously hired a tutor for him. I'd been stunned when the school counselor asked me if I was interested in taking the job.

"You have to do it," Janice had said when I'd told her about the offer. "Lord knows you aren't making enough working the morning shift here.

Besides, I see the way you look at him when he comes in here. There's a spark there."

I'd been quick to point out that my one-sided infatuation was not a spark, but in the end, I'd taken her advice. I needed the money. Getting to spend a little extra time in Quinn's company was the cherry on top.

It was only for one week, just to get him to pass one test, but what I discovered was everyone, including Quinn, had underestimated him. There wasn't anything subpar about him. He was as brainy as he was brawny. I suspected no one had ever told him that, though. Because of his size, he'd always been encouraged to focus on sports rather than his studies.

"Thanks for not treating me like I'm stupid," he'd said during our last session.

"Thanks for not *being* stupid."

He'd smiled as if he still wasn't sure he believed me. "I've always been more interested in things other than school, I guess. Classes came second to ball."

"You're smart, Quinn. You just needed someone to tell you that."

He'd nodded and smiled a goofy grin. "You think I can handle college? Not just the ball but the rest too?"

"I know you can."

When our week was up, I'd genuinely thought I had gotten through to him. I thought that one day he'd remember the odd girl from the diner as having made a tiny difference in his life. It had been a shock when, instead of picking a college, he'd announced his enlistment in the Army.

My finger trailed across the article to the photo of him in uniform. It hadn't been taken long after the other one, probably right after he'd enlisted. I wished the article had included a more recent one, but maybe it was all they had. Keeping your portrait portfolio up to date probably wasn't a high priority when you're hunting terrorists.

I wondered what he would look like today. Even if Afghanistan had marred his pretty face or robbed him of one of his able limbs, his eyes would be the same. They were what I remembered best. They were the color of emeralds—and not those shitty lab-grown stones they sell at chain stores in the mall. Quinn's eyes were a deep, dark green. When they focused on you, everything else faded away. The black and white photos in the newspaper certainly didn't do them justice.

The bell over the front door interrupted my thoughts, pulling me back to the here and now of the diner. I turned to greet the new customer but was struck by a wave emotion that nearly knocked me to the floor. I'd been lost in my own thoughts, reminiscing about Quinn, and I'd let the wall fall. I grabbed my chest and squeezed my eyes shut as I tried to erect it again. My head pounded.

Anxiety was always the hardest emotion for me to handle, and my new customer had a severe case of it.

Two

Quinn

THEY WERE ABOUT TO LEAVE. Their plates were empty, and their money was already on the table. After dodging them for months, they probably thought I'd planned it that way. If so, they'd be right. This was just a formality. I'd be gone soon enough.

I stood awkwardly next to their table, letting my three oldest friends greet me first. I was no good at this anymore. Three months and I still hadn't figured out how to deal with normal everyday tasks like conversing. Even with people I knew and loved, I was a lost cause.

Tim chuckled. "Well, look what the cat dragged in."

"Hey, man. Glad you made it." Bryson smiled.

In high school, Tim had been my best friend. We'd done everything together, but Bryson had been the one to reach out to me after I had returned to Woodland Creek. He was the only one to come to the house, which was a relief. I abhorred visitors, and I couldn't help but wonder if he'd warned the others to stay away after his one and only visit.

"Can I sit here?" I asked. I pointed at the only empty seat at the table. A cup of seemingly untouched coffee sat at the spot.

"Yeah, that's yours," Bryson answered, gesturing to the chair or the coffee or both. I wasn't sure. I sat down and pushed the cold mug away. He looked over his shoulder and gestured toward the back of the café.

Within seconds, a steaming mug of coffee and a menu slid in front of me. "I'll give you a few minutes and come back." Her voice was like music, soothing and melodic, but I ignored it.

I scanned the menu without really seeing the words. "Thanks, but I'm not really hungry."

"Are you sure?" she asked in her sweet singsong voice. Rage surged through me. If there was one thing I was tired of, it was people thinking they knew what I needed better than I did. "We've got chocolate mousse pie today," her voice wavered. "But I guess it's kind of early for that. Maybe just a bowl of oatmeal? It's pretty bland."

Janice's chocolate pie had always been my favorite, but not even that sounded good at the moment. My sour stomach was as angry as I was. "That will be fine," I answered through gritted teeth.

I handed the menu back to her and wished her away.

I reached for the cup of coffee at the same time she reached for a pile of trash on the table, and our hands collided. I finally looked at her and was instantly ashamed of myself. I knew her, or at least I'd known her, even it felt like a lifetime ago. I racked my brain for her name, knowing it was in there somewhere. These days, it seemed the bad memories were the only ones that hadn't abandoned me.

She peered back at me with an intensity that told me she wasn't having the same problem remembering me. She smiled faintly and turned to walk away just as it came to me.

Willow. Her name was Willow Ryker, and she'd tutored me in math once upon a time.

Relief swept over me, and she paused to cast another look at me over her shoulder. Her smile wider now, her eyes reflecting the same relief I felt— almost as if she somehow knew the inner turmoil I'd just gone through.

I felt like we'd just had a moment—the kind they make into Folger's coffee commercials.

"The oatmeal is bland?" Tim's mutter reminded me I wasn't alone. "Not really selling it, is she? Willow really needs to take some marketing lessons."

Tim's hatefulness made me further regret my own bad manners. She didn't deserve to wait on assholes, which was clearly how Tim acted.

"Cut her some slack, Tim," John said. "She doesn't look well." I looked at the back of the restaurant where she was slouched against the back counter.

Wow, she changed a lot.

Not as much as you, I reminded myself.

"Whatever. She's an odd duck." Tim certainly wasn't going to give her a break.

"A pretty duck, if you ask me," John countered. "And she's always so sweet."

That was my memory, too. "She *is* sweet." I felt the need to stand up for her after being so rude. "I used to know her."

"A lot changes in fifteen years, bro."

John smirked at Tim. "You're just ticked off she was giving you such a hard time earlier over The Monster."

"The Monster?" I asked.

Bryson scooted up in his chair excitedly. "Yeah, he's the latest beast we're all after."

"He has a name?"

"Not us. So far though he's been pretty elusive," John said. "But everyone's talking about him. Willow isn't really that hard on us, but you can tell she's not a big fan of our hobby."

Tim sneered. "The bitch needs to chill or I'm going to find somewhere else to eat. What we do with our free time is none of her business."

Wow. My back went rigid. I didn't like the way Tim was talking at all. It seemed like he had a real chip on his shoulder when it came to Willow.

"God, it's so good to see you again," John said, changing the subject to the awkward subject of me. "You look really good."

John had always been the peacekeeper in our group, something Tim and I frequently needed. Our similar personalities often landed us crossways with each other even though we considered ourselves best friends. John was good about stepping in and helping us settle our disputes, which generally revolved around our overlapping taste in girls.

He was a good guy, but on the subject of me, John was lying. I looked like hell, and I knew it. The dark circles under my eyes were a dead giveaway that I barely slept. I hadn't had a haircut since I'd come stateside, and the thick layer of fuzz all over my face proved I just didn't give a shit. "Sorry I'm late."

"Yeah, well, it's about time. We were beginning to think you were too good for us now that you're a big-time hero and all." Tim smiled as he spoke, but his voice was razor sharp. It was possible I'd offended him by not coming around sooner.

"I'm not—" I began before John cut me off.

"Of course not. Don't mind him. He's just jealous because you made the paper again. He still hasn't made it after all of these years. It was a great article, by the way." John smiled at Tim, who returned a glare. "Besides, you didn't miss anything this morning. I don't think there was a single buck out there."

"The fog was so bad I couldn't see more than ten feet in front of my face," Tim muttered. "I hope tomorrow is better. You going to make it out there this year at all?" He'd directed the last question at me.

My stomach pitched and roiled. I'd been stupid not to see this coming. Now that I'd shown my face, they would expect me to be around more. I scrambled for a non-committal answer. With my condition, putting a gun in my hands didn't seem like a great idea.

"I think the weather is supposed to be about the same tomorrow, so I may sleep in." John had offered me an out, and I appreciated it.

Bryson chuckled. "Well, you know you can come see me instead. You know where I'll be."

"Fat chance." Tim's obnoxious laugh was finally something that felt familiar, but as they continued to talk, I realized their familiarity with each other carved holes in the conversation I couldn't fill.

I had no idea where Bryson would be the following morning. I didn't know what Tim did for a living. I'd been a shit friend to these guys over the years. Of course, there'd been other things on my mind, important things like my boys and my job. They had required my undivided attention. But as I sat at a table with my oldest three friends, it occurred to me I didn't know anything about them anymore.

"Well, this has been real, gents, but I have to clean up and get to the office," Tim said, standing. I tucked away the little clue he'd given me. He had an office job—one keeping him busy enough to work on a Saturday.

"No rest for the wicked," Bryson said, laughing. "Let me know how you do tomorrow if you go out there again."

"Yup," Tim answered, digging in his pocket for his keys. "Go ahead and sleep in, boys. Fine by me. The mythical monster is mine." He turned to face me. "It was good seeing you, Dearborn. We're here every Saturday and some of us on Sundays, too." He threw a guilty look at Bryson, who laughed.

"No judgment here, man."

John scooted his chair back. "I have to get going too. I wish I could stick around and catch up, but I've been gone for five hours." He tapped his watch. "Gretchen has a whole laundry list of things she wants me to do around the house today."

Gretchen. John had a wife. Maybe I'd heard something about him getting married. I thought back to the girls in our class but drew a blank. I didn't remember a bossy Gretchen.

I forced a smile. "Maybe next time." *Now who is lying?* There wouldn't be a next time if I left town.

John squeezed my shoulder. "No worries, man. We know you have other things going on."

I nodded my response, hoping my expression didn't give me away. My biggest problem was I didn't have anything going on. My life and my purpose were still overseas.

My oatmeal arrived right after they left. Willow set it on the table in front of me so quietly I almost missed her altogether. "This will help," she said softly.

I nodded appreciatively, making an effort to look her in the eye this time.

Bryson waited until she left to speak again. "You look lost, man. Is there anything I can do?"

I stirred the oatmeal with my spoon. "Nah. I'm just still getting my bearings. Honestly, it's weird being back."

"I can imagine." I didn't think he could, but it was the right thing to say. People were good at saying the right things. "You'll get caught up on everything. I promise, not much has changed. As you can see, Tim is still just Tim, not worried about anyone but himself. John's still trying to please everyone. They're both great guys, though, with hearts as good as gold. With Tim, you have to dig a little deeper to find it, but it's there."

"Tim and I are too much alike."

"I disagree. Other than having everyone watching you and having the weight of the world on your shoulders, I never thought you were alike at all."

"What does he do for a living?"

"He's an attorney. Criminal defense work. Works all of the time." It explained a few things, like maybe why Tim seemed so jaded.

"Where will you be tomorrow?" I asked, changing the subject.

He looked confused for a second. "Oh, tomorrow morning? Yeah, the Woodland Creek Lutheran Church, my man."

"I guess you have a family? I'm sorry. I didn't even ask about them when you came to see me last time."

"No worries. I came to see about you, not to talk about myself, but yes, I'm married." He fiddled with a paper napkin, wrapping it around his finger as if he was suddenly nervous. "I'm sorry, Quinn. I really thought you knew. I married Hannah."

How had I not heard he'd married my high school girlfriend? "How long?"

"Twelve years now."

I considered this new information. "Do you have any kids?"

"Two. Elijah is three and Sarah is five."

I nodded slowly. "That's great, Bryson. I mean it."

"Yeah?"

"Really." Bryson was the kind of guy who was meant for all of that. During high school, he'd been loyal to one girl. I wasn't at all shocked to find out he'd settled down and started a family. I was a little surprised it was with Hannah but found it more interesting that I didn't care. I was glad she'd moved on after I'd left, but I would definitely be giving my mother a tongue-lashing for failing to deliver that information to me in advance.

"And I'm a Lutheran pastor too."

"What?" I asked, laughing. *That* was the most baffling yet.

"Seriously." He grinned at me as I tried to wrap my brain around the idea. "Hard to believe, isn't it?

The kid who snuck out of windows with you and drank beer behind the 7-Eleven is now a preacher." Finally, at a loss for words, I leaned back in my chair and pushed away from the table. "I started to tell you at the house, but I didn't want you to think I'd come to see you in some sort of professional capacity. And honestly, you said a few things that made me think you might stop talking to me if you knew."

It was probably true.

"Yeah," I said. "I don't know." My eyes drifted away from Bryson to the front of the restaurant. An older man, who looked vaguely familiar, struggled with the front door. I thought about getting up and helping him to avoid where this conversation was headed. As tempting as it was, before I could put my plan into action, the old man opened the door. He slipped through it, taking my exit strategy with him.

"I have you to thank for it, Quinn," Bryson said.

"I'm to blame for turning you into a preacher man?"

He laughed. "No, but you gave me the courage to answer the calling." I stared at him, confused. "I figured if you were brave enough to do what you were called to do, then I was brave enough too. I channeled my inner Quinn and accepted that I was meant to do this with my life. God, country, family, right? Isn't that your motto?"

I looked down at my boots. "I lost one of those in Afghanistan and left the other two to fend for themselves." It was the first honest thing I'd said in months.

"Do you want to talk about it? Not preachy, I promise. Just one friend to another."

I glanced at Bryson's concerned face. He meant well, but I didn't want to talk. "I don't think so."

"I understand. I get it."

My eyes roamed the restaurant looking for something else, anything else, to distract me. It was mostly empty now. Willow was behind the counter but leaning up against it, as if she was taking a minute to herself. Maybe she was enjoying the lull before the lunch crowd would start to trickle in. Or maybe she was trying to give us a little bit of privacy to talk. The small diner didn't provide much of that.

I watched her push off the front counter and then wobble a few steps. I started in my seat but stopped when she successfully made it to the back counter. She leaned forward on it as if she needed it to support her. John had been right. She didn't look well.

A narrow window separated the dining room from the kitchen behind it, and she appeared to say something to whoever was preparing the food in the back. A man stepped into view and peered back at her through the window, his face etched with concern. His forehead wrinkled as he said something to her. She shook her head, and he disappeared again. When she turned around again, her eyes met mine, and I looked away guiltily.

Bryson was watching me with interest. "You know what? I really need to head out. I have some folks to visit at the hospital this morning." He stood up to leave.

I remained seated. "Sure. I need to pay for my breakfast, and then I'm going as well."

"If you ever want to talk, Quinn, you have my number. Maybe you could come for dinner some night. I know Hannah would love to see you."

"Thanks for the offer. I'll think about it."

We both knew I wouldn't.

"Okay, well, don't be a stranger and don't make me hound you." He shook his head and chuckled. "You're going to make me hound you. I can tell."

"Nah, I'll be in touch."

"I'm going to hold you to it."

Bryson headed for the front door. Since Willow still looked pale and wobbly, I decided to go to her rather than make her come to me. I walked to the back, sat down on a stool, and set my phone and my wallet on the counter beside me.

"Ready to go?" she asked, already digging through the pocket of her apron.

"Willow?" I asked. For some reason, I wanted her to know I remembered her.

The man from the kitchen appeared from around the corner and stood wiping his hands on a grease-covered apron. He seemed to be about our age, but his face wasn't familiar to me. He was slightly shorter and stockier than I was, but from the way he was watching me, I knew he thought he could take me and was actually contemplating it. It was a pleasant surprise.

Willow waved him off. "I'm fine."

I didn't think either of us believed her.

He eyed her warily before narrowing his eyes at me again. He was protective when it came to his woman. I couldn't blame him. Willow had grown up, and she was gorgeous. If she were mine, I'd be protective too.

"Seriously, I got this. Go do your thing." He nodded at her once and disappeared again.

She slid a ticket across the counter to me. When she removed her hand, I couldn't help but laugh. It was the first time I'd laughed in months. It felt shockingly good and filled me with a tremendous amount of guilt.

"It's kind of early for marriage proposals, don't you think?" I asked. "I mean, you barely know me."

She turned as red as the ketchup bottles lining the counter and began digging through her apron again. She was flustered, but she didn't miss a beat. "When you know, you know, though I usually wait until after lunch to issue those."

She slid a second ticket across the counter and reached for the first one. I slapped my hand down on top of it, and she jumped. She was about the cutest thing I'd ever seen. "So you're saying you hand these out regularly? I shouldn't feel special?" I teased.

God, it felt so good to pretend to be normal for a second. Then again, I'd always liked being around her.

Despite her still pink cheeks and flustered demeanor, her eyes held mine, unwavering. "I always thought you were something special, Quinn Dearborn."

I cleared my throat, now equally uncomfortable. I wasn't the talented kid with the bright future she remembered. I dug through my wallet and threw a twenty down on the counter.

"Hang on. I'm out of small bills. Let me get you some change from the back." She walked away, no more steady on her feet than she had been before. It was kind of early in the season for the flu. I hoped it wasn't something more serious like vertigo or something.

As soon as she'd disappeared from sight, I turned and ducked quietly out of the diner, saving us both from any further embarrassment. As I got into my truck and drove away, I realized, even as awkward as it had been, I was glad I'd come and I wasn't going to drive as far as I'd planned.

It was time to do something with myself.

Three

Willow

RYAN WIPED HIS HANDS ON a towel before tossing it into the laundry basket I took home with me every afternoon. It would be another exciting night of laundry and studying unless I could coerce Ryan into coming over to work on our project. As sad as it was, *that* was the extent of my social life. At least currently.

"All right, you go first," he said.

I held up a finger to silence him. I needed a few more seconds of quiet concentration. When I'd finished adding up the day's intake, I smiled and looked up. Saturdays were always better than the rest of the week, but this had been a good day even by Saturday standards.

"Ahh, a good day, eh? Will it get you a new sink and bathtub?"

I closed my notebook, pushed it to the side, and nodded. "I think so. Janice would be pleased."

He leaned forward, his elbows resting on the counter. "No, Janice would be proud. You've turned the diner around and made it your own."

I grinned. "I'm going to hire someone to help us. Maybe two."

"I'm good in the kitchen by myself. I like it that way. But you need someone out here, even if it's just so you can have a day off now and then."

"I wouldn't mind having a couple of mornings off every month." The diner was open seven days a week. I couldn't even remember the last time I'd had a day to myself. "But I want the same for you. You need time off, too."

"No, I *need* the money." I looked away guiltily. I didn't know how he could afford to work here with what I paid him. It was peanuts. "Hey, I'm just kidding. I could use a day off every now and then, boss lady. As always, you know best."

I rolled my eyes. "If that's the case, then why am I letting you distract me instead of dissecting your problems?"

"I'm not distracting you. I'm praising you. People with manners say thank you when someone pays them a compliment."

I huffed at him. If there was a manners contest, I would definitely win. "So what's going on?"

"Nothing to tell." He stared at me, his eyes begging me to call his bluff. He wanted to talk about it. He *needed* to talk about it, but Ryan was a big, scrappy man's man. He wasn't going to beg for help or cry on my shoulder. Whatever it was, I would have to yank it out of him.

"Whatever. Your little note earlier this morning—"

"The one that caused you to make a fool of yourself in front of Quinn Dearborn?" He chuckled, amused by himself and my usual lack of finesse.

Good God, it had been embarrassing. To make matters worse, Quinn had snuck out while things were still awkward between us. Meaning, it would be awkward the next time he came into the diner, which I guessed would be sooner than later since he'd left his phone on the counter.

"Yes, that one," I answered. "Your note wasn't an offer. It was a cry for help that made me look like a jackass."

His weak laugh from before turned into a booming cackle filling the whole diner. "You make me laugh."

"You make me crazy. Spill it. Is she giving you the runaround again?" Ryan's on-again, off-again girlfriend was a flighty little thing who'd had serious commitment issues in the past. I really didn't want to have to hunt Vanessa down again, but I would. "Do you need me to break some bones again?"

He laughed, but this time it sounded pained. "Umm, no. That was like the worst night ever. And a completely mismatched fight, I might add."

"She could've flown away."

"Not after you broke her wings." He glared at me but could only hold the look for a second. She'd deserved it, and he knew it. Secretly, I think he liked that I'd stood up for him. "Besides, that was a long time ago, and she's changed her ways. *She's* not the problem."

"She better have. So it's your parents then?"

"Yep."

"They do realize you're a grown man, right?"

He snorted. "If I were eighty, wearing a diaper, and looking through Coke bottle-sized cataracts, they'd feel the same way when it comes to her and her family."

I sighed in exasperation for him. I didn't necessarily agree with Ryan's choice of women, but it wasn't for the same reason his family didn't.

The bear-shifting Balere family had deep-seated prejudices. Prejudices so old I didn't even think they could remember why they existed. It was silly. Anyone who'd been involved in the family feud had been dead for at least fifty years.

I didn't know what to say to make it better for him. All I could do was sympathize. "It's ridiculous, Ryan. Have your parents never seen *Grease, Beauty and the Beast*, or *Knocked Up*? Opposites attract. It's the law of nature. You're big. She's small. You're furry. She has feathers. You have four legs. She has two. So what?"

His eyes widened before shifting down. "According to them, I've dipped my wick in a pool of shame. They're using phrases like species dilution." His disappointment with his family wrapped around me, and I was equally enraged.

Ryan's grandfather dominated the Balere family. If he didn't approve of a family member's actions, they heard about it. There had been a fair amount of growling when Ryan had hooked up with Vanessa the first time. I'd thought Ryan was simply being young and rebellious, but Vanessa kept reappearing in his life, creating an ongoing riff between him and his family. Their disapproval was eating him up. It wasn't in his DNA to be a loner.

I reached across the counter and wrapped my hand around one of his giant ones. "That has to hurt, but we both know it has nothing to do with how many legs she has. Even if she were a fox, a deer, or a tiger, they wouldn't approve. All they care about is her last name."

"My dad said there's only room for one pecker in a marriage."

I let go of his hands, leaned back, and laughed. I couldn't help myself. "Sorry, but that's funny."

He smiled but dropped his head into his hands. "It is, but they said if I don't end it, they're going to throw me out of the family. Marrying her is out of the question."

I felt my eyes bulge. "But you're not even close to doing that, right?" Ryan and I'd had plenty of heart-to-hearts about Vanessa, but this was the first time he'd used the M word. "Right?" He ran his big hand down his face and didn't answer. "Oh my God. You are. You really are thinking about it, aren't you?"

"We're not getting any younger, you know."

"We're twenty-nine, Ryan. A long way from AARP and diapers."

"I want to marry her. That's not going to change. I love her, and she loves me." I must've looked at him warily. "She's the only person I know who can block me, but she chooses not to. She doesn't hide anything from me anymore."

"How do you know?"

"I just know."

In addition to his occasionally rebellious nature, one other thing sets Ryan apart from the rest of his bear-shifting family. He could read minds. Theirs. Mine. Everyone who came into the diner. Everyone except Vanessa when she didn't want him to.

It was how he'd known, when he'd written the first note to me in second grade, that I had no plans the day he wanted to swim in the creek. It was how he knew what people were going to order for breakfast even before they told me. It was why, even if we didn't look at each other like siblings, we could never be a couple. But it was exactly the reason he could be with Vanessa. She could block him out of her head when she wanted. None of us could figure out how or why.

"I love her, Willow."

My heart caved in on itself. My best friend wanted to get married, and the ramifications were endless. He was practically my only friend, and I didn't even get along with Vanessa. I knew she wasn't screwing around on him anymore, but I hadn't really believed it would get this far.

I was wrong.

I watched him run his hands through his hair. As hard as it was to think about losing him to her, his despair was greater than my own. I was choking on it. I needed to make a friend out of her, and I needed to do it soon. "Well, then I guess we have to figure out a way to make them see how ridiculous they're being."

He looked up. "You'll help me figure this out?" Instantly, the heavy weight pressing against my chest lifted.

"Of course I will."

His hope grew with every encouraging word. "But you don't like her."

"You do. That's enough for me. I'll grow to love her." He squeezed my hand. "Do you think she'll ever forgive me for the broken wings?" I asked.

"She already has. She knows she deserved it, and she knows we're a package deal. The real question is why are *you* suddenly being so forgiving?"

"If she's the one, then I have to accept it. Your family will too. Do you remember how mad my parents were when I gave up college to spend my life working in a diner? They came around though and yours will, too. It just takes time."

He stood up suddenly and walked around the counter. He wrapped his arms around me from behind and pulled me into one of his big bear hugs. "You're the best, and your parents are so proud of you now."

"They are."

The bell above the door dinged. "We're closed," Ryan growled.

We both turned toward the door, him with an arm still draped around my shoulders. I was glad for it. There were so many conflicting colors in the room, I could barely see. A cobalt haze of disappointment mixed with a green something or other I couldn't identify through the headache that had struck.

I didn't have to see Quinn to know he was there.

He cleared his throat. "I'm sorry. I didn't mean to interrupt. I think I left my phone on the counter when I was here earlier." His voice was thick and ragged.

I reached into the pocket of my apron for his phone. My knees buckled, and I sagged into Ryan. If he hadn't been holding me up, I would've been a puddle at his feet. Quinn took a few steps forward, but Ryan put up a hand to stop him. Ryan set me gently on the stool and snatched the phone from my hand. He met Quinn at the door, standing between us so his broad back blocked my view.

Not that I was seeing anything clearly anyway.

Seconds later, the bell rang again and Ryan was back at my side. He scooped me up and sat me on the counter, putting his arms around me once again, pulling me forward so he supported my weight. I rested my forehead on his shoulder and waited for the nausea to pass.

"What's going on, Willow?"

"Don't you know?"

"All I'm getting off you is confusion. You don't know what's happening, but you feel like shit. Every time he seems to be in the room, you ask yourself why you feel like complete and utter shit. You're nauseous. You're seeing things. You're confused because it's different from anything you've ever experienced."

"That pretty much sums it up. What about him?" I sat up straighter. The nausea had left with Quinn.

"You don't want to know."

I pulled back and met his gaze. "No, I do."

"I don't like your fascination with him. His thoughts are all over the place. He's angry. He's sad. He's disappointed. He's mad. He's jealous. And he's also rocking a severe case of confusion. The war has him all kinds of screwed up."

"I'm getting that, too. Tell me something I don't know."

"He doesn't understand why he feels any of these things. He's dangerous, Willow. Volatile. I don't like it, and I don't like the reaction you're having to him."

I sighed and slumped forward again, exhausted.

"Something's different with him. With everyone else, unless the feelings are really negative, I can handle it. Only when I pick up an intensely negative energy is it hard, but even then, my wall is good at keeping most people out. At least, it's bearable."

He nodded to spur me on.

"But Quinn's all over the place. He's a deluge of contradictory feelings and bright, vibrant colors. The colors are blinding. Beautiful but blinding. I think there's a link between what I'm seeing and what I'm feeling, but I'm not sure yet. When he came in earlier this morning to meet his friends, he was nervous, and everything was yellow and orange with maybe a tinge of red."

"*He* was nervous. They've been pestering him to meet them, but this was the first time he's done more than go to the grocery store. In three months, Willow. People make him nervous, and that makes *me* nervous."

It made sense. What Ryan was reading off him matched everything I was feeling. "Why did you read him? Were you trying to?" Ryan was generally as good at blocking people out as I was. Sometimes, he slipped, but sometimes, he eavesdropped for no other reason than he was bored.

"I didn't have to. He's a screamer."

That also matched what I was feeling. "And when he came in just now, he was, I don't know... what? Disappointed? Is that right?"

"Disappointed and jealous."

"Jealous? Of what?"

"Of me. He thinks we're a couple."

I laughed. "Quinn Dearborn wouldn't care about that. He was *never* interested in me." Surely, Ryan had misread him. Quinn was probably just being friendly.

Then again, Ryan was rarely wrong about people. It was kind of hard to get it wrong when you knew exactly what everyone was thinking.

"Well, he sure as hell is now. You're all grown up, and he likes what he sees. *That* is exactly what he was thinking."

I blushed. It wasn't fair that I knew what Quinn thought of me, but it didn't mean I didn't like hearing it.

"It's probably a good thing he thinks we're a couple," Ryan continued. "He's no good, Willow. Too conflicted. Dangerous."

Now, Ryan *had* to have that wrong. I refused to believe Quinn was a bad guy. "That's ridiculous, Ry. He's always been a good guy, and he's a hero, for God's sake. People are alive because of him."

Ryan shook his head. "And I'm sure plenty of people are dead because of him, too."

I shuddered. "You pulled that out of his head?" I couldn't imagine what Quinn had been through while he'd been away. War was an ugly, ugly thing, but whatever he'd done had been justified. Only a good man would have the guilt and regret he had.

"Look, I have a tremendous amount of respect for the man. I don't mean he's not good. I just mean he's not good for someone like you. He's a screamer. His thoughts were literally so loud that I couldn't hear anyone else in the diner, Willow. "

"Funny. That's how I felt about him, too, but I never got that sense when we were younger. He was never any different from anyone else."

"And today, you felt sick every time he came near. Maybe your abilities have grown."

"Not all the time. It only happens when he is upset. He was fine when he was talking to Bryson. Calm almost."

"I don't like it."

"He needs a friend. You of all people know that."

"He has friends. They were with him today. He doesn't need you. Whatever is going on here—" he motioned to my body, "—is not good for you."

"You know how it works, Ryan. You learn to adapt. Those are the cards we've been dealt. It's who we are." The wall hadn't worked today, but it just meant I needed to figure out where my weaknesses were and rebuild it so it was strong enough for Quinn.

"No, it's not the same. What you have to deal with is much worse than what I deal with. No one has *ever* made me physically ill."

I couldn't argue with that. Ryan considered his special ability a gift, but being an empath had always felt more like a curse to me. "So why do you think he's different? What do you think it means?"

Ryan stepped back, put his hands on my shoulders, and squeezed. "I think it means you need to stay away from him."

"But what if he's different for me like Vanessa is different for you?"

"Vanessa works against my powers. She nulls them out, and because of that, I find balance and peace with her. It's what makes us work." It was another unarguable point. Vanessa could escape Ryan's mind games and give them both a break when they needed it. "Quinn is working *with* your powers, amplifying them somehow," he continued. "I don't understand how he's doing it. Obviously, he has no clue it's even happening, but for whatever reason, you could barely walk when he was in the room."

I bit my lip and considered it. "He used to have such a positive energy." There'd been a time when his energy had been like a magnet, drawing me to him. His negative energy didn't seem to be any different, though I had to admit it didn't feel as good.

He dropped his hands from my shoulders and sighed. "You're not going to stay away from him, are you?"

I couldn't make a false promise when Ryan could pick the truth right out of my head. I made a joke instead. "All my life, I've been waiting for someone to knock me off my feet. What if this is it?"

"Prince Charming shouldn't make you vomit. Just be careful, okay? I don't want you to get hurt."

"I promise I won't seek him out. How's that?"

He shook his head. "As good as I'm going to get."

Four

Willow

AS SOON AS THE LAST words of the lecture left my professor's lips, I slammed my notebook closed and shoved it into my bag. My mind should've been on my professor. He was going to teach me everything I needed to know about business and hospitality law, which was something I would need someday soon, I hoped.

Unfortunately, someone a few rows behind me had hijacked my attention for the last forty-five minutes.

Concentrating during class was difficult at times. Most of the university's students were younger than I was. They had more friends than I did. They had more fun than I did. But they also had a lot more drama in their lives. With drama came an overabundance of emotion. Even the quiet of the library was a cacophony in my head.

Sometimes, I wished I could read minds like Ryan. Everyone around me was a puzzle, but I only had half of the pieces. Even when I tried to force them together, I still came up with only half a picture. I had to remind myself constantly that I was on campus to learn. Getting wrapped up in the peripheral noise of other people's problems was not an option. Yet that was exactly what I'd done today.

The girl behind me was grieving, but I didn't know why. A person? A pet? A love gone wrong? It didn't matter. I'd spent the last forty-five minutes wiping at my stinging eyes, taking deep calming breaths, and forcing myself not to put my head down on the desk and bawl with her. I was exhausted.

I followed the flow of students out of the building and onto the sidewalk. Heading toward the parking lot, I cut across the lawn leading away from the throng of chattering students, hoping to save a few steps and a shred of my sanity.

I tapped out two text messages, one to Pizza Pi and one to Ryan, who would already be waiting for me at home. For the price of an occasional dinner and a whole lot of beer, he was helping me renovate my old house. We'd already finished the first floor and were moving on to the upstairs tonight.

The first wave of nausea hit me as I got close to my car.

He was nearby.

It had been almost a week since I'd seen Quinn. He hadn't come back to the diner, but I hadn't expected him to. That didn't mean I hadn't been thinking about him. Out of sight, out of mind was not working for me.

Get in your car and get out of here, my Ryan-guided common sense urged me. I knew from the weekend before that distance would bring relief. As soon as Quinn had driven out of the parking lot of the diner, I'd felt instantly better. The headache had lingered, but he took the nausea with him.

The smart thing to do was to ignore the pull, get in my car, and go home. But there was a louder voice coming from somewhere deeper inside me. It overpowered the voice of reason and propelled my feet to walk right on past the refuge of my car.

The nausea took a turn for the worse as I approached the back of the parking lot, telling me I was heading in the right direction ... or the wrong one, if I was to believe Ryan.

I didn't doubt Ryan's intentions. He was looking out for me as he always had. But he could be overprotective at times, and I didn't really believe Quinn was dangerous. I couldn't reconcile Ryan's warnings with what I knew about him—Quinn had been a good kid who'd sacrificed everything for the good of his country and gone on to become a hero.

I found him in the back row of the parking lot, slumped over the steering wheel of a beater of an old truck. If not for the arc of color radiating from him, I would have thought he was injured or passed out ... or worse. The halo of oranges, yellows, and blues emanating from the truck told me otherwise.

I'd never seen anyone project color like Quinn did. Every now and then, I could see a light hue around someone if they were a strong projector in an intense moment. More typically, though, the color association was entirely in my head. I sensed purple in response to anger, a light lovely red for love and adoration, and yellow for fear. The grieving girl in class made me think a dark cobalt blue, but I didn't see it.

Though I knew no one else could see them, the colors around Quinn were not just in my head. Color bathed him. It should have been off-putting, but it had the opposite effect. The colors were beautiful, their glow stunning against his skin. The effect was magical, making something in my chest flutter despite the unease in my stomach.

I scrambled to erect the wall, even though I knew it would be mostly ineffective against him. I tapped on the window. "Quinn."

His head immediately popped up, and I was blasted with the same crippling anxiety I'd felt when he had walked into my café. His emerald eyes were dark, and depicted every emotion I sensed visibly.

My legs threatened to buckle.

I thought I might have to sit down in the parking lot or open the door to the truck and crawl inside. That would be something to explain. *Excuse me, Quinn, as I crawl across you and try not to vomit on your lap.*

Fortunately, I didn't have to. Anxiety was replaced with recognition. With a few blinks, his expression changed from tortured to wary yet welcoming. The red morphed into a Caribbean turquoise, and the worst of my discomfort disappeared.

Did I have the same calming effect on him that he had on me during high school?

He rolled down the window. "Hey there, Willow." His voice was hoarse as if it was the first time he'd spoken all day even though we were well into the afternoon.

"Are you okay?" I placed a hand on the window frame of the truck, more for support than anything as I waited for his answer. He looked at it as if he wasn't sure about my proximity, and a hint of yellow snuck back in again.

There goes my calming theory.

I let go of the truck and took a step backward, nearly laughing out loud. I was the one who couldn't get within a city block of him without getting sick, yet he was the one eying me like he thought I might rob him.

He turned his gaze to the front window of the truck and seemed to focus on something he found out there. His fingers drummed nervously on the steering wheel. "Yeah, I'm fine. I was trying to figure some things out, I guess."

I tried to think of something—anything—that would ease the awkwardness between us but came up short. "Figuring things out is good." I nearly rolled my own eyes at the ineptness of my answer.

He shrugged, his eyes still focused on anything but me. "A necessary evil, I guess. Woodland Creek seems so different to me now." A rich blue entirely replaced the yellow. Drowning in it, I had the urge to lay my head on his shoulder and bawl all over it.

What was it like to be Quinn? He'd put his life on hold, sacrificed everything, and risked it all. What would it be like to devote yourself to your country with such purpose? And then, in a flash of an eye, be dumped back into your old life? My guess was Quinn couldn't simply pick up where he'd left off. Life in Woodland Creek had moved on without him. His young dreams of playing professional football were long gone. While he'd been away fighting for our freedom, someone else had cashed in on his dream and taken his place.

I had a sudden desire to know him—really *know* him. To know what he'd given up. To know what he'd gone through. To know everything about him.

Considering my churning stomach, it defied all logic, and Ryan would not be a fan of this new plan.

"So are you coming or going?" I asked

"Coming." His jaw ticked with determination.

"Are you taking a class?"

"No. I have an appointment with a course counselor. Do you know what time it is?"

I looked at the phone in my hand as it vibrated with an incoming text. "Almost five-thirty." I quickly read the message from Ryan. *Sorry, can't make it tonight. Will come by later and explain.*

I knew his explanation somehow related to Vanessa. I sighed, knowing I needed to get used to being second in line.

"What's wrong?" Quinn asked; his green eyes filled with a concern I felt all the way to my bones.

I forced a smile. "Oh, it's nothing. Ryan was supposed to help me with a project tonight, but he can't make it now."

"Oh." Quinn ran his fingers through his hair, as he seemed to mull something over. The rainbow shifted around him as his conflicting emotions warred with one another. I tried not to stare, but his emotional instability was one of the loveliest, most awe-inducing things I'd ever seen. It all stabilized when he came to a decision. "Is it anything I can help you with?"

"Trust me. You do not want to get involved with me."

He laughed, his eyes sparkling with a lightness that had been missing before, but then the rainbow surrounding him suddenly disappeared. My brain scrambled to figure out why but found Quinn to be a blank slate. He cocked his head, his lips quirking upwards into the first real smile I'd seen from him. He probably thought it was hilarious. Odd little Willow still had a crush on him after all of these years.

And it was a ridiculous notion. I told myself that my interest in him stemmed purely from curiosity. I simply wanted to know why he had the effect on me he did, why he seemed to magnify the curse I'd been living with my whole life, and find a way to deal with it. If he had this effect on me, there would surely be others.

Right.

Why are you even thinking about this? He's clearly a head case too. He's avoiding his friends. He eats oatmeal because his stomach is a wreck—and that's nothing compared to what he does to yours or what is going on in that head of his—and now he's sitting in his truck avoiding his future.

Nope. I wasn't interested in him. Not like that, anyway.

As much as I'd wanted it to, dating normal guys had never worked out for me. So dating one who made me sick every time I was near him was out of the question. I'd never be able to put up the façade of normalcy. Ryan was right. I needed someone who was different like I was different. Sure, Quinn was a walking rainbow, but he wasn't the kind of different I was looking for even if the view was lovely.

"I meant, involved with this project," I continued, rolling my eyes at the additional layer of awkwardness I'd interjected into our conversation. As if we really needed any more. "You don't want to get involved in this project. It's huge and doesn't pay well." I laughed. "Or at all."

"I'll be the judge of that. I can do huge." He winked at me, and suddenly, those eyes gleamed as if he was eighteen again with none of the burdens of the last fifteen years behind them. My heart stuttered to a stop, and my cheeks caught on fire. He was a big man. I was sure he could do huge. His eyebrows arched. "The project, of course."

I gaped at him and backtracked. "Don't you have a meeting to get to?"

"I missed it an hour and a half ago. I'm sure she gave up on me by now and is probably heading home. You said it's after five."

Geez. He's been sitting in his truck for an hour and a half?

I should've heard warning bells. They should've been clanging as loud as a Catholic church when the pope comes to visit, but it was silence all around me. My nausea had completely passed, and the Dearborn rainbow was conspicuously missing. Could we work together without it making me feel as if I was going to collapse? Maybe Ryan was wrong. Like Vanessa, Quinn seemed to be able to block me at times. I needed to find the loophole.

I also really wanted to work on the bathroom. I had goals. A schedule to keep. "Do you really want to help me?"

He nodded. "More than anything."

I laughed. "Do you think, maybe, you're using me as an excuse to avoid your future?"

He nodded again. "More than anything."

"You should talk to someone about that."

"I'll look into it."

I looked down at my phone again. "I ordered a pizza. I need to pick it up on my way home."

"Dinner's included, too? What a deal."

"Of course. Dinner and beer. I don't expect you fellas to work for free."

His face fell ever so slightly. "What *about* Ryan? Will he care?"

Most definitely, he would. "Not at all. He'll be glad you took his place."

"Oh, I'm not taking his place," Quinn said quickly. "I don't want him to think that. I just thought, you know, you helped me out once when I needed it. I want to return the favor."

"Well, that's entirely unnecessary. I was paid to help you out, and I enjoyed it."

"I wouldn't have gotten to play the championship game without you. I want to do it. I can pick up the pizza and meet you."

"Are you sure?" I dug through my purse for some money. I felt bad letting him pick up the pizza, but I could use a few extra minutes to pick up the house before he got there.

"I'm sure. Where am I going? Pizza Pi?"

"The one and only." As in literally. It was literally the only pizza place in town, though if Quinn hadn't been anywhere but the grocery store in three months, he probably didn't know that. I pulled out a twenty and held it out to him.

He shook his head. "No way."

I reached through the open window and dropped it on his lap then immediately started backing away so he couldn't hand it back. "I pay for dinner or there is no deal."

He cocked his head but put his truck into gear. It let out a big groan in response. "Where to after that?"

"The green and purple house next to the diner."

He nodded and the truck began to inch forward. "See you in a few."

"Oh, and Quinn?"

He stopped suddenly and the truck lurched. "Yeah?"

"Ryan is only a friend."

His smile as he drove away had a more devastating effect on my jelly legs than anything else he'd inflicted on me.

It was only after he'd turned the corner and his truck was out of sight that I realized he hadn't even asked about the project. He was helping me and going in blind. I had a feeling this was not a new concept for First Sergeant Dearborn.

Five

Quinn

I SAT OUTSIDE THE PIZZA place gripping the steering wheel of the truck as if I could choke answers out of it. How was I going to make it through an evening with Willow if I couldn't even force myself to go inside and pick up her dinner? It was a terrible idea.

I twisted my hands back and forth around the worn leather wheel. *You can barely help yourself. How are you going to help her?*

I had to find a way. I was messed up in the head, but I wasn't so messed up I didn't know what I wanted.

I'd been ready to bolt from this town. There was something about it, something that made it hard to escape from Woodland Creek; something that yanked you back even when you did. I was proof of it. I'd come to visit my mother and ended up staying three months even though I wasn't myself here.

All it had taken was one look from Willow to put my escape strategy on hold.

I'd packed my bags. I was ready to roll. I went to the diner planning to say my goodbyes before I'd even said hello, but I hadn't expected her. I'd been so worried about meeting with the guys I hadn't even considered the fact that Willow might be there, too. Then again, why would she be there fifteen years later?

She'd been smart—super smart, in fact. Hell, she'd tutored me in math when I was a senior and she was just a sophomore. She should have left this two-bit town and never looked back. Working in a diner and going to school at night didn't seem like a big enough life for a girl like Willow—correction—for a woman like Willow.

She was all grown up now, and I wasn't sure which side of her I liked more. While working, she'd pulled her dark hair up into a messy knot on the top of her head. Food splatters had covered her Creek Café shirt and grease streaked her apron. Tonight, she'd left her hair down and long brown ringlets fell down her back. She'd swapped her t-shirt and apron for something that showed off a few more assets. I guess I liked both sides. She was the sexiest thing I'd seen in fifteen years, and I'd seen a lot.

I'd gone home from the diner and finally unpacked my bags.

There was something about those almond-shaped eyes, the color of dark honey, wide and sparkling, that held me captive and made the prospect of staying a little more bearable. I just needed to keep my shit together long enough to have a normal conversation with her.

Not that I could pull anything over on her.

When she looked at me, I could tell she saw it all. The madness, the misery, and the hopelessness all reflected in her eyes. She knew exactly how messed up I was.

But I could see something else reflected in them, too. She remembered the boy I'd once been, so innocent, eager, and full of life. She looked at me as if she thought there was still a piece of that kid somewhere inside of me—but I knew better. He was a mirage that vanished as soon as you reached for him.

A part of me wanted to duck my head and hide all the awfulness from her. A part of me wanted to bare it all to see if she could help me find him again.

Willow

I SCRAMBLED THROUGH THE HOUSE, grabbing shoes and stray clothing as I went. I threw them into my bedroom without even looking and pulled the door closed behind me.

The kitchen was next. The open cereal box went back in the cabinet. I stashed the dirty dishes in the dishwasher where they belonged. With everything put away, I began wiping down the countertops and kitchen table. The house wouldn't have gotten this kind of treatment for Ryan. He would have eaten pizza on top of my crumbs without complaining, and I would expect that of him. But I couldn't ask the same of Quinn.

I tossed the rag into the sink, hoping the kitchen looked like I actually lived this way and not like I was trying to impress him.

On my way to the front door, I worked on my wall, reconstructing it brick-by-ineffective-brick. I reached the door at the same time as the doorbell rang and forced myself to count to five before opening it. He didn't need to think I was standing by the door waiting for him. He was more agitated than he had been at the end of our conversation in the parking lot, but it wasn't nearly as bad as when I'd found him with his forehead pressed against his steering wheel.

I welcomed him in, and whatever inner conflict he had felt when he stepped onto my porch passed. He stepped into my entryway draped in a faint seafoam hue as calming to me as he felt. As he shrugged off his jacket, I took a moment to look at him. He wore cargo pants like you would find at a department store. A plain black t-shirt stretched nicely across his chest. The jacket he threw onto the hall tree appeared to be military issue. The combination was telling, as if he'd tried to make an effort to look like a normal civilian but couldn't completely surrender to it. Once a soldier, always a soldier. Was that how it worked?

He glanced around the entryway with genuine interest. "I've always thought this house was so cool."

"Really?"

"When we were kids, everyone thought this house was haunted and that Janice Crabtree was a witch, mixing spells in the basement. I never really bought into that nonsense though."

I nodded and swallowed the lump in my throat. It was a rumor perpetuated by the kids from the newer side of town where Quinn had grown up. Because I was from the old part of town, I knew better. The house wasn't haunted, and Janice hadn't been a witch. There was no such thing in Woodland Creek.

There were a few wizards scattered around though, and the rumors about Janice mixing spells in her basement were not too far from the truth. Not that she minded them. To the contrary, I'd always suspected she'd painted her house lime green and purple to feed the rumors. The old Victorian monstrosity—complete with round room and turret—looked like a witch should live there. Experience had taught me that there was a grain of truth at the heart of every rumor, no matter how seemingly outlandish.

"Hmm. I'm sure they probably say the same things about me now," I said, laughing.

"Nah, you're too pretty to be a witch. Not that Janice wasn't pretty in her day. I'm sure she was," he added quickly. "Is she here?" His gaze traveled up the grand staircase leading to the second floor.

"No. She died a few years ago." Guilt-tinged grief washed over me. I was glad he didn't suffer from the same affliction I did, so he couldn't feel it too. It had been almost six years since her heart attack, but I still missed her terribly. "Come on," I said, trying to change the subject. "We can eat in the kitchen."

I turned in that direction, but he stopped me. He looked at his hand as if he was surprised he had touched me, and both his expression and his touch caused my stomach to do flips. This time, in the very best way. "I'm so sorry, Willow. I know you two were close." Melancholy wafted off him, matching my own.

He gave my arm a squeeze, and then I watched his hand fall. I was sure my expression gave me away, too. It had been a while since a man other than Ryan had touched me, and even longer since one had made my heart stutter and race as his touch had. I led him through the house, fighting the urge to grab his hand and pull him along simply so I could touch him again.

"I know people thought Janice and I were an odd match. They couldn't understand why I would want to hang out with someone fifty years older than I am, but she was one of my best friends."

"There are no rules when it comes to friends. Besides, even witches have a family, right?" He laughed at what he still considered an absurd notion. "I figured she was an aunt or something since you were always here and helping her at the diner."

In the kitchen, I took the pizza from him and placed it on the table. I pulled some plates out of the cabinet and set them down too. "We were family in all the ways that mattered. I was all she had, and when she died, she left me the house because she knew I loved it."

He looked at me incredulously. "Really? She gave you her house?"

"And the diner, too, though I think she considered it a payment for an old debt." I opened the door to the refrigerator. "Beer?"

"That would be great. What kind of debt?"

I ducked my head into the refrigerator. "Thanks for picking up the pizza," I said, changing the subject. I'd already said too much. If I kept it up, he'd know all of my secrets before we were done with dinner, and I'd be in a heap of trouble.

"Not a problem."

I pulled two beers from the refrigerator and turned to find him standing almost at attention behind a chair he'd pulled away from the table. He gestured for me to take a seat. Only after I'd sat did he sit down too. Then, in a second act of chivalry, he reached across the table and twisted the top off my beer before opening his own.

Flustered, I popped open the pizza box and gestured for him to take a slice. "I hope you like sausage and mushrooms. I ordered it for Ryan before I knew he wasn't coming."

His eyes clouded over, and I wondered if the sausage and mushroom pizza had turned him green or if the mention of Ryan had. "It looks good," he said in a neutral tone that gave nothing away. "I'll pretty much eat anything. I stopped being discerning years ago."

"Is the food bad over there?"

"It serves a purpose, and they do the best they can. So what's the project for tonight?" he said, changing the subject quickly, obviously not wanting to talk about his time in the service any more than I wanted to talk about my odd relationship with Janice.

I thought about the bathroom I wanted to do first, and the task suddenly seemed too big and imposing. I should've never even considered asking him to help. "Well, Ryan was going to help me tear out an upstairs bathroom tonight," I said, my voice tentative and shy. "But I don't actually expect you to help me. It's kind of a big job."

He nodded, chewing thoughtfully. "So you're renovating."

"Yes, we've already finished the first floor."

He appraised the kitchen. "I can tell. It looks really good. Did you do all of this by yourselves?"

"I hired someone to do the countertops in here, but we did the cabinets and floors ourselves."

"Is it some sort of stone?" he asked, pointing at the shiny, bronzed countertops.

"It's actually polished concrete. I was worried granite or marble would seem out of place in here. Too fancy for this house, if you know what I mean?"

He nodded but shrugged. "I don't know anything about decorating, but they look good to me."

"I don't either. I'm learning as I go. I really wish we'd gone ahead and put a built-in microwave above the oven." I looked wistfully at the ugly microwave sitting on the counter. "That thing is an eyesore and takes up valuable countertop space I need when I'm making pies."

Something flickered in his eyes at the mention of pie. "So fix it."

"Nah. It's taken us three years to get this far. I don't want to backtrack now."

"Why so long?"

"We open the diner at five every morning, and I have class most afternoons. In the evenings, we can get a little work done, but I also have to put together the lunch special for the next day. I also try to remember that Ryan has a life, too. His girlfriend squawks a lot if he spends too much time over here." Technically, woodpeckers didn't squawk so much as chirp, but the comment still made me giggle.

"He has a girlfriend?" His lips turned up into a half smile, though I could barely see it through the scruff on his face.

Quinn's beard wasn't the intentional scruff gracing the pages of *People* magazine's Sexiest Men edition. It was at least four or five days beyond that, pulling him out of the I-Manscape-to-Look-Falsely-Rugged category and landing him squarely in the I-Don't-Give-a-Shit category. I thought he wore the category well though, and once again, I had the awkward desire to reach out and touch him.

I squashed it, and instead, loaded each of our plates with another piece of pizza. "Yeah, her name is Vanessa Birdwell. She's younger than I am, which would make her quite a bit younger than you. You probably don't remember her from school."

He shook his head. "Doesn't ring a bell. So who are you dating? Would I know him?"

I blushed furiously. If I were to believe what Ryan told me, then Quinn was just as interested in me as I was in him. There was some peace of mind in knowing that. It took away a bit of the does-he-or-doesn't-he-like-me guessing game we would otherwise play, but knowing it also left me jittery and nervous. "No boyfriend here. I dated your friend, Tim, a few years back though."

Though Quinn's expression gave nothing away, a flash of dark, woodsy green shot through the kitchen turning my stomach rancid. I fought the urge to flip the kitchen table and put my fist through the wall and hoped he did, too. Neither one of us needed to put a hole in my newly painted and textured walls. Certainly, Tim Reyburn didn't warrant such a reaction.

"You just turned green," he said.

It sent me into a momentary state of confusion. Maybe he could see the Dearborn rainbow, too. Maybe it wasn't all in my head. Was there a vein of magic running through his blood as well? "What do you mean?" I was cautiously hopeful. If he could also see the jealousy hanging in the air, I would kiss his face and ask him if he knew why it was so hard for me to be around him even though it was all I wanted to do.

Circling a finger in the air, he gestured to my face. "Your face. It was green for a second." He looked puzzled. "It looks normal now. Was it the pizza or the subject of Tim?"

"Must be the pizza." I pushed it away and took a sip of beer to hide my disappointment. I was glad I hadn't made a fool of myself by asking him about the rainbow he projected. "The thing with Tim happened years ago, and trust me, it didn't last very long. For some reason, I'm drawn to men I don't have a lot in common with."

"He's not right for you." The definitive tone of his voice made me a little swoony.

"I found that out pretty quickly, actually. But why do you say that?"

"He was never very nice to girls in high school, and it doesn't seem like he's changed much."

"We live and we learn, right?" I stood and went to the refrigerator for two more beers, glad the nausea had passed as quickly as it had come on.

Again, he reached over and popped the tops off both our bottles, starting with mine. "Do I need to kick his ass? I feel like maybe I do."

I laughed. "No. I'm pretty good at taking care of myself, but thank you very much. Besides, he's *your* friend."

"*Was* my friend. Saturday was the first time I'd seen him since high school, and if he treated you wrong, then my only interest in him right now is kicking his ass." I rested my chin on my fist and wiggled in my seat. Though I certainly didn't mind it, it was a fierce reaction. "Women have always been our problem," he continued.

"Sounds like there's a good story here."

"Not really. In high school, we always competed for girls. I think he knew I had a thing for you, actually."

My heart thundered in my chest. I didn't dare speak, or I'd give away that I'd *always* had a thing for him.

"You look surprised," he continued. "The week you tutored me was the same week of the fall dance. Do you remember?"

I didn't remember the dance. All I remembered about that week was him. "You had a girlfriend," was all I could manage.

"We'd broken up the week before, and I needed a date. I was planning to ask you, but all week long, you said you weren't feeling well. Then you didn't come to school on Friday, so I figured you had the flu or something."

That part I remembered. I hadn't had the flu though I had felt queasy the night before. Janice had plugged me full of some herbal tea, curing me instantly. I'd stayed home on Friday for no good reason at all. Had I really come that close to a date with Quinn?

It suddenly dawned on me that he might have been the reason I was ill. What if it had been what I now called the Dearborn Effect, and I just hadn't known it at the time? "Who did you take?" I asked, thankful I didn't sound as breathless as I felt.

"I went alone." His mouth quirked into a less than happy smile. "But I saw Hannah there, of course. We patched things up and didn't break up again until after graduation."

Regret laced around my heart, binding it and squeezing it.

I didn't know what to say. I wanted to ask what he regretted more—going to the dance alone or getting back together with Hannah. But what if it was more complicated than that? Because not long after, he'd left town, and then in his absence, she'd married his friend. Maybe his regret ran deeper than a fall dance and the what-could-have-been. Maybe he regretted losing Hannah.

That was the curse I lived with—I knew what he felt but not the why of it. What's worse, I shouldn't know anything of his regret. I was a window to his soul, but he didn't know that. If he wanted me to know where his regrets lay, he would have to tell me on his own.

"I suppose everything happens for a reason," I offered, for lack of anything better to say. It was a crappy, generic response. Something you say to someone when you can't think of anything better.

"Maybe," he said, smiling thoughtfully. "But it makes you wonder, doesn't it?" My heart stopped, and I held my breath waiting for him to continue. "What would have happened if you hadn't gotten sick, and I'd taken you instead? What would have happened then?"

I would've said yes! I would've jumped your bones, and you wouldn't have left. You would have played football at some college, and I would have cheered from the stands. Today, my purple and green house would be filled with lots of little Quinnish babies.

Of course, I didn't really believe any of it was true. One little dance wouldn't have changed the course of everything that happened afterward. Would it? I knew a fortuneteller I could ask, but I knew better than to walk down that road. I didn't need my own regrets when Quinn was already suffocating me with his.

He pushed away from the table and stood up. "Why don't you show me that bathroom? I think I'm going to enjoy tearing some shit up tonight."

"THIS PIECE IS REALLY HANGING on." I crammed the crowbar further under the baseboard and winced when the sheetrock crunched under the pressure. "Uh-oh."

"Good thing you want to replace that, too," Quinn said with a laugh.

"Most of it is loose, but I can't get the end to let go."

"Here, let me help." He maneuvered into the space next to me, squatted, and took the crowbar. "Pretty cozy in here, isn't it? I feel like I know you better already." He winked, and my insides went all gooey.

This bathroom was one of the smaller ones. My lingering guilt over suckering him into helping me had prompted me to pick it instead of the larger one down the hall. I was trying to give him a break but had gotten a bonus for myself. All evening, we'd practically worked on top of each other. Bumping arms. Brushing backs. Every touch sent an electrical current through me. I was hyper aware of his every movement and found myself orchestrating our collisions rather than trying to avoid them.

"Hold onto that end there. You just need some extra muscle."

I gripped the free end. "Got it."

Since he'd brought up the subject of muscle, I decided he'd sort of given me a pass to gawk at his. While he shoved the crowbar back under the board, I marveled at his arms and shoulders. Every inch of him flexed and pulled beneath his t-shirt as he moved. I wondered what he would look like without a shirt on. I was sure he would be magnificent.

"I'm going to load all of the big stuff in the back of my truck unless you have other plans for it," he said.

Before I could answer, he shoved downward. With an efficient pop, the board sprung free, catapulting me backward. I landed on my backside with an oomph. Quinn was immediately over me. Not hard in a room the size of that one. "Oh, wow. I didn't mean to knock you off your feet."

Funny. That's all you've done since coming into my diner.

"I'm fine," I said laughing.

He offered me a hand, and I took it. He pulled me up, and once again, we were practically on top of each other, with only a broken board and a few inches separating us. Emerald eyes sparkled down at me. The paper definitely hadn't done them justice. They were every bit as deep in color as I remembered. His chest rose and fell, and his breath hitched.

His gaze fell to my mouth, and my already gooey insides incinerated. He wanted to kiss me. I could see it in his eyes, in the way his lips twitched. I could feel it in the room now colored magenta with desire. His desire. I wondered what shade mine would be if it had a color.

"Is that okay?" he asked. His jaw ticked beneath all that fuzz.

What would it feel like? Would it be rough? Scratchy? Leave a mark on my face? I wanted to find out. "Yes." He didn't need to ask permission to kiss me.

"So you don't have any plans for the wood?" he asked.

Well, now ... *that* was pretty forward, but then again, I'd technically already asked him to marry me. I laugh-snorted at the thought, and his lips twitched up at the corners as if he'd read my mind. "Yes," I mumbled, still staring at his mouth. I had plans for the wood.

Do it. Kiss me.

To my complete and total disappointment, he stepped away from me instead and out into the hall. "So I shouldn't haul it off then?" he asked, pointing at the pile of scrap wood accumulating there.

My cheeks flared bright enough to rival the color of the room. I was sure I hadn't misread his emotions though I'd surely misinterpreted his words. I turned away embarrassed, glad he couldn't read my mind or emotions right now. "I can use it for firewood."

"Good idea. Do you have a pile somewhere?"

"Out back."

"All right. I'm going to take a load down."

"That would be perfect. Thanks." Frustrated, I picked up the sledgehammer and swung at the wall. The hole in the sheetrock instantly made me feel better. According to Ryan, he was interested in me, and my emotional barometer confirmed it. Yet he'd passed on the perfect opportunity to kiss me. Confused, I took another swing at the wall.

He was gone a long time, maybe having a hard time finding the woodpile, and by the time he got back, an entire wall was missing. A few hours later, the entire room had been demolished. The old cabinets and fixtures were loaded in the back of Quinn's truck for him to haul away. We'd torn the walls down to the studs, and I had a list of things to order from the lumberyard the next day.

After our awkward moment, I'd carried most of the conversation, yammering on and on about anyone he might know and filling him in on what had happened while he was away. From the blank slate in his head, I gathered he was content cracking tile and listening to my endless chatter.

When we finally collapsed in the formal living room, me on the couch and Quinn in my favorite wingback chair, we were both exhausted. "I'm so tired." I sighed.

Quinn raked a hand through his hair. The dark circles under his eyes were more pronounced than they had been earlier. "I'm filthy and probably shouldn't be allowed anywhere near your furniture," he said, running his hands down the arms of the chair.

I laughed. "Oh, please. I'm not any better. Besides, I purposefully picked all of the furniture to be super durable."

"So what exactly is your plan for this place? Obviously, you have something in mind."

I nodded, a wide smile spreading across my face. I leaned forward, grabbed a magazine from the coffee table, and tossed it into his lap.

His forehead wrinkled as he studied the snow-covered house on the cover. "*Peaceful Getaways* magazine?"

"I'm taking hotel and restaurant management classes at the college."

"You want to turn this into a hotel?" he asked, flipping fast through the pages.

I swallowed the lump in my throat. Ryan was the only other person I'd told about my dream for the place. I certainly hadn't made it public knowledge yet. This town already had one inn, so I wasn't sure how well my idea would be received; not that anyone could stop me at this point. "A bed and breakfast, to be exact."

"Oh, yeah," he said nodding. "This house is perfect for that. It's certainly big enough. What have you got—four rentable rooms?"

Earlier in the evening, I'd given him a tour of everything but my room on the first floor and the basement below. My room was a mess from the quick cleanup job before he'd arrived, and the basement was still full of Janice's more eccentric belongings. Balls, chalices, daggers, and cauldrons. Jars of things, which I was too scared to think about. Things like horny goat weed, skullcap, horehound, and dragon's blood incense, just to name a few. I didn't know what she did with the ingredients or how to dispose of them.

Eventually, I would have to go through it all because I had plans for the basement, too, but it would have to wait until I'd finished the rest of the house. Honestly, as weird as her stuff was, I wasn't in any hurry to rid the house of the last remaining traces of Janice.

"There are the four rooms you saw upstairs. There's also an apartment over the garage. Janice fixed it up for me after I graduated from high school. She was getting older and thought it was a good idea to have someone close by. I needed to get away from home, so it made sense at the time."

He nodded, seeming to consider something. "I understand that. There definitely comes a point when you're too old to live with your parents."

"The apartment's nothing fancy. It could use a little sprucing up, but it's another rentable suite."

"It has its own bath?"

"It does. I have two ideas, and I really haven't been able to decide which way to go. I have a while to think about it though since this is the longest renovation in the history of ever."

He sunk further into the chair to get comfortable. "Lay it on me."

"Okay, so the first idea. Do you remember the board game Clue?"

"Sure. I used to play it with my mom." His lips curled into a smile. "Colonel Mustard in the library with the poison."

"Exactly!" This idea had me particularly excited. "I had the game when I was a kid, too … wish I still had it. Anyway, I heard about this bed & breakfast in Louisiana that has a Clue-themed dinner theater every evening."

He looked confused. "What does that even mean?"

"I'm thinking I'll serve a five-star dinner and then the guests get to act out the game. One person is designated as the victim, and everyone else are potential murderers."

He laughed. "And since everyone in town already thinks this house is haunted …"

"Right. And maybe when I'm not full, local people will make dinner reservations, too. The more the merrier."

"I think it sounds like a great idea. What's the other one?"

"Okay, another option is to decorate each of the bedrooms upstairs with a different theme. I was thinking one could be an enchanted forest and one could be *1,000 Leagues under the Sea*. Maybe with some mermaids. It sounds stupid when I say it out loud though." I was suddenly very nervous again. The only other person I'd told my ideas to was Ryan, and he had been kind of 'meh' on both, but he didn't really have a vision for it. He'd have to see it finished before he'd actually get it.

Quinn leaned forward and clasped his hands together. "It doesn't sound stupid at all, but why not do both?"

"Both?" I asked, bewildered. I hadn't thought of that.

"Why not? All of the bedrooms are on the second floor, and all of the rooms you need for Clue are on the first floor, right?"

"Yeah? Well, I'm pretty sure the original Clue game had a bedroom as one of the game rooms. The only bedroom on the first floor is mine, and I don't really want guests tromping through my room every night."

"Hmm ... yeah. That's a problem, but this is such a cool idea. It's definitely different from anything else in town."

"Well, there is only one other inn in town, so it won't be hard to stand out. I figure, between the tourists the park brings in and the visitors to the college, it will do okay." I didn't tell him I thought it might also be popular with some of the more eccentric in town.

"I think so too." He leaned back in the chair again, deep in thought. Suddenly, the room was alight in rosy pink and hyperactive orange, and my nerves were buzzing. "You could have an Arabian Nights room and make the bed float like a magic carpet. Another room could be a jungle theme with a stuffed bear in the corner."

I hid my shudder. This was as excited as I'd felt Quinn get. I didn't want to discourage him, but taxidermy of any kind was out of the question. "No bears, but I love the magic carpet idea. I'll have to do some research to figure out how to do that."

"I can help you. Now, you only need one more theme."

"Two. There's the garage," I reminded him. "Maybe I could move into the garage, but I feel like it might not be close enough to the guests."

"Okay. A few problems to work out but still doable."

I was silent while I let him brainstorm some more. Whatever he was thinking about, it wasn't upsetting to either of us. "You'll still keep the diner, right?" he finally asked.

"Absolutely. I love the diner, and I have to serve them breakfast somewhere, right? Since it's just next door, I think it works. I might rename it, though."

"What about Candlestick Inn and Revolver Diner?"

"Oh, my God, I love it. Hold that thought for a second." I stood up and walked the short distance to the entryway. I threw the door open to find Ryan's hand extended to knock. Gaston, Janice's Russian blue cat, snaked between his legs before disappearing into the house.

"Took you long enough. I thought maybe your Ry-dar was broken. Hell, with the state I'm in, you should've felt me coming a mile away."

I threw a finger over my lips and hissed at him. "Shhhhh. I have company."

His eyes narrowed and he sniffed. "Who? Now that you mention it, I'm getting a weird vibe from this house tonight."

"Come see for yourself," I said, careful not to say the name of my visitor in my head.

In the living room, Ryan nodded curtly at Quinn. "Dearborn. Good to see you again." Then he turned and gave me a look letting me know how he really felt about finding him here.

Quinn muttered a hello as Ryan sat down next to me on the couch, much closer than was customary for us.

The room was full of aggression, and I found it curious. Ryan wasn't usually so territorial and couldn't make a claim on me anyway, and Quinn ... well ... I didn't know what to make of him. I didn't know him well enough even to venture a guess.

"Quinn helped me tear out the first bathroom upstairs," I said, filling the awkward silence.

"Yeah?" Ryan turned to Quinn and sized him up.

Quinn seemed unconcerned. "She said you were tied up tonight, so I thought I'd help out."

Ryan dismissed him with a nod, but I could feel his disapproval diminish a bit. "Listen, Will. I'm really sorry I stood you up. I've had a hell of a night though."

"What happened?" I asked.

"I spent the evening at Pond & Duck with Nessie."

Ahhhh. Here it is. A trip to the most expensive restaurant in town could only mean one thing: changes were on the horizon. Ryan only took her there when they had something big to discuss. It could only mean one thing.

"So you asked her then?"

His face twisted in disbelief. "No, *she* took me there. *She* asked me."

"To dinner?" I asked hopefully.

He snorted. "No. To marry her."

"She asked *you* to marry *her*?"

"Yep. I was as shocked as you are."

I laughed. "I guess she was tired of waiting for you. I have to give it to her. For such a little bird, she's got big cojones." She obviously didn't care about his family's feelings toward her. I wasn't sure how I felt about that. I wanted to be impressed by it, but it was going to cause many problems for Ryan. Regardless, I had to give it to her. She got things done.

Ryan looked briefly at Quinn, weighing something, and then shrugged dismissively. "I guess it's going to be public knowledge soon anyway. She's pregnant."

I jumped up from the couch and stalked across the room, trying to put as much distance between us as possible. Whipping around, I stared down at him. "Say that again."

Quinn stood, too, and moved into the middle of the room. "I should be going. You guys need to talk."

"It was an accident," Ryan said, ignoring him. "I didn't mean for it to happen."

"Accident, my ass. There are things to prevent these types of *accidents*, which makes them not accidents but acts of stupidity."

Ryan jumped up and pointed a finger at me, and streaks of violet and purple instantly bathed the room as Quinn reacted, too.

Anger. Disappointment. Shame.

Three competing states of mind pummeled me at once. I couldn't tell where one stopped and the next began. Which one was mine? Was I angry or disappointed? Lightning bolts of searing pain shot through my head, and I crumpled into a chair in the corner. Instantly, Quinn was in front of me, standing guard between Ryan and me.

If I hadn't been so sick, I would've been amused. I knew Ryan better than the back of my hand. We understood what it was like to be different. Our arguments often got heated, but I was never in any danger with him. Even if he shifted, I was safe. The same couldn't be said for Quinn. He had no idea how dangerous Ryan could be. Yet, here he was, standing guard over me.

Ryan backed down first, sinking back onto the couch. I knew he had just pulled something out of Quinn's head and that something had changed Ryan's opinion of him. I'd seen it flash through Ryan's eyes. I felt his disapproval turn into something more attune to acceptance.

He looked at Quinn as he spoke, the expression on his face something between surprise and awe. "I would never, ever hurt her, man. Never. You don't have to worry about that."

They stared at each other a moment longer, as if having a silent private conversation where I wasn't allowed. I knew it wasn't really fair since only one of them knew what the other was thinking, but Quinn seemed to be holding his own.

I could ask Ryan for a rundown on Quinn's thoughts the next day at work, but I wouldn't. I already liked Quinn too much to violate his privacy like that. Whatever Quinn thought about me—or anything else, for that matter—I wanted him to tell me himself. Secondhand would never be good enough.

Their standoff ended, and Ryan turned to me. He shook his head before dropping it into his hands and threading his fingers through his hair. Tears sprang into my eyes, my sorrow a reflection of his. "I didn't think *you* were the one I had to worry about, Will. *Someone* has to be in my corner, and I need it to be you."

I looked at his fallen face and slumped shoulders and melted.

He's going to be a dad.

He was nearly thirty years old. He had someone who cared about him. She might not be my choice, but he was definitely in a better place than I was. The only guy I'd been attracted to in at least three years made me sick on sight.

All I had was a cat—and not even my own cat, since I'd inherited him with pretty much everything else I owned. I was doomed to grow old; a lonely spinster in a house full of strangers … and that was only if my bed and breakfast was a success. Ryan, though … he had a family now.

I rubbed my temples and forced a smile through the headache. "Of course, I'm on your side. What do we do next?"

"Plan a wedding?"

"What kind of wedding?" The two-natured typically had two weddings—one they could invite their human friends to and one for their immediate family and pack or clan, as the case might be. The latter was an intense ceremony requiring the bride and groom to exchange vows first in human form and then in shifted form. The group's leader typically performed it. In Ryan's case, that meant his grandfather. His parents would also have a role, so without his family's support, there would be no such a ceremony, and they would remain unmarried in the eyes of those who mattered most to them.

"She doesn't care that she's knocked up. She wants an old-fashioned white wedding with a reception afterward," he said, answering my question.

"Ahh. Where?" Woodland Creek was short on party venues, but there was the community room at the library and the ballrooms at the university.

Ryan ducked his head and winced. "I kind of told her we could do it here."

I narrowed my eyes at him. "Ryan! The house is nowhere near ready for guests, let alone a party."

"When?" Quinn asked, showing a sudden interest in Ryan's predicament.

"Six or seven weeks, but it's perfect, Willow. Think of it like a sneak peek for people to see the magnificence of what's coming to Woodland Creek."

"In the backyard?" I asked, hopefully.

He looked exasperated. "It's going to be freezing cold in six weeks."

"We'll get tents and those heater things. And swans." I thought about one of my favorite movies as a little girl. That was how they'd done it, and how I'd always imagined my own wedding would be. There was nothing more romantic than swans.

"You're such a sap," he said laughing. "We don't know any swans."

"True." I snuck a glance at Quinn to see if he'd caught Ryan's reference to the two-natured, but Quinn seemed lost in his own thoughts.

I was just thankful the room was a normal hue and whatever he was thinking about wasn't affecting me. I was too zapped to even try to construct the wall again. I suspected I would be a wreck the rest of the evening, so it would help if everyone could get along.

"I actually told Nessie we could have the wedding in here, and she could walk down the staircase. She wants a grand entrance."

I rolled my eyes. *Of course, she did.*

"What if people want to go upstairs? There's no way it can be ready in six weeks."

"That's cool. Seven's fine."

I glared at Ryan.

"I can help," Quinn interjected.

Oh, man. I wasn't sure how I felt about that. There was no way I could spend the next six weeks sick as a dog. Then again, I hadn't been worried about it at all when I'd been begging him to kiss me upstairs. When it came to Quinn, I was in a constant state of confusion, torn between needing to get as far away from him as possible and wanting to pull him closer.

I tore my eyes from Quinn to find Ryan scowling at me, probably because I'd just admitted to wanting Quinn to kiss me upstairs. He had to understand that I couldn't accept Quinn's offer. "That's so sweet of you to offer, but I can't ask you to do that. Besides, I'm sure you have better things to do with your time."

He shrugged. "I really don't."

"And I can't afford to pay you much … if anything."

Ryan piped up. "I can vouch for that. She's been abusing me for months, but she'll feed you well and keep you in beer." I narrowed my eyes at him. Why was he suddenly so supportive of this idea?

"That's payment enough for me. I'm not supposed to work yet anyway."

"Why?"

"Medical reasons."

That concerned me. "If you're still healing, then this is definitely a bad idea. I don't want you to hurt yourself."

I could feel him shutting down on me. "It's nothing like that. This will be good for me. At least, it will get me out of my mom's house for a few hours every day."

"Sounds like the perfect solution," Ryan said, "because I need to get a real job."

I went into full glare mode. "You're not even going to help?" I was going to put the hurt on him next time I saw him when Quinn wasn't around.

"I'll help, but I need to make some extra cash in the evenings. I have a baby on the way."

"Do you realize what a pain in my ass you are?" I asked him before turning to Quinn. "Are you sure about this?"

He nodded happily. "I'll get started tomorrow."

I didn't need Ryan's help to know Quinn's intentions were genuine. I chewed on the inside of my cheek while I considered his offer. If I could manage to stay on my feet when he was around, it could work out well for everyone. Vanessa would get her wedding, and Ryan would get to play her savior. Quinn would have somewhere different to go every day, which seemed important to him. And I might be able to open my bed and breakfast years before I'd planned.

It would work.

Maybe.

Six

Willow

QUINN'S TRUCK WAS PARKED AROUND the back of the house, sitting in front of the garage as if it belonged there. The sight of it filled me with equal parts apprehension and excitement.

This whole situation still felt like a disaster in the making, but how could I say no? Ryan hadn't left me with much of a choice. It was going to take someone working nearly full time to get this house ready for a wedding in seven weeks.

As much as it should be Ryan's problem, I knew he couldn't do it. He'd spent this afternoon combing the streets looking for a second job. I couldn't pay him enough at the diner to support a family. Maybe if we stayed open for dinner too, but that would mean giving up my dream. I couldn't be at the diner every night and run a bed and breakfast. Even if they were next door to each other, I couldn't be in two places at once.

My bigger fear was that I was going to lose him completely. If he found a job that paid better than I could, I was sure he'd quit the diner altogether. Good cooks were hard to find, so the thought terrified me, but I'd decided not to dwell on it for the time being.

After all, I had another problem to focus on—Quinn Dearborn.

He was in my house.

He'd spent all day working upstairs, and I'd spent all day preparing myself for the roller coaster ride of emotions I'd have to deal with when I got home. Both his and mine.

I'd decided to take a proactive approach. Before I'd left for the diner this morning, I'd gone down to the basement to hunt for the tea recipe Janice had used when I'd come down with the Dearborn Flu during high school. Luckily, Janice had always kept meticulous records of her concoctions. The basement shelves held stacks and stacks of journals. Some of the pages read like recipes while others read more like diary entries, but all had dates. It hadn't taken me long to find the book most likely to have the information I needed.

I'd flipped quickly through the October entries during 2001 until I'd found a page titled 'Willow's Tea.' The ingredients were common enough, and I found the chamomile, ginger, and cinnamon bark I needed in Janice's jars of weirdness.

Before I'd left for work, I'd made a big pitcher of the vile smelling tea and gulped down an even more vile tasting glass of it. I'd put the rest in the refrigerator, knowing I was going to need to mainline the stuff when I got home from school. I parked my car next to his truck, grabbed dinner off the seat, and ran around to the front steps with that in mind.

To my surprise, he was standing in the kitchen eyeing the microwave. "Oh no, I was really hoping you hadn't eaten yet." I held up the bag of Chinese food.

"I haven't." He shifted on his feet as if he wasn't entirely at home standing in my kitchen. To be honest, I wasn't entirely comfortable with it yet either.

"Were you looking for something to drink?" I stepped around him, opened the cabinet, and pulled two glasses out.

"Uhhh, yeah."

Gosh, I hope it's not going to be this awkward for the next seven weeks. The night before we'd been completely at ease with each other, but now, we were both acting as if we'd never met.

"What would you like?" I opened the refrigerator and pulled out the pitcher of tea.

The smell hit him not long after it hit me. His eyes grew wide, and he covered his nose. "Not what you're having."

I giggled. "I don't blame you. You know what? There's still some beer in here. Would you like one of those instead?"

"That would be great." He went to the refrigerator to get it himself. While he dug around for a beer, I frantically drank my glass of tea. I did my best to keep my expression level but coughed midway through when the wretched stuff went down the wrong pipe.

"Why *are* you drinking it, if it's so bad?" he asked when I'd finally stopped barking like an asthmatic seal.

"It's sort of medicinal."

"Does it cure more than it hurts?" he asked with a wince on his face.

"Let's hope so."

He cocked an eyebrow at me and clinked my glass with his bottle. "Down the hatch then. I hope it makes you feel better."

"If it doesn't kill me first," I muttered.

We stood in my kitchen and tipped our drinks up like a couple of college freshman, finishing about the same time. "Another?"

I grimaced and shook my head. "How did it go here today?"

His mood was suddenly a bright blushing pink. "Excellent. I made some real progress on the big bathroom."

"I can drink to that." He returned to the refrigerator, and I began to unpack the food. "I took some liberties with dinner based on your proclamation last night that you'll eat pretty much anything." I popped open a container. "Mongolian beef seemed manly enough for you."

He grinned and pounded on his chest, causing me to giggle. "And what's the lady having?"

"Orange chicken but I'll switch with you if you prefer."

"Nah, you eat your froufrou chicken. I'll keep my manly beef. You know what I find even more interesting than your gender-specific selections?" He slipped a pair of chopsticks out of the paper wrapper and pointed them at me.

"What?"

"This is two nights in a row you've eaten takeout."

"So?"

"It just surprises me. Obviously, you know how to cook. But when you're at home, you don't even bother to get out a plate."

I pushed my chicken around the Styrofoam container and laughed. "We ate on plates last night, and you've seen my refrigerator. It's not like my cupboards are completely bare," I added, even though they were a bit of an embarrassment. All I really had was what I needed to make the lasagnas for tomorrow. "The thing is, I serve food to people for eight hours every single day, seven days a week. Tonight, I have to put the lasagnas together for tomorrow's special, and I have to get up at the crack of dawn to throw together some desserts."

He nodded. "I get it. The last thing you want to do is cook for yourself."

"Right. They say the best tasting food is anything cooked by someone else. I make my living based on that principle. I live by it too, I guess."

"No judgment from me, lady. That's a pretty tough schedule."

We ate in a comfortable silence, the awkwardness permeating the room when I'd first gotten home gone. After a few minutes, Quinn finally spoke. "So last night you said you inherited the diner because of a debt. I've been wondering about that all day."

I nodded and swallowed. "I really shouldn't have said that. I think Janice felt like she owed me, but it's not exactly true."

I weighed my next words carefully. How much was I willing to share with this man I barely knew? How much did I want to know about him? The answer to both questions, I feared, was everything. As a teenager, he'd been the most outgoing, gregarious guy I knew. For me, he'd been a positive light in a world of muddled emotional upheaval. I knew he now battled a darker side, but there were still traces of the boy I remembered in there. Maybe if I opened up to him, he'd open up to me. "Do you want hear the story?"

"Only if you want to tell me."

"I do, but nobody knows this but Ryan and my parents, and I'd like to keep it that way."

"I'm good at keeping secrets, Willow." His forehead furrowed with sincerity. It wasn't hard to imagine the kind of secrets he'd kept during his fifteen years in the military.

"Okay, well, Janice was a bit of a free spirit." He nodded and set his chopsticks down to give me his undivided attention. "She went through a phase where she didn't agree with the direction our country's politics were headed. As a conscientious objector, she exercised what she believed was her right not to fund the government in endeavors she didn't support."

He visibly bristled. "What does that mean?"

"She didn't pay her taxes."

"At all?" Disgust colored the air a russet brown.

Quinn was a patriot. After devoting his life to protecting the same government Janice had disavowed, he was not okay with what she'd done. I didn't actually agree with her decisions either, but Janice was Janice. I loved her regardless.

"Not at all. For about four years."

"What four years was that?"

"The Reagan administration. She was unhappy with the Iran-Contra affair."

He shook his head. His disapproval had the effect of amplifying my own feelings about it. "But see that's not really the way it works."

"I know, but Janice was different," I continued. "Right or wrong, she operated under her own set of rules. She did start paying them again when the first Bush was elected but then began rethinking things again with the Clinton disaster."

Quinn let a tiny smile slip. "I guess she wasn't partial to one party then was she?"

"Nope and she wasn't much of a money manager either. When the taxman came in 2003, she couldn't pay the fines. The diner wasn't doing all that well at the time, and she nearly lost it."

"But?" he asked.

"But someone stepped up and paid them."

His jaw fell. "*You* paid her back taxes? How? You were, what? Eighteen?"

"I had a nice little college fund my grandmother had set aside for me. I used that."

"I can't believe your parents let you do that, Willow. You were the smartest girl I knew. You could've gone to any college you wanted."

I'd heard all of this before. A million times over. And that was from my parents alone. It was one of the reasons I'd never told anyone. "I didn't really give them a say in it. It was my money. That was the real reason I moved out of their house and in with Janice. Unfortunately, for a while, moving in with her only made things worse. They thought I was under her spell or something. It took them a few years to realize that it was my choice and I made the right one."

"I also can't believe *Janice* let you do that."

"She didn't know. She didn't find out until a few years later. Believe me, when she did, she wasn't very happy with me, and Janice was not someone you wanted to piss off."

"That's one of the most generous things I've ever heard. I can't believe you gave up college to help her out."

"She was like a grandmother to me. To me she was no different than family."

Quinn shook his head in awe. "You're one of the most quietly amazing people I've ever met." Red-hot adoration poured out of Quinn, warming me all the way to the tips of my toes. Better than any tea, I wanted to bottle it so I wouldn't forget what it felt like.

"When I was young, I didn't have a lot of friends. For many reasons, I was different than most of the girls in my class. Dorky. Quiet. I loved reading and animals and was happy to play by myself."

Sorrow fell over me, but it wasn't mine. "Don't look so sad, Quinn. I had Ryan and Janice. I had a couple of cousins. And—" I said, pointing a teasing finger at him, "once upon a time, there was this really cute and popular boy who was nice to me and really liked my pie. I even heard that he almost asked me to a dance once."

"The chocolate pie is your pie?"

I laughed. "Surprised?"

"I always thought it was Janice's pie. Wait, wasn't it called Janice's Chocolate Mousse Pie?"

"Yeah. Because she ate every leftover piece of it."

"Hard to believe there were leftovers. How'd you meet Janice anyway?" It wasn't an unusual question.

I pointed at the window above the kitchen sink, which looked out over the backyard. The property line ran along the creek. "I used to walk along the creek and play in the woods on the other side. She had an herb garden over there no one knew about." Even though I'd already divulged a little about Janice's penchant for illegal behavior, I decided not to get into what she'd grown in her little garden. I didn't need to tell him all of my secrets in one day. "It didn't matter that she was so much older than me or that she was even stranger than I was. She taught me life's about quality, not quantity."

"So when she was in trouble, you bailed her out."

"That's what friends do."

"I need friends like that." A faint smile played at his mouth.

"You *have* friends like that."

He looked skeptical. "I did."

A cloud of sapphire settled between us. I fought to ignore it and picked up my chopsticks. "Well, that's my story. What's yours?" I looked at him pointedly, practically daring him to divulge something—anything—about himself.

He chewed slowly and swallowed heavily. I felt his reluctance slip away. "The athletic department lost my paperwork for the physical I'd gotten the summer of my senior year. I had to get it redone or I wouldn't be able to play football that season." His eyes sparkled in a way that grabbed my full attention. "I was in the waiting room of Dr. Parker's office when the first tower fell. I could take you there now and show you the exact spot where I was standing when my life changed. For the next few months, all I could think about was that. All those families destroyed by a few well-orchestrated and barbaric acts. I knew I had to do something."

My eyes watered at the passion in his voice. "So you joined the Army?"

"Right before Christmas. I was already eighteen. My mom couldn't do anything to stop me. I didn't even tell her until Spring Break."

"Well, weren't we a couple of headstrong eighteen-year-olds."

"Like your parents, she was not happy. She chewed my ass until I walked out the door the last time." He laughed at the memory of it.

"It takes a pretty special kid to give up his dreams for such a noble cause."

"I didn't give up my dreams, Willow. I changed them. But it doesn't make me special. Almost everybody who's joined the armed forces since 9/11 can tie their decision to what happened that day. All of my boys were there for the same reason." There was a softness in his eyes when he said 'my boys.' I knew without him telling me that they were his family.

I reached across the table and touched his arm. "Then you were all special. You chose to do something most people can't even imagine. That's incredibly honorable."

He shook his head. "No more honorable than what you did."

I leaned back in my chair, wishing I had an excuse to keep my hand on his arm. "Uhh, not even close to being the same thing. I gave up college for a few years. You risked your life for what you believed in."

He sighed heavily. "I'd still be over there if I could. Coming home isn't what I thought it would be."

"Why?" I asked.

"Maybe it's because I didn't come home on my terms. Or maybe it's because I didn't have anything to come home to. Most of us have two lives. One over here and one over there." He closed his eyes for a second and then continued. "They have wives, kids … something to fight and live for. I didn't … don't. Aside from my mom, my platoon was my only family."

The melancholy blue cloud seemed to pulse between us, growing in intensity until it threatened to engulf us both. "Now, I'm home, living with my mom again, as if you can just erase fifteen years. It's not good for either of us."

"I'm sorry, Quinn."

He'd slipped into an almost trance-like state while he'd been talking—almost as if he had to distance himself from the story to be able to tell it—but in a flash of a second, he was back. He sat up straighter, annoyed and on the verge of angry. "I need to get on with it, I guess."

He tossed his chopsticks on the table, and I flinched at the sound of the chair dragging across the floor. He pulled another beer out of the refrigerator and popped the top off. "If it's okay with you, I'm going to rip out the sink in the big bath before I go."

"Sure."

His heavy boots clomped up each step of the staircase. I shoved my dinner away and laid my head down on the cool tabletop. I banged my head on the wood surface in time with his footsteps and internally argued with the voice whispering the beginnings of a plan in my ear. *He's helping you*, the nagging voice said. Hadn't I just told him he had the kind of friends who would help him out if he needed it? Who had I been talking about? Tim? The thought made me snort.

Was it really such a bad idea? I sat up and took stock of my current state, realizing I felt fine. Mentally, Quinn always worked a number on me, but physically, I felt okay. No nausea. No headache. I looked at my empty glass sitting on the counter where I'd left it. Maybe the tea actually worked. Maybe I'd found a way to combat at least the worst parts of the Dearborn Effect.

That hypothesis would require further testing, and my heart pounded at the prospect of it. I was going to do this.

"Quinn," I yelled, taking the stairs two at a time. "I have an idea."

"Hang on," he yelled back. A few bangs, a plethora of four-letter words, and the unmistakable whoosh of flowing water followed. Way too much flowing water.

I flew around the stairway railing. When I reached the bathroom, I gaped at Quinn, who was lying on the bathroom floor. Water poured out from under the sink as he sputtered and grunted beneath it. The bathroom cabinet hid his head and chest while his lower body extended out into the room. He shifted and his shirt hiked up a little, showing just enough of his abs to get my heart racing for a whole new reason. I gaped openly at him and momentarily forgot about my wet feet.

After a few more curse words and pounds, he groaned. "I'm sorry, Willow. My mind was elsewhere, and I forgot to turn off the valve. Can you get some towels?"

I ran back down the stairs and grabbed as many as I could from my bathroom. When I got back, I found a dry spot for the stack of towels and then got down on all fours to begin mopping up the water around him. When the first towel was soaked through, I leaned over him to reach for another one. He chose that moment to emerge from under the sink and sat up so we were practically nose-to-nose. Wet tendrils stuck to the side of his face, giving him what would have been a sweet, boyish look were it not for the fuzz all over his jaw. The combination was like pouring fuel on my already racing heart. A bead of water fell from his beard and onto his already drenched shirt. It was plastered to him, no longer concealing the broad chest and curved shoulders beneath. My heart officially went up in flames.

"You're all w-w-w-wet," I stammered.

He chuckled, low and throaty. "Yeah."

When I forced my eyes back to his face, I found him carefully watching me as if he was trying to gauge what I was thinking. A small smile pulled at the corners of his mouth.

"Let me help." My voice was breathless. I needed to get a grip. He was just a man.

A very wet, very handsome, very sexy man. But still just a man. It wasn't as if I'd never been around a man before.

I blotted at his face with the dry towel, taking care to get the water out of the fuzzies of his beard. The towel slipped from my fingers, but they remained on his face, brushing lightly against the coarse bristly hair. The feel of them against my fingertips was as if someone defibrillated my already racing heart.

I stared at the lips he'd denied me the night before.

They twitched as desire coiled around us, begging one of us to make the first move.

It would have to be him. After last night, I wouldn't make the first move.

Kiss me, Quinn. Kiss me so I'll know. Don't turn away again.

He sat still as a tree, and I held my breath, waiting for him to bend. My hand slipped from his beard and trailed down his neck. Apparently, it hadn't gotten the memo that we were waiting for Quinn to make the first move.

"Willow?" he muttered.

It was only my name, but it held every question I didn't want him to ask, every doubt I didn't want him to acknowledge.

"No." I wouldn't let him go there.

"You had an idea?"

"No."

"You didn't?" He looked confused. "I thought when you came up the stairs you said you had an idea."

I did? I couldn't think. He'd muddled my mind with his proximity. I racked my brain finally coming up with the answer. *Ahhh, yes.* It was sounding better and better, so I went for it. "Move in with me."

"What?" He scrambled away from me, the spell between us broken, and hit his head on the edge of the cabinet.

Wincing, I sat back on my heels and rubbed my own head. "Ouch. That had to hurt," I said to cover for myself.

He cocked his head at me curiously. "I may have a concussion, but I swear you just asked me to move in with you ..." his voice trailed off.

"Yes, that's what I said. Move in here." He looked at me as if I was speaking Greek. "What you said downstairs got me thinking. If it's not working out at your mom's, then move in here until you're finished working on the house or until you find something better. There's plenty of room."

He looked around at the destroyed bathroom. "No, there's not. I've torn everything apart. I haven't even begun putting it back together."

"The garage apartment is in good shape. No one's stayed out there since I moved to the house a few years ago. It needs a good cleaning, but it has a bathroom and a small kitchen. You don't even have to see me if you don't want to."

He looked wary. "I don't think this is a good idea."

My heart tore apart. Two nights in a row, he'd come close to kissing me but hadn't. I'd all but thrown myself at him. Now, he was turning down my offer to move into an apartment where he wouldn't even have to see me if he didn't want to. To cover my disappointment and shame, I returned to the task of soaking up the water all over the floor. "I understand."

"No, you don't," he said, grabbing my arm. I looked at his hand until he dropped it. "It's not you, Willow. I have zero hesitations when it comes to you."

Yet, you hesitate every time. I nodded to the floor. "It's fine, Quinn. No offense taken."

He sighed, deep and heavy. His gaze fell to the floor. "What can I say to make you understand?" His hands fisted in frustration. "*I* have issues, Willow. Weird, scary issues that I'm trying to work through. I don't want to pull you into them. It wouldn't be fair to make you deal with my problems."

"I've been dealing with weird and scary my whole life, Quinn. I can handle whatever you've got."

He sat quietly, watching me wipe up the water around him. "Are you sure about this?"

I met his gaze. "I'm sure. I've never been more sure." I held my breath as he mulled it over. I didn't know if I could take any more rejection from him.

After a few torturous seconds, he finally spoke. "Okay." That one word changed his entire expression. His emerald eyes were bright and shining and reflected the hope glimmering and fluttering all around us.

Seven

Quinn

I THREW MY DUFFLE BAG onto the bed and it squeaked. Grimacing at it, I sat down on the edge, and it groaned in response.

I looked around. This was Willow's old room. Had the squealing mattress been hers too? I imagined her curled up, her dark hair spread across the pillow. Both times I'd been near her, she'd smelled like vanilla and sugar cookies. I imagined myself lying next to her, pulling her closer, burying my nose in her hair, and getting lost in her delicious scent.

Something inside of me stirred to life, just as it had the night before.

Twice, I'd come so close to kissing her but choked at the last second. Both times, it was clear she'd wanted me to. Her eyes had practically begged me to do it, but I'd somehow managed to pull together all my self-control and resist. I was a broken man. A head case who looked like a lumberjack. Willow was the exact opposite. Levelheaded. Completely put together. She ran her own business and was starting another, for God's sake. She deserved more than a stolen kiss in a deconstructed bathroom.

I had a plan though.

If I were a better man, I'd stop my scheming and back off completely. But I wasn't and I couldn't. Already, it seemed I couldn't stay away from her, and now, she'd given me the best reason not to—I was moving in.

I bounced on the bed and it argued back. I added stopping by Mattress Express to my list of things to do. Sleeping was hard enough without an argumentative mattress. Willow was going to need a new one anyway if she was going to rent this room out eventually. Maybe if this arrangement worked out, she'd let me stay on a long-term basis. With guests around, it wouldn't be a bad idea for her to have a man around in case something needed to be fixed or someone got out of hand.

My mom was my only family, and I'd do anything for her, but we'd both known our current living arrangement was temporary. I was a grown man, and she still treated me like a kid by constantly hovering over me. I didn't need someone to make my bed for me. I didn't want anyone folding my underwear. If I had a beer or two or three or five at the end of the day to help me sleep, I didn't need my mom counting my bottle caps to decide if I'd had too many.

She'd looked a little sad when I'd set my packed bag by the door this morning, but I'd seen a trace of relief in her eyes too. I kept her awake at night. We both knew it was better this way.

I looked at my watch. It was a little after noon. Willow would be at the diner for a few more hours before she came home to get ready for school. After she left again, I would have until seven to get everything I wanted to get done. I jumped up from the bed ready to earn my keep.

I had a few errands to run before I could get started on the afternoon's projects. I needed to go to the lumberyard for some plywood and trim for the little project I wanted to do this afternoon. After that, I needed to hit the hardware store for a nail gun and to pick the owner's brain about the mechanics of plumbing since last night's disaster had proven I didn't know what I was doing. Then I had a few other stops to make. Finishing it all before I needed to clean up for the day was going to be a challenge, but I'd pulled off massive military operations in less time. I would make it work.

I took a quick spin around the apartment. Out of habit, I opened the refrigerator as I passed it. An untouched chocolate mousse pie sat on the top shelf. A folded note welcoming me to my new home sat on top of it.

I smiled at Willow's surprise. I had one for her too.

Willow

WHEN I GOT HOME FROM school, Quinn's truck was parked out back again. It was something I would get used to, I supposed. I raced up the front steps hoping I could sneak to my room without getting caught.

We had plans. Or maybe we didn't. I wasn't entirely sure.

When I'd come home between work and class, I'd found Old Man Hansen's breakfast ticket from Saturday. It was sitting on the kitchen table with the backside facing up.

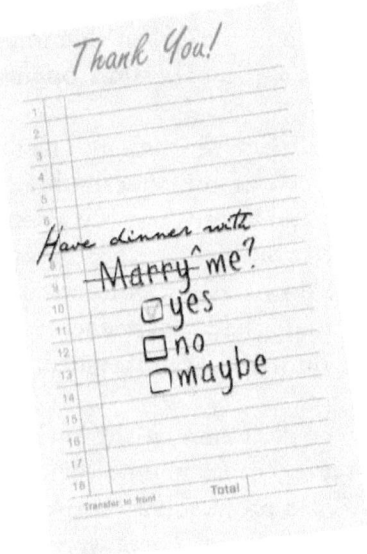

I hadn't even realized Quinn had made off with Ryan's note, but the fact that he had and then hung on to it made me smile. I'd poured myself a tall glass of tea while I considered his offer—though 'considered' was probably not the right word. There was no way I was *not* having dinner with Quinn.

I'd checked the box for yes before grabbing my backpack and heading out the door for class. I shouldn't have even bothered going since I didn't hear a word of the professor's lecture, and this time, I couldn't even blame it on my classmates. My head was in the stars, and it had everything to do with the man in my house.

I opened the door and the smell of the lasagna I'd cooked the night before smacked me in the face. I quietly slipped into the foyer and listened for any noise upstairs. The only sounds I heard came from the back of the house rather than above. There was a couple of thumps and then humming. Was that Quinn? It had to be. The grin on my face spread wider.

I slipped down the hall as quietly as possible, careful to skip all of the squeaky boards I knew by heart. I was nearly to my doorway when he called out. "Willow, is that you?"

I looked down at the coffee stain on my shirt, something that had happened while I was daydreaming during class and sighed. "Yeah. It's me. Where are you?"

He hesitated. "Umm … the kitchen. But can you give me just a few more minutes before you come in? I'm working on a project. It's a surprise."

"Sure," I called out. There were a couple of more thumps, a bang, and then something clattered to the ground. I couldn't imagine what he was working on in there. The kitchen was finished.

In my room, I found a black shirt in the closet and slipped it on. I took a few minutes in front of the mirror to tame my hair and freshen up my makeup. I was trying to keep it simple enough so it didn't look like I was trying to impress him.

It was all an allusion since impressing him was the only thing on my mind.

We'd already had dinner together twice, so the note could only mean one thing—we were going on a real date. It both excited and terrified me. It had been a while since I'd let a man have this kind of effect on me.

When I was satisfied with what I saw, I stepped away from the mirror and backtracked my way down the hall again, purposely hitting the squeaky boards this time to give him a warning I was coming.

"Can I come in now?" I had asked before I took the last few steps. Asking permission to enter my own kitchen seemed kind of odd, but I didn't want to ruin the 'surprise.'

Something hissed in the kitchen. I looked at the stream of light on the floor in front of the doorway for some kind of clue as to what was happening in there. If he were taming a rattlesnake in my kitchen, the front door would be where I headed next.

He muttered a curse before answering, "Okay. I'm ready."

I bounced around the corner with a grin on my face that matched my mood. "Honey, I'm home." I giggled at my silly joke as my eyes darted around the room, taking in the now empty spot where the microwave had been and its new location built into the wall over the stove. It wasn't the biggest surprise, though.

He was.

He almost looked like a different person—not that I'd minded how he'd looked before. The rugged, mountain man thing had worked for him as far as I was concerned. But the new look did too.

My eyes lingered on his face before traveling down the rest of him. He'd shaved the beard, revealing a smooth jaw much more defined than it had been when I'd last seen it. Of course, he'd been eighteen at the time. Still just a kid. Now, he was a man.

He'd dressed up in jeans and a white button-down, which he'd then attempted to protect with Janice's 'Keep your hands off my buns' apron. A spaghetti noodle hung off the ladle in his hand, and there was a tomato red smear across his chest. The nervous energy in the air was the only verification I needed. I'd just walked in on our first official date.

"Nice apron."

He arched an eyebrow at me. "Not exactly manly, is it?"

"Oh, I disagree." Quinn could make a tutu and bunny slippers look manly. The noodle dropped to the floor, and he stooped to pick it up.

"You made us dinner?" The awe in my voice was apparent.

"Spaghetti. Sorry, it's really all I know how to make." He grinned, a lopsided smile that made my heart pitter-patter a little bit faster. "Let's hope what you said about stuff cooked by someone else is true because your lasagna smelled pretty good this morning. It's going to be hard for my spaghetti to compete with it. I probably should have taken a peek in your recipe book." He gestured with the ladle to Janice's recipe book, which still sat on the counter.

"Probably better that you didn't," I said, giggling again. "That was Janice's, not mine."

"She was a good cook, too."

"Oh, she was, but when she wasn't cooking for the public, she put together some really weird stuff." I needed to put the book away before he learned more about Janice than he needed or wanted to know. I also needed to remember I wasn't alone in the house anymore. I couldn't leave things like that sitting around. Having Quinn around was going to be good practice for when I actually opened the bed and breakfast and needed to put on a constant air of normalcy.

"Can I pour you a glass of wine?" he asked. "Tonight's your night to be served."

I thought about the pitcher of foul-tasting tea in the fridge and decided I didn't need it. Quinn's mood was infectious. The only thing bothering my stomach was butterflies, and it was a very welcome feeling. "Allow me," I said, looking for the bottle.

"Nope. That's not the deal, remember? I'm serving you."

"It won't be good if I get used to being spoiled. I can be a real handful."

"I'm counting on it," he said, chuckling. He turned away from me to pour wine into two glasses he must have found in the dining room. They were the good ones, presents from Janice and her husband's marriage.

While I waited, I went over and inspected the microwave. It was perfect, and a surge of excitement ran through me. He was clearly detail oriented and had even added trim around it to match the cabinets. If he put this much effort into the upstairs, it was going to turn out beautifully. "This looks great, by the way. I'm really impressed."

He handed me a glass of wine. "I'm glad. That's what I was going for."

My cheeks flushed and burned. I was glad I'd taken the extra two minutes to change my stained shirt. "Well, mission accomplished."

"I'm sorry I didn't get it painted. I ran out of time and didn't know where the leftover paint was. I kind of felt bad snooping around your house." He looked at me and grinned guiltily. "I mean obviously, I snooped some," he said gesturing to the apron and then dinner simmering on the stove. "But I didn't want to go through all of your things. I thought maybe we could paint it after dinner, though."

"Sure," I said, running my hand across the smooth wood around the new opening. "I really can't tell you how happy this makes me."

"It's the little things, right?"

I smiled and sighed contentedly. "Yeah, it really is." I was already picturing the assembly line of pie building I would put in the new open space.

It had been a long time since someone had done something for no other reason than to put a smile on my face. Ryan was great, but I usually had to beg and bribe him to get him to do anything for me. I also had to be really explicit with my instructions. He would never do anything like this without discussing it with me first. Quinn had done this on his own simply because he knew it would make me happy. From the vibes he projected and the smile on his face, making me happy gave him pleasure. *That* gave me pleasure.

He slid his glass onto the table and untied the apron from around his back. He pulled it off over his head, tossed it onto the counter, and turned to face me. "Little things are good, but sometimes it's the big things, too. Dinner's ready, but I want to take care of something first."

"Something big?" I teased.

"I hope so." In three long strides, he'd closed the space between us. "Drink," he said, nodding to the glass in my hand. I took a sip but didn't take my eyes off him. By anyone's standards, he was acting strangely. When I pulled the glass away from my lips, he took it from me. With his other hand, he grabbed my hand and pulled me across the room until we were standing next to the open space of the counter. He set the glass down and pushed it away from us. Then in a move taking me completely by surprise, he put his hands on my waist and lifted me to set me on the counter, too.

"What are you doing?" I asked, my heart racing in anticipation.

"I want to get this out of the way right now. Otherwise, it will distract me all night." He put his hands on my jean-covered thighs and gently nudged them apart. A surge of electricity shot through my body, leaving me humming. I watched him curiously as he stepped closer and, in a bold move, settled himself between my legs.

Everything about this was weird. There was an air of intimate familiarity between us that wasn't warranted. As if I might find him cooking dinner for me every night. As if it was no big deal he was nestled between my legs, his hips pressing so purposely on the inside of my thighs. Yet, the truth was, we barely knew each other. I knew who I thought he might be based on the boy I'd longed for years ago, but he wasn't that boy anymore. He was a man and a complicated man at that. There were times he seemed so broken and lost that he could barely function, and times when he seemed perfectly fine.

This Quinn—the one who'd positioned himself between my legs—was functioning fine. Warm green eyes looked back at me with lustful determination.

'Trust me,' they seemed to say. A blanket of calm confidence fell over me. I didn't know whether it belonged to him or me, but I didn't care.

Without another word, he took my face in his hands. I barely had time to think, *he's actually going to kiss me this time*, before his lips brushed across mine. They were soft and gentle, but there was nothing timid about his kiss. It was tender but deliberate. My eyelids fluttered closed, and I memorized the moment. A first kiss could never be recreated. You only got one shot at it, and Quinn's lips felt like they belonged on mine. I sighed against his mouth.

He pulled away slightly, and I peeked to find him intently watching my mouth with a slight smile on his face. I hoped he wasn't done because I wanted more. Lots more. Hungry for him, I licked my lips.

Kiss me again. Kiss me more.

He exhaled heavily and his lips parted. A hand slipped around the back of my head and pulled me closer. He ran his tongue across the seam of my lips and I opened for him. His tongue slipped inside and mine welcomed his. He tasted of spaghetti sauce and wine and something else delicious I knew was inherently Quinn.

The electric hum that had been buzzing through my body since he'd first touched me grew more insistent, settling between my legs. I needed to touch more of him. I slid my hands up his chest, more than vaguely aware I liked what they found there. I wanted to linger and explore, but I forced my hands up to his shoulders and around to the back of his neck. I threaded my fingers through his hair; a safer, more appropriate spot for them for a first kiss. His tongue tangled with mine, and I became a broken electrical wire, the end sparking with every whip in the wind. There was nothing safe about it.

It no longer felt like a first kiss. It felt like *the* kiss. The one that grabs on to your heart and shoves you firmly into life-altering, all-consuming infatuation. Quinn's mouth made me dizzy. His touch made me crazy. I never wanted it to end.

But it had to. He pulled away, leaving me needy and breathless. I opened my eyes to find the room bathed in the same crimson desire that had burned behind my closed lids, which confirmed he felt it too.

"Well, that was certainly worth the fifteen year wait, wasn't it?" he said, chuckling.

"Let's do it again." I smiled hopefully.

He laughed. "Oh, we will. I have a feeling it's all I'm going to want to do from now on."

"Mmm." I agreed. I ran my fingers up the back of his head. The short hair bristled against them, and I realized the beard wasn't the only thing he'd trimmed. "You got a haircut today?"

"Another attempt to impress. How'd I do?"

"Done, done, and done," I murmured, still slightly breathless.

"Speaking of done, the garlic bread is probably more than done." He offered me a hand and helped me off the counter. He led me to the table and handed me my glass of wine again.

A few minutes later, he slid a plate in front of me loaded with spaghetti and what appeared to be homemade sauce. A slice of only marginally burned garlic bread topped it off. "Sorry about the bread," he said.

"It was worth it."

"Indeed."

My heart hummed. "Quinn," I said, as he sat down beside me with his plate. "This is truly wonderful. The dinner, the haircut … it's all … wonderful … but I want you to know you didn't have to do it. I wanted to kiss you last night and the night before that. You look amazing, but I liked you the way you were, too."

"I know."

Loving that he didn't pull any punches, I smiled. "Okay. I just want you to know you can be yourself with me."

He shrugged. "I don't think I can be anything else, but I do recognize there's room for improvement here," he said gesturing to himself. "You were staring at my beard last night. I figured it was a good place to start."

"I was wondering what it would feel like against my face."

He chuckled. "I guess you're still wondering then."

"Kind of but this was good, too." *Better than good. Fantastic. Perfect. Amazing.*

"Here's the truth. I'm messed up, Willow."

Not wanting to confirm I already knew that, I kept my expression stoic and let him talk. "I'm not right, but something about you makes me want to be. I watched you look at my beard last night, and I decided you deserved better than that."

"Better than a beard? I really didn't mind it. It kind of worked on you."

"You have your shit together. You own your own business. You're about to open another one. You're sweet and beautiful and funny. Any man interested in you should want to be his best because

116

you deserve it. You're the kind of woman who shouldn't have to settle for someone who's just getting by."

My heart, which had been so full a few minutes before, broke.

"That's why I didn't kiss you last night even though I really wanted to. To be worthy of you, I needed to be more than just getting by."

"But you barely know me, Quinn."

"I know enough, and I know you deserve better than me." He smiled another lopsided grin. "As you can see though, I'm not very good at denying myself what I want."

"And you wanted to kiss me?" I said, a bit giddy.

"I did, and after dinner, I'm going to do it again."

I never ate so fast.

Eight

Willow

"LET'S FINISH THIS TOMORROW," I said when Quinn reached the corner. We were nailing new crown molding to the sheetrock around the top of the bathroom.

He climbed down the ladder and spun around to capture me in his arms. "I agree. It's Saturday night. Let's do something fun." His lips brushed against the hollow just below my ear, and I melted into him.

"You have something in mind, perhaps?" My cheeks flushed pink. "I should probably shower first." Though he didn't seem to mind, I smelled of sweat and dust and hard work.

The last few days had been a dream. That might be the ravings of a lunatic so lost in desire she couldn't see straight, but it wasn't an exaggeration. Since it couldn't possibly last, I gave myself a pass to be quietly and privately crazy about him.

We were head over heels in lust. Every sideways glance seemed to mean something. Every little touch sent a zing through my body. Every beam of color radiating around us made me realize how black and white my life had been before Quinn stepped back into it. Even the colors warning of his darker moods were bearable if only I could touch him.

The tea and his touch seemed to be the best ways to combat the Dearborn Effect. Even just a touch of my hand on his arm seemed to ward away the worst of the nausea, so I touched him a lot. Luckily, he seemed more than okay with it.

Every day, when I came in from work and went upstairs to check on his progress, he would drop whatever he was doing and kiss me. Because he'd missed me, he said. When we could pull ourselves away from each other, I'd invite him down to eat whatever I'd brought back for him for lunch. Afterwards, he would kiss me because he was grateful. When I left to go to school, he'd kiss me for luck. Every single one was better than the last, but it always stopped there. I was supremely happy with where things were headed, but with every touch, I wanted more.

The feeling was mutual. An upside to the curse I lived with was that I didn't have to guess how he felt about me. I could see it in the air around us when he kissed me at the back door each night. He was being the perfect gentleman, but he didn't want to be. It was getting harder and harder to let him walk out the door.

"I do have something in mind. I need to grab a shower too. Meet me in the living room in twenty minutes?"

I let my imagination run. The thought of where the evening might lead made my knees weak. "I can't be fixed up and pretty in twenty minutes."

His teeth grazed along my earlobe. "I'm sure you're beautiful sopping wet. No need to get fixed up tonight, doll. We're not going anywhere."

There was no need to get fixed up *any* night. We never went anywhere. Quinn was a workhorse, preferring to stay in and work on the house to doing anything else. He'd probably work all night if I'd let him. I couldn't complain. After all, the renovation was the reason he was here. While he worked on the house, I worked on giving him more reasons to stay.

"If you'd like to see me sopping wet, I'm sure I can arrange it. You could shower here and save water." I was taking *that* approach with Quinn. It was a little forward, but he seemed to need the encouragement. Hell, I'd endured two days of rejection before his first kiss, but it had been more than worth it. Rejection is easier to take when you know it's unwillingly.

His eyes flashed dark and the room flashed red as he considered what I was suggesting. But as usual, instead of taking me up on it, he let me go and backed his way out of the bathroom. "Twenty minutes. In the living room. Bring your game face."

I rushed through my shower, shaving my legs just in case bringing your game face included smooth legs. I threw my still damp hair into a messy bun on the top of my head and pulled on a t-shirt and yoga pants. Exactly nineteen minutes after I'd received my instructions, I was perched on the couch waiting. Janice's old cuckoo clock ticked the time away. Five minutes passed and then ten. I went to the kitchen to pour myself a glass of wine and snuck a peek out the window. His apartment lights glowed.

Returning to the living room, I settled back in to wait. I reached for a magazine on the coffee table, and his phone, which sat next to it, caught my attention. It was lit up, and the string of missed text messages taunted me. I forced myself to look away, but my curiosity was already piqued. I'd spent almost a week with him and had never even seen him look at his phone. After a few seconds, I succumbed to my curiosity. Was it still an invasion of his privacy if I didn't have to pick it up? I wasn't doing anything wrong, I justified. The messages were right there on the screen for me to read.

Meet us at Tim's if you're interested.

Sorry, we missed you. Tim didn't get him, so there's always next week.

The chances of him coming on my land are nil.

He was last spotted on the reserve.

That was a week ago. He's probably halfway to Canada by now.

Quinn can track him. He's like a trained bloodhound.

The Monster. Every hunter in town was now tripping over his feet trying to get a chance at him. In a matter of a few weeks and after a few more sightings, he'd become a legend even though I suspected only two or three people had actually laid eyes on him. If it had been more, he would've already landed himself on someone's wall. It was reminiscent of a darker time. The thought of it made me more nauseous than Quinn's worst mood.

I wasn't crazy about Quinn going hunting—and I certainly didn't love the idea of him hanging out with Tim—but I couldn't help but feel bad. He'd spent his whole Saturday working on my house even though his friends had apparently invited him to do something more fun.

I jumped at the sound of the back door opening and closing and pushed his phone away guiltily.

"Close your eyes," he called from the back part of the house. Though I couldn't see him, I could feel him. He was twitchy with excitement. It was such a new and different emotion from Quinn that I forgot my guilt.

"They're closed," I said, squeezing my eyes shut.

He was closer when he spoke again. "Okay, open them." When I did, I found the room bathed in a rosy pink that matched Quinn's mood. He was as happy as a kid on Christmas morning. With an arched eyebrow, he held the Clue box up and shook it so the contents rattled inside.

"Where did you get that?" I asked in awe.

"My mom's house. This was mine when I was a kid. I thought we could play. In the name of research, of course."

I'd had other ideas for how we might spend the evening, but this sounded fun, too. Besides, he was so pleased with himself; there was no way I could say no. "Of course."

"Let's do this then," he said sliding off the lid.

I grabbed the stack of hotel and decorating magazines from the top of the coffee table to make room for the game. Quinn reached for his phone, which lit up again as soon as he touched it. He barely glanced at it before tossing it onto a nearby side table.

"It went off while you were gone," I admitted.

He shook his head in frustration. "I don't think they're going to give up."

"Your friends?" I asked, playing dumb.

"Yeah." He sighed.

"Well, they're glad you're back. Can't really blame them."

The cheerful room turned to a dismal gray.

"Okay. So who do you want to be?" I said, trying to change the subject back to the happier subject of the game. "The incredibly brave and cheerful Colonel Mustard?" I held up the yellow game token. "The intensely intelligent and excitable Professor Plum?" I shook the purple one. "Or the dashing though occasionally jealous Mr. Green?"

Quinn's mood improved immediately. "Mr. Green, please," he said, holding out his hand.

I dropped the green game piece into the palm of his hand. "Excellent choice though I had you pegged as a Colonel Mustard."

"Green is one of my favorite colors."

I looked into sparkling emerald eyes. "Mine too."

"Now, let me guess," he said, plucking the red piece from the game board. "You want to be Scarlett."

"How'd you know?"

"She's the movie star. Every girl wants to be Scarlett."

"True. Maybe I should be Ms. White since she never gets any love."

"Nah," he said, placing Scarlett in the middle of the board. "White's too bland for you. Scarlett is vibrant and sexy. You're definitely a Scarlett."

I beamed while setting up the game. Quinn pulled a chair over to sit across from me, and the downside to spending Saturday night playing a board game became immediately clear. There would be no canoodling while we played. No snuggling on the couch or trying to coerce him into breaking all of the unspoken rules he'd made for us. *Unless you can get creative.*

After warning him about what happened to cheaters in my house, I let him select a card from each stack and slide it into the secret pouch. We turned up a suspect card and a room card and immediately knocked out Mr. Green in the Conservatory as a possibility. "Ah-ha! I knew I didn't do it. But you," he said, shaking a finger at me, "are still on my list of shady characters."

I shuffled the remaining cards. "You better not take your eyes off me."

"As if I could." His sly grin brought out my own.

After an hour of pointed accusations and fierce card guarding, the murder was still a mystery and nobody was smiling. "Does it feel like this game will never end?"

I groaned. "It is dragging. Or maybe I am." I'd been up since four that morning. "I tell you what. I will strip naked and run down the street if you'll show me all of your cards," I begged.

Quinn barked out a laugh and threw his cards face up on the board. "Consider the game forfeited. Though you don't need to run through the streets. I'd prefer my own private show."

"Done." I stalked around the coffee table, stopping when I stood directly in front of him. "I win," I said, lifting the hem of my shirt slightly and then letting it drop again. "But for the record, I think it was Scarlet in the living room with the rope. I think Mr. Black tried to use it on her before she turned the tables on him and killed him."

He leaned back in his chair and watched me. "It seems like a plausible theory. A sexy woman with a rope is a dangerous combination."

"Could've been in fun if it hadn't ended in murder. Now, are you ready for your consolation prize?" I raised my shirt a fraction of an inch at a time, giving him a peek of what was to come if he was willing. I had no idea how far he would allow this new game to go, but I knew how far I was willing to take it.

His jaw ticked and his eyes narrowed. The room was awash with the magenta desire that seemed to follow us around these days. I raised my shirt a bit more, and my heart jackhammered in my chest as I watched him for a reaction.

With his eyes still riveted to the skin I'd exposed to him, he wrapped an arm around my waist and pulled me closer. "You're making it very hard for me to be good, Willow."

"I don't want you to be good, Quinn. I want you to touch me."

His hand snaked its way under the hem of my shirt. The pads of his fingers brushed against my bare skin. "Like this?"

"Yes," I breathed.

He pulled my shirt up to expose a little more skin. "You smell and feel so good. I know you'll taste even better." He brushed his lip against my bared stomach. Uttering a sigh, I threw my head back and rocked into him. "But I don't want to rush this," he continued. "It feels important."

I groaned. "I've been good my whole life. With you, I want more. I want to make rash decisions and live in the now. I don't want to think. I want to act on emotion alone." *Yours and mine.* The room was so full of need; I thought we'd choke on it if we didn't do something about it.

I threaded my fingers into his hair and pulled on it gently.

"No mistakes with you," he mumbled as he continued to plant kisses across my stomach. His hand slid up my side and a thumb skimmed the underside of my breast.

Need flooded over me. It took root in my soul, implanting itself so I couldn't tell where mine ended and his began. "I've been dreaming about what you'll feel like, Quinn."

"You dream about me?"

"Yes," I breathed, closing my eyes. "And we do the most amazing things together." I brushed a kiss across his forehead because it was the only place my mouth could reach. "What do you dream about?"

For whatever reason, the question had been a glacial mistake. The air turned icy around us as he pulled away. He was out of the chair before I knew what was happening. "I'm sorry, Willow. I have to go home."

I listened, dumbfounded, to the sound of his retreat. Footsteps clomped down the hall. The back door opened and shut. A key turned in the lock.

Home.

I ran through the house to the kitchen window that looked out at the garage. His truck remained parked in front of it. The lights in the apartment above burned bright. I stood there, watching for any sign of movement; my wall torn down by my own choice. I used every receptor I had to feel Quinn's presence out there. Self-hatred and disappointment filled the air between us.

I waited long enough that I was sure he wasn't going anywhere, and then I wrapped my arms around myself and walked to my room.

I took solace in two things—Quinn wasn't happy about what had just happened and his home was in my backyard.

Nine

Quinn

I HELD THE BOTTLE OF beer in front of my face and watched the condensation slide down the blue Rocky Mountains. I moved my thumb to allow a particularly ambitious drop to make it all the way to the bottom. It held on to the ribbed edge for a few long seconds before dropping onto my chest. Even though I knew it was coming, I still flinched from the cold.

When did you turn into such a pussy, Dearborn? I could practically hear my boys laughing at me.

There was no logical reason I was hanging out alone in my apartment. Willow had offered herself to me on Saturday night, and I'd run away. All because she'd asked about my dreams. She didn't know the dreams were the problem. They stole my nights, filling me with a fear and rage I wouldn't be able to hide from her. It was a side of me I didn't want her to see.

She'd kissed me the next morning and had told me that slow was good too, but I still felt like a jackass. Five days had passed and I still hadn't pulled myself together enough to give her what we both wanted.

My boys would have a field day making fun of me if they knew what a pussy I'd become.

My boys.

I shrugged off the thought as I picked up my phone and reread Bryson and Tim's text messages from earlier in the day. They were going out again Saturday afternoon. I typed out a message and accepted.

Because it went so well the last time you hung out with them.

I ignored the nagging voice predicting another failure. If I was going to find normalcy, I needed to make an effort to do normal things. I had two days to prepare myself.

A flash of lightning outside lit up the room, and I jumped. Maybe we'd be rained out on Saturday. *Not likely. Real men aren't afraid of the rain.*

Jimmy Fallon told a joke on the old box television and canned laughter filled the room. The joke, the punch line—it was all just background noise; static that would eventually make me sleepy if I was lucky. I wasn't really paying attention anyway. I had one thing on my mind. Or rather one person. My mind never seemed to venture too far from Willow. I glanced out the window at the small patch of grass separating her bedroom window from mine.

In a perfect world, I'd be in there with her, our legs entwined with the heavy scent of sex lingering around us, and we'd fall asleep to the sound of the rain beating down on her metal gutters. I shifted on the bed, and it groaned in response. I still hadn't made it to the mattress store. I kept telling myself maybe tomorrow.

But sometimes there isn't a tomorrow.

I shook them out of my head again and crawled out of bed to replenish my now empty beer. Nothing covered the windows so I should probably worry about walking around naked, but Willow's light had been out for more than an hour.

When I was lucky enough to catch some sleep, clothes were out of the question. They were too restrictive, twisting and tightening around me with every toss and turn. Even when I fell asleep in my boxers, I almost always woke up naked. Apparently, even my subconscious hated underwear.

Jimmy announced the guest band, and the audience cheered as I walked to the fridge. I'd had two glasses of wine at dinner with Willow. One more beer and I would be out like a light. For the whole night, I hoped.

I climbed back into bed and Fallon's guest band began their set. One chord and the room flashed brighter than the Afghan sun.

This summer's gonna hurt like a motherfucker.

I wasn't fond of the band, but that particular song had become something of a mantra for us. The boys had sung it at the top of their lungs as we approached the gate. My usual team of Sgt. Derrick Matheny, Cpl. Mark McGraw, Pfc. Donald Jamison was with me, and Pfc. Grant Oliver was driving. Their off-tune voices died off one at a time as we left the safe zone of the wire.

We were the third position in the three-vehicle convoy of thick-skinned vehicles, traveling together on a mission that would have us back well before sunup. No one wanted to miss the celebration the next day. There wouldn't be a cookout or a parade or even the ice-cold chest of beer I dreamed about, but there would be pizza. Real pizza. Or the closest thing to it. The Fourth of July was a reason for excitement no matter what continent you were on.

The heavy vehicle hit a bump, jostling me into Matheny, who didn't even notice. I was on edge and didn't know why. There wasn't anything unusual about what we were doing today. It was a typical operation. Get in, grab the target, and get out. I replayed our directive over in my head as we traveled to our destination.

"Do you think a puppy is an acceptable alternative? Could buy me a few more months." Matheny finally broke the silence. He was thinking about his wife. I didn't know for sure, but I imagined it was hard not to at times like this.

I couldn't see his eyes through his dusty goggles to determine if he was serious, but I knew he wasn't. I'd been side-by-side with this man for almost three years and knew him better than he knew himself. It was all posturing. He was going home in a few weeks, for good this time. Arguing about his future was his way of planning for it. "No," I answered. "She wants a baby. Get her a puppy and you'll have a puppy and a baby. Nobody wants that." I'd seen pictures of his wife. He'd shoved them in my face nearly every day during his first six months in Afghanistan.

"Maybe if I just show up with it," he grumbled.

"Or maybe you use that dick of yours for more than a hand warmer," Grant said from across the truck. He was a cocky bastard who always had something to say. But when we needed it, like now, the comedic relief was appreciated.

"He has a —"

A thunderous roar ripped through the vehicle, tossing us into the air. I had the vague sense of being upside down and then it was roll after roll before the lights went out.

My eyes shot open as another blast rocked through the upturned MRAP. Had I been unconscious? If so, it couldn't have been for more than a few minutes. Comprehension hit me full on, and I was instantly juiced.

We were on fire and under fire.

Something exploded in the distance. Based on the rumble and quake of the vehicle, it should have been louder than it was, but nothing could compete with the ringing in my ears. My eyes adjusted to the darkness. Even through my goggles, there was too much smoke to make out more than vague outlines. I reached my arms out to hunt for Matheny, aware I was happy to find them still attached to my body.

Crawling on my knees, I hit something. "Dearborn, is that you?" Matheny sounded as if he was talking through a tin can, but the sound of my best friend hit me in the chest.

"Yeah, man. Can you walk?" I shouted, assuming he couldn't hear well either.

"I don't think so."

Another flash of light revealed a hole in the side of the armored wall of the vehicle. It was probably my best, if not only, exit strategy at this point. I hoisted Derrick onto my back and pulled us to the opening. There was the pop of gunfire and another explosion in the distance, and we both went facedown into the dirt.

I popped up on my knees again and looked down at my chest, halfway expecting to see it torn open. I was covered with blood, but it wasn't my own. Everything on me hurt, but nothing hurt enough to account for the amount of blood I *saw*.

Had I lost more time? I wasn't sure.

Nothing around me looked as I expected, but what I assumed was enemy gunfire got me moving anyway. There was cover off to the side of the road. My feet flew over the ground, and I couldn't believe how weightless I felt, considering the load on my back. Where were all of the rocks? Dried dusty leaves crunched under my feet.

"Derrick? Derrick?" He didn't answer, but I couldn't hear anything anyway. "Hang in there, my man," I said, hoping the message was received.

I stopped as soon as the brush line hid us. "I'm going back for the others," I said, rolling him off my back and into the brush. I patted his face, but he didn't answer. His eyes stared back at me blankly, and I knew it was too late. I didn't understand. He'd been right there with me a second ago. I was sure of it. My eyes traveled down his body and stopped where the bottom half of him should have been.

My best friend was gone. I looked up at the moon, and rain pelted me in the face. When had it started raining? It hadn't been raining when we loaded up. Had it been raining when we crawled out of the MRAP? I couldn't remember, but there was always about a fifty percent chance of rain at this time of year. I'd never hated Afghanistan more.

Lightning cracked again, followed by a boom of thunder off in the distance. When I looked back down at Derrick, he was gone—not half of him, but all of him—and the ground under my feet wasn't Afghan ground. Relief surged through me though it was immediately chased by a healthy dose of debilitating guilt and then confusion.

I sunk to my knees. My bare skin seemed unnaturally bright against the maple leaves and pine needles covering the ground. I looked up to the sky, thankful for the rain and clouds obscuring the moon and any light it might have cast over the forest.

None of this made sense. I covered my face with my hands and wondered why this kept happening, when it would stop, and which way was home.

Willow

WITHOUT TURNING ON THE LIGHT, I found a glass in the cabinet and filled it with water. A flash of lightning momentarily illuminated the kitchen. That and the rolling grumble of thunder outside pulled me to the window.

I expected the windows over the garage to be dark at this hour. Only the certifiably insane were up at 4:00 AM on a Friday, but Quinn's uncovered windows glowed and flickered, making me wonder if maybe the television was on. More than once, he'd mentioned he didn't sleep well.

Oh, Quinn, you are such a puzzle. My heart flickered and sparked with the lightning outside.

Gaston jumped onto the counter, and I turned on the water for him. Weird cat that he was, he liked to drink directly from the faucet. When he was done, I turned it off again and absentmindedly scratched the top of his head. "You like that don't you, old boy?" I asked.

He purred his answer and watched out the window in quiet consternation.

We stood together at the sink enjoying the early morning together as we did most days. In a few minutes, I would have to get dressed, load my car with the two pots of chicken and dumplings that were today's lunch special, and make the fifty-yard drive to the diner. Any other day I'd simply load my little red wagon and drag it over there, but today, the rain was coming down in sheets.

Gaston hissed suddenly at the window, and I leaned forward to peer out with him. Even through the pouring rain, I could see something move in the brush beyond the creek at the edge of the property. I leaned forward to get a better look.

The land on the other side was mostly undeveloped. It wasn't unusual to look out my window and see a fox or a bobcat or even a family of deer wander over from the national park. Once or twice, I'd even had brown bears rooting through my trashcans. Of course, I'd teased Ryan, but he swore he didn't need my scraps.

Another flash of lightning lit up the yard, and nausea hit me like a freight train. I closed my eyes and tried to fight it off, but it was too much. There was too much darkness. Blue and black and every shade of dismal gray threatened to grab me and pull me into a pit I hadn't seen since Janice had died. Tears of grief welled in my eyes, but they weren't my tears.

Quinn.

There was a shift of movement in the darkness, and Quinn bolted across the creek. My heart skidded to a stop. My breathing went ragged, and my foggy early morning brain jolted awake. I gripped the edge of the counter so I could stay upright. My stomach roiled and twisted, but I couldn't look away. Even through the haze of despair separating us, Quinn was a beautiful sight.

The man wasn't wearing a stitch of clothing. His bare-naked skin practically glowed against the black landscape.

It wasn't something I hadn't seen before. Men frequently ran naked through the woods around Woodland Creek. Two-natureds were common in the area; it was bound to happen from time to time if you knew when and where to look. Most planned ahead though and left a pile or bag of clothes hidden out in the woods to avoid being caught. It had nothing to do with embarrassment. For the two-natureds, being naked was as natural as running on four legs or flying. However, precautions had to be taken. Most humans in the area had no idea, and no one wanted to land themselves in jail for indecency.

Quinn sprinted for the garage, his legs and arms pumping, his body taut with purpose. Naked or not, there was nothing indecent about him. The planes and curves of his body were blurred perfection as he ran. When he reached the stairs at the side of the garage, he hurled himself over the railing and took the stairs two at a time.

My heart beat with such ferocity I thought I might stroke out.

I'd seen him—every glorious inch of him. He couldn't possibly know I was watching, but I could feel his embarrassment as clearly as if he'd whispered it in my ear. It defied his magnificence.

When he closed the door behind him, I sagged against the counter. The relief was his, not mine. Even in my compromised state, I could've watched him run like that all day. Even if the sight of naked Quinn induced vomiting every time I laid eyes on him, it was worth it. Though I had to admit that maybe it was a good thing we hadn't slept together yet. If I threw up all over him the first time he undressed in front of me, things could get awkward.

I dumped out my water, opened the refrigerator door, and poured myself some of Janice's special tea. I gulped down a glass and then poured another before sitting down at the table to get my bearings. His projections were already fainter, my intuitions dimming as he calmed himself down inside his apartment.

I sat in a stupor, my head full of questions and my heart full of doubts. Why was he running naked through the woods? He had no business being out there, especially in his current state of mind, which was another thing I couldn't make sense of. The woods were full of mischief at night. Only a month before, I'd lost a cousin to the dangers out there. I didn't want Quinn running into the wrong types of creatures too.

And why was he making me sick again? We'd had several good days, and I'd decided moving into the garage had done him some good. I'd thought that maybe in his own space he was finding some peace and dealing with his past. I'd allowed his quiet to lull me into thinking again that this was possible, that *we* were possible. But now I found myself just as susceptible to his moods as I had been the first time he came into the diner.

For every step forward, it felt like we took two steps back. And every time I got close to reaching him, he pulled away again. Of one thing I was sure—Quinn was hurting.

I didn't know how or even if I could help him.

SEVERAL HOURS LATER, I WAS feeling much better. Maybe it was the tea. Maybe Quinn had settled down or even gone to sleep. Or it could have been the physical distance between us. The diner seemed to be far enough away from the house that he couldn't reach me. Whatever the reason, I was glad for the reprieve for one very specific reason—I was trying my best not to think about what I'd seen earlier that morning.

I delivered breakfast to table number six and was at the window again just as Ryan hit the bell. "Order up."

"What's on tap for the weekend?" I asked him.

"Wedding stuff," he huffed. "Apparently, throwing a wedding together in six weeks is a challenge."

I gave him a hard look. "So is throwing together a house."

"I know. I'm sorry. I owe you big time."

"Not me. Quinn. He's working his ass off."

"You are, too."

I shook my head. "Not as much as I should be. He won't let me. By the time I get home, he's usually done for the night."

"How's it coming along?" Ryan looked nervous.

"You should come by and see it. He's pretty amazing. Yesterday, he finished tearing apart the last bathroom *and* had dinner on the table when I got home."

He arched an eyebrow at me. "And after dinner?" Since we pretty much discussed every aspect of our lives, Ryan was well aware that Quinn's and my relationship was at a physical standstill.

"And then, as usual, we both ran to our prospective corners." My mind drifted where I didn't want it to. I couldn't help myself. The mere mention of Quinn running brought back the image of him earlier that morning. Toned and buff in my backyard.

Naked.

Ryan shielded his eyes as if the image pained him. "Whoa. But you've clearly seen him naked."

"Get out of my head!" I glared at him. This was the very real and inconvenient downside to having Ryan as a best friend. I grabbed the plate from the window and spun away from him. It was too late, though. I'd already let too much slip.

"Where was he? Looks like I need to come back over and get back in *his* head."

I turned abruptly around again. "Mind your own business, Ryan. I mean it. Something is up with him, but I'm not pushing him. He'll tell me when he's ready."

"Or I can cut through the red tape."

"No tape cutting. I want to hear about it from him, not you."

Ryan looked displeased. "I told you before he was dangerous."

"And then you changed your mind when it suited your purposes." I mocked him, "Gee thanks, Quinn.

You're willing to work on the house and get it ready for my wedding so I don't have to? Awesome. Appreciate it. You're going to hang around Willow every day? I don't trust you, but that sounds great." My hands were shaking, I was so livid.

"Settle down, Willow. I would never let him hang around if I thought for one second he was a threat to you," he growled back at me.

I stood tall and glared fiercely at him. "Yet you did."

"No. I *let* it happen because I picked up every single thing going through his head that night. He was like an open book, and he was so easy to read. He thought *I* was going to hurt you, and he stood between us. *Me*. He wanted to protect you from me." Ryan let out a little laugh.

"Then you know he's not going to hurt me, and you can give him the privacy he deserves," I said defiantly.

He leaned forward so his face filled the entire window. "His heart seems to be in the right place, but what if he can't help it, Willow?"

"Stay out of his head. And stay out of mine." I turned on my heel and stomped away.

"There are no rules when it comes to your safety," he called after me.

I was still fuming when I got to Old Man Hansen's table. The plate clattered on the table and a slice of toast slid off the plate and onto the table. He looked up at me with genuine surprise but didn't say anything. Instead, he picked up the toast and placed it back on the plate. He gave me a rare smile, and I tried my best to return it. I could still feel his eyes on me as I walked away.

Rounding the counter again, I ignored Ryan, who was still watching me through the narrow window. I flipped open my order tablet and flipped through the tickets. When I found Clive's, I ripped it in half and tossed it in the trash. "Your fault," I said over my shoulder. "I practically dumped his breakfast in his lap."

"Stop being so dramatic," he huffed.

The bell over the door rang, and I looked up to see Quinn walking into the diner. "Oh, for the love of God and all that is holy," I muttered. This was not good timing. I was so mad at Ryan I was nearly in tears. My wall was a pile of rubble, and even if I could get it up again, I knew it stood no chance against him. I didn't want Quinn to see me like this. I didn't want to see *him* like this.

The last time I'd seen him, he'd been naked and wet. That was the image still running through my head as he stood in front of me.

"Hi," he said, his voice unsure. "Everything okay?"

"Uhh, yeah," I said, flustered. *You have clothes on so maybe. Or maybe not. Take them off and let's see.*

I heard Ryan laugh behind me, and I whirled on him again. "I'm warning you," I said, pointing a finger at him. "You're not the only one who can play this game. Do you want to know everything Vanessa is feeling right now? Pregnant women are a lot of fun," I said with a healthy amount of sarcasm.

"Nooooo," he said, putting his hands up in surrender. He turned back to the stove and started whistling.

"That's what I thought, you coward." When I turned back to Quinn, he looked thoroughly confused. "Don't mind us. We were arguing about something before you came in, but it's all good now." I smiled to put his mind at ease. I didn't need him flying off the handle right now. "What's up?"

"I came by to ask you about the fixtures in the bathrooms. I took some pictures of what's at the hardware store, but I don't think you're going to like what I found. We may need to order something."

I nodded. Apparently, Ryan wasn't the only one who could read someone like a book. I already knew what was at our local hardware store, and there wasn't anything I wanted there. The fact that Quinn was already getting a feel for what I liked and disliked warmed me in all the right places. "You could have texted them to me."

"Well, I thought about it, but unbelievably, I don't have your phone number."

"Yeah, you do," I said, sheepishly. "I put it in your phone when you left it here by accident." So much had changed in the course of a few weeks.

"Really?"

I shrugged. "I thought you might want to talk sometime."

"You're kind of sneaky, aren't you?"

"I can be." I leaned forward, my forearms on the countertop. "When I want something." I looked up at him and blinked innocently.

He arched an eyebrow at me. His green eyes seemed to sparkle brighter than they should in the fluorescent lighting of the diner. He pressed his hands on the countertop on either side of me and leaned forward slightly. "And you wanted something from me?"

The air between us thrummed with sexual tension. The image of him naked flitted through my mind again. "Just all of you," I said, throwing caution to the wind.

He studied me for a second, his expression suddenly serious. "I'll keep it in mind."

"Please do." I looked down, suddenly nervous. What was I doing? Was I pushing too hard to make this into something more than it was? I didn't want to spoil what seemed to be developing organically between us, but this seemed natural too. "We could go to Louisville," I blurted.

"Louisville?" he asked, confused again.

"For the downstairs bathrooms, I drove to Louisville and bought everything there."

"Support local businesses," Ryan called out from behind me. "They support you."

I whipped around and practically growled at him. I was serious about not wanting him listening to every single thing that was said or thought between Quinn and me. "Mind your own business," I hollered at him. "Or better yet, get your own."

He laughed. "You need me here."

I couldn't argue with him. I was already worried about how I would handle the diner without him if he found a better job, but I was in no mood to concede anything to him. I waved him off and returned my attention to Quinn.

"Why not Cincinnati?" he asked.

I shrugged. "I found what I wanted in Louisville. Why go any further?"

"We could go this afternoon. You don't have school, right?"

"I can't. I can go tomorrow after I get done here, but I'm interviewing a girl this afternoon."

Quinn was suddenly very happy. The entire diner glowed pink. "Someone to help out here?"

"Yes. Some girl Ryan found."

"Another waitress is a great idea. Maybe this will work out and you'll be able to take a day off now and then."

A laugh came from the kitchen. I waved it off. "Ignore him. He's trying to stay on my nerves today. We could make a day of it. Well, an afternoon of it. I can't leave until after I close up tomorrow." The excitement in my voice was unmistakable. The prospect of getting out of town for an afternoon made me almost giddy.

His face fell. "Oh, I can't go tomorrow. I already told the boys ..." He paused and a rainbow of emotion hit me in the gut. "I told Bryson and the guys," he continued, "that I'd go out with them tomorrow afternoon. There are only a few weeks of bow season left, and they've been after me since it started."

A new kind of tension pulsed in waves around me, causing my stomach to flip and tumble. I walked around the bar to where he stood and sat myself down on the closest stool. I waited for the orange and blue waves to recede. When they didn't immediately, I realized he had more on his mind than clearing his calendar for our trip to Louisville.

My position on hunting would never waver, but for the first time in my life, I felt obligated to remain silent. I didn't want to discourage Quinn from spending time with his friends. I didn't know what he was going through exactly, but they had known him longer than I had. They'd been better friends with him and spent more time with him. There was a chance they could reach him and help him before I could.

I watched guiltily as Ryan walked by with two plates to deliver them to a table I was ignoring. Everybody needs friends. I might never be able to support Quinn's hobby, but I could still support him. "We could go Sunday instead," I offered.

Quinn studied the floor as if he still wasn't sure what to do.

"Or next week. There's no rush," I added.

He answered without looking up. "No, let's go Sunday. That will work."

"Hey, Quinn?" His head snapped up, and he finally met my eyes. "Are you okay?" If he kept this up, I was going to need to take a gallon jug of Janice's tea with us just to get through the trip. Or sit on his lap the whole time. Sitting on his lap sounded better.

"Yeah, why?"

"Seemed like I lost you there for a second."

"Oh … yeah. I'm sorry." He cocked his head and really looked at me. "Wait. Are *you* okay?"

Just like that, a whole new buffet of emotions were laid out for me. These I could handle. Unsurprisingly, his concern for me felt good reflecting back at me. "Yeah, I'm fine."

He looked unconvinced. "Is it your stomach again? How's your head?"

"I'm fine. Promise." Ryan walked by again on his way back to the kitchen and gave me a disapproving look. What did he want me to do? Tell Quinn about the mysterious Dearborn Effect? *Not going to happen.* "I do need to get back to work, though."

I started to get up, but Quinn's hands on my shoulders pushed me back down onto the stool. "Okay, but will you please think about going to the doctor. This stomach virus seems to be hanging around."

"I'll think about it." He huffed quietly and then leaned down and gave me a chaste though tender kiss on the lips. "Would you look at that? I feel better already," I said.

"If that's all you need, I've got plenty more where that came from."

"Dr. Quinn, Medicine Man to the rescue."

He laughed hard. "Oh, my God, no. Don't ever make that joke again."

"It was pretty awful, wasn't it?"

"The worst."

We were stalling. He was not ready to go, and I was not ready for him to leave.

The bell over the door rang again. "I better get back to work," I said reluctantly, turning to greet the new customer.

The man was tall with dark exotic looking skin. He breezed through the diner with a gracefulness that didn't match his size, stopping directly in front of Quinn and me. He stuck his hand out in greeting. "You must be Willow. Ryan told me all about you."

I stuck my hand in his. "I'm sorry, but I'm afraid I don't know who you are." I searched his face, wondering if I should know him from somewhere. Gorgeous amber eyes sparkled back at me. They were second to only one.

"I'm Les. I'm early. I hope it's okay."

"Oh!" I said, laughing awkwardly. "You're Leslie! I'm sorry if I seem thrown. I wasn't expecting you until later." *And I was expecting you to be a woman.* I looked down at our still clasped hands as the room turned a murderous red. Quinn did not like this man touching me. I retracted my hand and smiled at Quinn.

"Leslie, this is Quinn. Quinn, this is Leslie. He's the new hire I was telling you about."

"My friends call me Les."

Quinn's eyes narrowed, but he took Leslie's hand, shook it once, and then dropped it as if it was hot. "It's nice to meet you, *Leslie*. I guess I assumed a woman was applying for the job."

Les eyed Quinn and some unspoken threats and silent chest beating were lobbed back and forth before he finally turned to me, dismissing Quinn. "I've waited tables in Columbus for the past six years. Like I said, I know I'm early, but I thought the best kind of interview for this job is a working interview. If you're game, I can help you out with the lunch rush and then we can do the interview afterward if you like what you see."

Despite Quinn bristling beside me, I thought this was a great plan. "Works for me."

Ryan was laughing under his breath again when he strolled around the counter. Unexpectedly, he threw a bottle of syrup at Les, who caught it easily. Ryan clasped Les on the shoulder in the male version of a hug. "Glad you're here, man. We sure can use the help." He turned to Quinn and me. "Les is an old friend of mine, and as *you* can see, Willow, he has cat-like reflexes—something that will surely come in handy if he's going to keep up with you."

I nodded in response to his hidden message and wondered if Les was a panther or some other big cat.

I'd never met one before and had to admit I was a little enamored with the idea.

"He's also an artist," Ryan continued, "and moved here because of the beautiful landscape."

Les smiled at me. "There's certainly no shortage of beautiful sites around here."

Quinn made a choking sound. The room was full of purple rage, and he looked like he might spontaneously combust at any moment. I was glad I'd had a healthy helping of the nasty tea this morning but reached for his hand because it was the best medicine.

"Well, we should probably get to work then," I said, cutting the conversation off. "Ryan, can you get Les an extra apron from the back and an order pad from the office?" I turned to Quinn. "What are you going to do this afternoon?" I asked a little more softly.

His shoulders were back, his chest out. All of this He-man posturing was incredibly sexy and endearing and touched some instinctual need I had inside. "I almost have two rooms ready for paint, so I'll finish them and wait for you to come *home*." I didn't think his emphasis on the last word was for my benefit.

With Les watching, I raised on my tiptoes and gave Quinn a quick kiss on the mouth. "I can't wait. Maybe we can do something fun tonight."

"I'll figure something out." Quinn leaned in and kissed me one more time before heading reluctantly for the door. As I watched him get into his truck through the window, I grinned. There was never a dull moment when Quinn was around. Either I felt the best I ever had—as if there was nothing in the world I couldn't handle—or the worst I ever had. It was like throwing a dart with your eyes closed. You never knew which you were going to get.

"All right, let's get started," I said to Les. "Almost all of our customers are regulars, so you'll be familiar with everyone in no time." I grabbed the full coffee pot from the counter and handed it to him. "I've been a bit neglectful this morning, so if you wouldn't mind making a spin through the room to freshen up mugs, that would be great. Save the old man in the corner for me. I'll deal with him myself."

Les needed no further instruction. I watched him for a moment before taking another pot for myself. I made a beeline for Clive. "I'm sorry about nearly tossing your food in your lap earlier," I said as I refilled his cup. "Breakfast is on me today."

"That's not necessary," he grumbled. "Are you feeling better now? That boy certainly has an effect on you."

I laughed. "Yes, Ryan definitely knows how to push my buttons, but I shouldn't take it out on one of my best customers."

Clive's eyebrows knitted together. "Not *that* boy. The other one."

"Oh, you mean Quinn?" I couldn't stop the grin from spreading across my face.

"One's never stood up for what he believes in and the other's never done anything else. I'm talking about the one who knocks you off your feet and makes you see stars."

My eyes widened, and my jaw went slack. I was torn between wanting to defend my best friend's honor and being flat speechless. Clive had never spoken more than his breakfast order to me.

Before I could make up my mind, he stood up and pushed his chair in. "That's contrived love for you. It's fire and ice. Leaves your head spinning so you don't know which way is up or what's right from wrong. Then again, sometimes love is pure magic and doesn't need any help at all. I guess it remains to be seen what yours is."

He shuffled toward the door, mumbling Janice's name under his breath like it was a curse word. I immediately walked to the kitchen and reversed everything I'd said before. "I changed my mind. I want you to pick someone's brain for me."

I recounted the exceptionally strange conversation I'd had with Clive in case he'd missed it. "So what do you think his connection is to Janice?" I asked. "Do you think they had an affair? She never said anything about him."

Ryan sighed heavily and shook his head. "I don't know. Clive's a tough one for me. He's like Nessie. I only get what he wants me to get, and I'm pretty sure he knows it too. This morning when he came in, he spoke directly to me as if he knew I was listening. Then he went radio silent until just before he walked out the door."

"What did he say?"

"Earlier, he told me thanks again for the hash browns and let me know that Aristotle died yesterday. Then when he was leaving, he said, 'just read the damn books,' but I'm not sure who the message was for."

"He was mumbling Janice's name on the way out the door. I wonder what it means?"

"Who knows?"

"What if he was madly in love with her and ate here every day because he couldn't stay away from her? How romantic is that? I should ask him when he comes in tomorrow. Or maybe we should go see him." My mind raced with the made-up romance I'd already conjured up in my head. Janice had been a widow all of the years I'd known her.

"Or what if he had some crazy vendetta against her and he's going to turn us into toads just for gracing his doorstep? I rather like being a bear. I'm masculine and scary."

I rolled my eyes, but Ryan's steely gaze told me he wasn't going to bend. He wanted no part of visiting Clive. If I wanted to go see him, I'd have to go alone.

"No. You will not."

I huffed in exasperation. "Get out of my head, Ryan."

"Stop giving me a reason to be there."

"When I look at Clive, I see sweet."

"And I see sinister."

"Speaking of sinister," I said, leaning in and pointing at him. "You could have warned me about *Leslie*."

Ryan chuckled. "I don't think you were the one who needed the warning. That boy has it bad for you."

"Did you do that on purpose?" I asked incredulously. "Seriously, don't poke the bear, Ryan. He has enough problems."

Ryan rolled his eyes. "Don't poke the bear. Very funny. More like don't poke the human."

"I think the effect is the same in his case."

"No joke. He was still worked up about Les when he left."

It was so tempting. A part of me wanted to ask what Quinn had been thinking about when he left, but I thought I had a pretty good idea on my own even without Ryan's brain-picking skills. I really didn't want to cross that line with Quinn. It felt wrong. I was keeping enough secrets from him as it was.

"I don't want to know," I said, stomping away from him for the second time that day.

"Okay, but dress up tonight," he called after me.

Ten

Willow

IT WAS LATER THAN I'D hoped when I pulled up to the house. Not because I'd gone by Clive's house like I wanted to—I'd skipped that because I made it a life policy never to completely ignore Ryan's warnings—but because hiring Les meant a ton of paperwork. I'd spent the afternoon filling out tax forms, a reminder of why I preferred to work alone.

Clive's order ticket was on the entry table inside the door, right next to a small, grocery store variety bouquet of flowers. They were bright and cheerful and perfectly out of season. They made me incredibly happy.

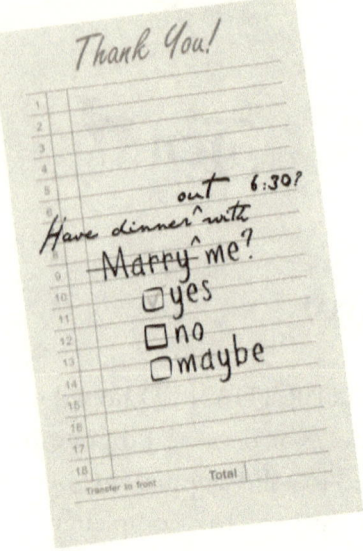

Quinn had erased my yes answer from the time before, but it was still slightly visible. I checked the time on my phone. While I would have loved to hand deliver my answer, there was no time. If I was going to be ready by 6:30, I needed to get moving. He had to know I was going to accept anyway.

Nearly an hour later, I emerged from my room with a few minutes to spare and not a trace of diner smell or grease anywhere on me. I left my hair loose since it was usually in a ponytail and going out in public with Quinn was definitely a first and a special occasion. My heels tapped across the wood floor of the hallway on the way to the kitchen for a tall glass of magic tea.

I rounded the corner and nearly screamed. Quinn was leaning up against the counter with the recipe book in his hand. My heart skidded to a halt. *No.*

He snapped it shut and tossed it on the counter before meeting me in the doorway. "Hey, I'm sorry if I scared you. I didn't mean to."

I looked at the refrigerator and then back at him, not sure which one I wanted more. "It's okay. I just wasn't expecting you yet." A woodsy aftershave that smelled good enough to make me forget my name and my good sense wafted all around me.

"Want me to go away and come back?"

"Not at all." *Yep. It's him. I definitely want him more than the tea.*

He took a step backward, away from me. "You know what? This is all wrong." He spun on his heel, and before I could even register what was happening, the back door clicked shut behind him. I listened, shell-shocked, to his feet thunder across the old wood porch. Then there was only silence. I stood, frozen in disbelief, and wondered what had just happened and if I'd run him off. I looked down at my simple black dress. *That couldn't be it.* I looked at the recipe book on the counter. *That definitely could be it.*

I ran across the room and grabbed it. I opened the closest cabinet door and tossed it inside harder than necessary. Frustrated, I slammed the door shut. I looked at the back door again, unsure of what to do. I took a step to go after him, but the doorbell stopped me. I flew through the house, my smile growing wider the closer I got to the front door, which I threw open to a grinning Quinn.

"Hi."

"Hi," I breathed, noticing for the first time he was also dressed up. When combined with his delicious scent, Quinn in dress pants, a button-down shirt, and fancy leather loafers gave new meaning to the Dearborn Effect.

His eyes traveled down my body, lingering here and there. My body heated under his gaze. "You dressed up," he said, echoing my own thoughts.

"And you smelled up," I responded. His brow quirked in confusion. "I only meant that you smell good."

"Ahh. Well, Eau de Sweat didn't seem appropriate for a night on the town." He gestured behind him. "Should we go?"

"Sure." *Or we could stay.*

"We have reservations."

"We better go then." *Or we could cancel them.* He met my eyes. He was as determined to go as I was to stay. "I'll get my coat."

A few minutes later, he pulled into the parking lot of Pond & Duck. He'd insisted on driving my car because his truck was a dirty mess. Knowing my projects were to blame for it, I'd gladly handed over my keys.

"This is too fancy, Quinn."

"No, it's not. This is where I would have taken you."

"Huh?" I asked somewhat mesmerized by the romantic glow of the lights streaming from the windows of the restaurant.

"If I'd taken you to the fall dance, this is where we would've come for dinner."

Oh.

Once again, I was speechless. Pond & Duck was the nicest restaurant in town. All the high school kids brought their dates here when they wanted to play grown-up. "It's probably been about that long since I've been here, to be honest."

"Well, then you're overdue for a nice dinner."

He unfolded himself out of my tiny car and walked around to open the door for me. With his hand on my back, he led me through the front door. As soon as we were inside and he removed it, the air around me shifted. It was a Friday night, and the restaurant was packed. A few couples stood waiting around the hostess stand. Quinn bypassed them all to ask about our reservation.

The hostess led us through the crowded dining room. The best tables sat along the back wall and looked out over the pond. Quinn's mood plummeted with every step. By the time we sat down, I was thoroughly confused and my head was beginning to ache. I didn't understand where the good mood in the car had gone. I needed to touch him.

The hostess handed us menus and disappeared.

I reached across the table for his hand. As soon he wrapped his around mine, I felt marginally better. "I can tell this is hard for you," I offered.

He squeezed my hand and smiled weakly. "Honestly, it's the way people look at me. It gets to me."

"You mean like they adore you?" I was confused. As we'd walked through the restaurant, plenty of people had recognized him and smiled. No one had looked at him crossly as far as I knew.

His face tightened, and he cleared his throat. "Like I'm something I'm not."

"But you're a hero, Quinn. For most of these people, you're the closest thing to a superhero they'll ever get."

"Trust me. I'm not."

"In our minds, you are. It's nothing to be ashamed of."

"Please don't say that, Willow. Don't be one of *them*, too. I like being around you because you look at me the same way you always did. Like nothing's different."

I shifted in my chair. *It's because I adored you before. Nothing has changed.* "Why don't we go somewhere else?" I offered. "We can pick up some fast food, go home, and have a carpet picnic."

He squeezed my hand again and let go. He leaned back in his chair. "No. We're doing this."

I nodded as the waitress showed up to take our drink orders. I ran through the tea recipe in my head and then browsed quickly through the menu before ordering a cup of chamomile tea, a Moscow Mule, and a water. The waitress looked at me like I was crazy when I ordered a side of baked cinnamon pears as an appetizer.

Quinn's face shone with amusement. "Thirsty much?"

"You have no idea."

"I get it," he said, his eyes suddenly wide. "You're trying to recreate that awful stuff you drink, aren't you? What's it called? Willow's Tea. I saw it in Janice's recipe book."

I was stumped. How could I share the truth with him without completely freaking him out? I didn't want to hide who I was from him any longer than I had to, but I didn't want to scare him off either. My secrets would do that. I feared it would be a long time before I could be completely honest with him, but maybe I could start with something small. Maybe if I gave a little of myself, he'd open up too and explain to me why his heart was so heavy. Maybe he'd explain why he'd been naked in the woods that morning.

"That's exactly what I'm doing. I can't get enough of the vile stuff."

"You said it's medicinal. What does it do for you?"

"I've had a lot of stomach issues recently."

"That virus," he said, nodding. "You really need to go see a doctor."

"The tea actually helps quite a bit." I took a deep breath. "It's not a virus. It's just … I have an extremely sensitive stomach. Being around people can be very difficult for me." *Namely, you.*

"You suffer from anxiety?"

"Sometimes. It depends on what's going on around me." *And how you feel.*

I knew my answers were vague, but there wasn't really another way to answer him honestly. "Anyway, the tea helps soothe my stomach and calm my nerves. It's something Janice came up with when I was in high school."

"You've been drinking this stuff since high school?" he asked in disbelief.

"No. I guess you could say I've been in sort of a relapse." *Since you walked into my life.*

He leaned forward, his eyes earnest, his heart full of sincerity. "I have PTSD." He cleared his throat and shifted uneasily in his chair, and a few of the Quinn puzzle pieces fell into place for me. "They diagnosed me after the …" His already quiet voice trailed off to nothing.

I held my breath, waiting for him to finish his sentence. When it became clear he wasn't going to, I tried to fill the empty air between us. "I'm sorry, Quinn. I really can't imagine."

He shook his head. "But it sounds like you can. I get anxious in places like this, too." He'd assumed it was everyone else in the room who made me anxious rather than my present company. "It's not just the way people look at me. I have triggers, and I'm worried something is going to happen that will trigger a bad reaction. My therapist said I'm a walking time bomb."

"If that is your therapist's clinical diagnosis, then I think you need a new therapist."

He smiled. "Well, I may have paraphrased a little. You know, put it in layman's terms. It's severe enough they forced me into a medical retirement. Obviously, I can't go into the field if my boys can't count on me. So I'm now a washed-up soldier, of no good to anyone at the age of thirty-one. I can't even help on the training side." A full spectrum of grays surrounded our table.

"I'm sorry, Quinn."

"It's just … it's all I know. It's all I've ever done. I'm not sure what to do now. I don't know how to leave it behind."

"You'll find a new reason to move forward. There's something else out there for you. I know it."

"Maybe," he said as our waitress returned with our drinks. When she walked away a few minutes later, she had food orders even though we'd barely glanced at our menus. "Let's talk about something else. How was the new guy this afternoon? Did you hire *Leslie*?"

I smiled at his apparent annoyance with the guy. "Is he the reason why we're here?"

"What do you mean?" he asked with feigned innocence.

"I mean, he was obviously hitting on me this afternoon, and now we're at the nicest restaurant in town. I just wondered if maybe he had something to do with it."

His eyes widened, and then a big grin spread across his face. "Are you really just going to call me out like that?"

"Yep," I said, grinning back at him over the top of the copper mug containing my Moscow Mule. "I really am. If it's the reason we're here, I'm okay with it. I thought it was cute."

"You thought he was cute?"

"No. I think this jealous streak is cute."

"Does it scare you?"

"No. The men in my family are all very possessive. I'm used to it."

He nodded and leaned back in his chair. "Good because I'm afraid there's probably more where that came from."

"You're not sure?"

"I've never done this before, so no, I'm not sure."

"Done what before?" I teased.

"Dated a woman."

I snorted. "I do not believe that for one second, Quinn Dearborn. I know for a fact you've dated women. I remember one pretty clearly."

"She was just a girl. We were kids. This is a new ballgame for me."

My skepticism had to be written all over my face. "Are you really trying to tell me you haven't had a girlfriend during the past fifteen years? How gullible do you think I am?"

"If you hired *Leslie*, I'm hoping you're not gullible at all."

I rolled my eyes. "Don't change the subject." Our waitress set our salads in front of us, but we barely noticed. "Tell me about your last girlfriend."

"She was about five-foot-seven, a hundred pounds sopping wet, and usually on the top of the pyramid at my high school games. I saw her at the 7-Eleven a few days ago, and she has a whole gaggle of kids who look an awful lot like Bryson."

I was starting to get annoyed. After all, I'd freely disclosed my quasi-relationship with Tim. "I do not like liars, Quinn." As soon as the words left my mouth, I immediately regretted them. I wasn't being completely honest with him either. I'd only begun to divulge the depth of my secrets. "I'm sorry ... I have a hard time believing Hannah was your last girlfriend," I backpedaled.

"She was. I swear. I've seen ladies from time to time, but I've had more understandings than relationships, if you know what I mean." He looked sheepish. "My priorities have always been elsewhere."

"Do you regret it?"

He sat taller in his chair. "Never."

"I didn't think so."

"Speaking of suitors," he said. "Did you hire Mr. Exceptional Reflexes or not?" He wasn't going to let this go.

I answered him with a sweet smile and a good teasing. "Yes, I think he's going to be really good for the diner, and he's quite charming, don't you think?"

"Don't poke the bear. He wakes angry."

I giggled. "I said the same thing earlier to Ryan."

"There's no shortage of beautiful sights in Woodland Creek," Quinn mocked. "Did he really think that would work on you?" He narrowed his eyes. "It didn't work on you, right?"

I laughed. "No, it didn't work on me. See, there's this guy, and I kind of only have eyes for him. Turns out he hasn't had a girlfriend in over a decade so he has no idea what he's doing. It's a fun ride, though."

"Willow Ryker, are you saying you'd like to be my girlfriend?"

My face flushed. It hadn't been what I'd been saying at all, but now that he mentioned it, I realized it was exactly what I wanted.

Someday.

After we'd worked through some of his issues and I'd come clean about all of mine.

"You don't have to answer that," he continued. "I'm just giving you a hard time. We're not there yet, but I want to stake my claim before the guy with the pretty eyes and fancy lines tries to steal my girl." He leaned forward and touched my arm. "Because you need to know something about me."

"What?" I asked and then held my breath.

"I'm in like with you, Willow Ryker."

It didn't matter what else happened the rest of the night. I knew I'd still have a smile on my face when I went to bed. "I'm in like with you too, Quinn Dearborn."

I STEPPED INSIDE THE DARK foyer and put my purse on the table by the front door. When I turned,

Quinn was still standing in the open doorway, his massive body backlit by the porch light. "Are you coming in?"

I could vaguely make out the shake of his head. "No, not tonight."

We were both disappointed in his decision. "Are you sure?"

"Yeah. It's late and you have to get up early tomorrow. I have to go to my mom's in the morning to get my hunting gear together."

Excuses. Another example of one step forward and two steps back.

If he wasn't going to come inside, I was going to get one hell of a good night kiss before I let him go. I walked back to the doorway and ran my hands up his chest, a decision that made us both happy. "Tonight wasn't so bad, was it?" I asked.

"Well, I hope not," he murmured. He ran an arm between my dress and coat and pulled me closer to him. "Bad wasn't really what I was going for."

My fingers, ever eager to explore, skirted over his shoulders and around to the back of his neck. "My salad was good. You barely touched your steak, but neither of us flipped out on anyone or made a scene. All in all, I'm declaring it a success." I didn't add that I'd learned a few things about him, confessed a few things myself, and was still glowing because he was 'in like' with me.

"You know the steak just didn't taste good to me. Weird." He shook his head thoughtfully. "But I know this—I had good company tonight. She made it easy."

I raised up on my tiptoes to give him a reason to stay. "I couldn't agree more."

I didn't give him time to argue or overthink it before my mouth was on his. The slide of my lips against his begged him to stop pushing me away. My kiss invited him in and pleaded with him to stay.

He parted his lips and his tongue found mine. They belonged together. My fingers gripped his hair. My body melted into his. I never felt so whole and at peace as when I was touching him.

Don't stop.

His breath was ragged as he stole mine. The hand around my waist belied his determination to leave, gripping me instead as if he would never let go. My body buzzed and hummed in response to his touch.

I am so in like with you, Quinn Dearborn. So, so in like.

Far too soon, he pulled away with a determined sigh. "I wish I could take you with me tomorrow. You make everything better, Willow. You make me feel like anything is possible."

I took a step backward, my legs still wobbly from my favorite part of the Dearborn Effect. "What are you worried about?"

He looked at the ground instead of me. "I should've just canceled and gone to Louisville with you. It's not as if we even hang out together while we're out there. Hunting is not a group sport. We each have our own tree stand. It doesn't matter whether I'm there or not."

I'd hoped sending him out with his friends was a good thing. I was supremely disappointed they wouldn't all be hunkered down together having quality guy time while they waited for the mythical beast to wander by. It was only for the betterment of

Quinn's mental psyche that I could let go of my hatred for the 'sport.' I didn't see how hanging out in a tree stand all by himself was going to help him, but I didn't want to change his plans now. I planned to check in with my family. Since Quinn had stepped into my life, I hadn't spent any time with them. Taking him with me was not an option.

"Won't you guys go out afterward? Dinner? Drinks?" I asked hopefully. "The guys usually come into the diner to talk about their conquests. Since we'll be closed, I assume they'll have some sort of backup plan."

"I'm sure you're right. I just wish I could skip straight to that part. Beer drinking, I can handle. The rest, I'm not sure about."

"Why don't you come in and we'll talk about it?"

He laughed. "We both know if I come in, we won't do any talking."

"Do you think I have no self-control at all?" I teased. "I can keep my hands off you. I promise." I wasn't sure it was entirely true, but I could certainly try.

"It's not *your* self-control that concerns me." He looked at the floor again and then turned sullen. "I guess I'm worried about being out there with nothing but my own head to keep me company." His gaze traveled up the stairs. "Working on the house has been good for me because I'm busy and thinking about what I'm doing ... and you. I spend a lot of time thinking about you."

"If you have a bad feeling about it, don't go." It wasn't the encouragement he needed, but his ominous mood made me wary. If he was walking into it with misgivings, I was worried too.

"I already told them I was coming. I don't go back on my word."

I nodded, knowing his word was more important than anything was. His unwavering integrity was part of what made him who he was, and one day, I hoped that the promises he would keep would be for me. "Okay, well, promise me one thing." I stepped back to him and put my hand on the side of his face. His shadowed eyes met mine. "When you're in the tree stand, if things get to be too much, close your eyes and imagine I'm right there with you. Just think about me, and I'll be there to make it better."

I kissed him one more time before I let him go.

Eleven

Quinn

A FRONT CAME THROUGH DURING the night. The air was crisper and colder than before. It was a perfect day for deer hunting.

If you were somebody else.

From the start, my heart and my mind weren't in it. It was exactly what I'd feared—too much quiet in which to think. Too much time in which to remember. Sitting in rural Indiana with only the sounds of nature to keep me company felt all too familiar.

Different geography, but still just a waiting game.

Hours had passed, and I was jumpy and distracted. My knee bounced hard enough to bring down the entire structure. I'd expected the tree stands we'd used as kids, but these were fancy. Tim had said there were eight of the elevated blinds distributed over the 80-acre property. He had too much money, I'd decided. There was even a portable, gas-powered heater in the corner though I hadn't bothered to turn it on. It was cold but not unbearable.

We were all spread out, each on our own separate mission. I hadn't seen or heard anything from the other guys since Tim had unlocked the gate and assigned us our positions, mine being in the remotest corner of the property.

My equipment was outdated. Nothing like the modern weapons they had. My bow had no sight on it, leaving me with nothing but a pair of good old-fashioned binoculars and my own eyes to watch for my target. I'd worked under worse conditions.

I pulled the binoculars to my eyes and peered out through one of the screened windows, looking for any movement. It was one pine after another for as far as I could see.

The enemy was hidden and quiet. Evasive fucker that he was. My patience was wearing thin. I wanted to unfold myself out of this coffin in the sky and go get a beer somewhere. I needed something to take off the edge.

I was scoping out the thickest portion of the forest when the first gunshot sent me scrambling. Equipment flew around the small enclosure. I covered my head with my arms but still took a few hits, one to the face.

I was too high and too exposed in the blind. I threw myself through the small doorway, diving for the ground six or seven feet below. My body bounced and rolled across the rocky terrain.

I'd heard only the single shot, but I didn't waste time getting my bearings, crawling instead with one leg dragging behind me. My eyes were set on the area I'd just canvased. It would be a good spot to lay low and wait it out.

Once there, I hunkered down and assessed the damage. I'd lost my weapon, and I was reasonably certain I had at least one broken bone. I tried to stand just to verify my suspicions and was disappointed to discover I was right. My ankle was broken. It would be the second time for this ankle.

Something warm trickled down the side of my face. My hand instinctively found the cut on my forehead and found it to be sticky. Based on the amount of blood alone, I needed some butterfly stitches. I emptied the pockets of my jacket in hopes I might find a first-aid kit, but then coughed out a laugh. I was hunting deer, not terrorists. I hadn't packed for injuries.

Another shot rang out and I went flat again. Covering myself with leaves under a low-lying pine, I prepared once again to wait but blacked out instead.

MY HAND WAS WET. IT was the first thing to come to mind as I woke up. The sky was darkening and my hand was wet.

"Dearborn," a voice called.

I puffed out a breath. Whoever it was, he was too far away to help anyway.

Something nudged my hand hard enough to move it, and my eyes flew open. I blinked as they adjusted to the darkness. Two large brown eyes blinked back at me.

She's beautiful.

She was nestled into my side, almost on top of me, in fact. Her warmth seeping into me even as the cold ground fought against her presence. Something scurried through the underbrush nearby, and her head turned suddenly. She snorted and her large ears perked up, intent on not missing a thing.

After a few minutes, she turned back to me again and met my eyes. I wasn't dreaming. The doe was the most beautiful, graceful creature I'd ever seen, and I was instantly in love with her big brown eyes.

I couldn't imagine any man who'd come into the forest with the intention I had—the intention of killing one of her kind—ending up in the position in which I found myself.

She stuck her wet nose in my hand and snorted again, this time just for me.

I smiled despite the pain. "What are you doing here, beautiful girl? You're going to find yourself in a whole world of trouble if you stick around." She rewarded me with a lick to my palm.

"Dearborn." The voice was closer now.

"They aren't looking for you, but you'd better get out of here just the same."

She blinked slowly, unmoved by the situation.

"Dearborn."

Suddenly, she let out a bleat and bolted up on four legs. With one last long look, she was gone.

WHEN I WOKE UP AGAIN, there was no warm body lying next to me and no reassuring nose pressing into the palm of my hand.

The room was artificially cold and a less than melodic beep rang in my ear.

"Mr. Dearborn has a broken ankle, but I'm more worried about the possibility of a head injury."

"First Sergeant Dearborn," a melodic but mighty voice corrected.

I loved that voice.

I have a head injury? I tried to focus on the ceiling because it seemed like an appropriate test.

"He's awake," Willow said, rushing to my side. Her hands were in a hundred places at once as if she needed to make sure I still had all my parts. "Doctor, he's awake."

Another shadow fell over me, this one larger and not as welcome. "That was quite a tumble you took, *Sergeant* Dearborn."

Based on his tone alone, I didn't feel any need to answer.

A tumble? I didn't remember it that way.

"I'm going to do a quick check of your vitals, and then I'll let you rest for a while."

I opened my mouth to speak but found it was filled with invisible cotton.

Willow leaned down and whispered in my ear. "I'm so glad you're okay. You really scared me, Quinn." Her lips brushed across my forehead and then she laid the side of her face against the side of mine. "I'm going to step outside so he can do his examination. But I promise I'm not going anywhere." She ran her fingers down my arm and across the top of my hand before stepping reluctantly toward the door.

"It's after visiting hours, Ms. Ryker, but you can come back tomorrow after nine."

"The hell," I said, finally finding my voice. "I'm going home." I threw my legs over the side of the bed and attempted to stand. My head felt like it split wide open and my ankle throbbed. Standing suddenly didn't seem like such a good idea.

"You have a concussion, Mr. Dearborn. Please lay back down."

"People walk out of hospitals with concussions all of the time. I once drove an MRAP over one hundred and fifty miles with one. I think I can manage being driven home by my girlfriend."

Willow took a step forward, her face glowing. "Please lay down, Quinn. I promise I'll bust you out of here as soon as they let me."

The disgruntled doctor shook his head in disagreement and then looked at the clipboard in his hand. "You won't be going home tonight, Mr. Dearborn. Based on the dilation of your eyes, you hit your head pretty hard. You're also running a fever, and we haven't put a cast on your ankle yet. When did you get the scar on your forehead?"

I ran a finger across my forehead until I found the barely raised line. "Early July."

"Well, it healed nicely. It's barely detectable now."

"Yes."

"It looks like your ankle is broken, but we'll know for sure after the X-ray. The nurses will come to get you in a few minutes."

"You better tell them to hurry because I'm headed home. I'm not sleeping here tonight, and I have plans tomorrow."

"Quinn, please cooperate. Louisville can wait," Willow said before slipping through the curtain.

The doctor's expression softened. He stepped up to the bed and inserted the ends of the stethoscope in his ears. "Let's see what we can do to get you out of here."

Several hours later, the doctor had relented, and we were on our way home. My head had checked out with only a minor concussion and the fractured ankle would heal in about six weeks. I could wait until Monday to get a cast. "I was thinking you could sleep in the house tonight," Willow said. "I'm not sure you can manage the garage stairs." She glanced down at the boot on my foot. "And I'd feel better if I can keep an eye on you."

"I'll be fine out there," I promised. "Who found me?"

"Tim and Bryson. I have your phone in my purse, by the way. It's been blowing up with messages from them. They were at the hospital but left after I got there. Bryson said he'd check on you tomorrow."

I looked out the window at the blackened woods along the highway leading to Willow's house. "Did they tell you what happened?"

"They weren't exactly sure but said there was some poacher firing shots and you fell out of the deer blind. What happened out there, Quinn?"

I slumped against the car window. "It went exactly as I thought it would. It was too quiet. My head was a mess. I probably could have kept it together, but the gunshots messed with my head somehow. It's bow season. No one should've been hunting with a gun."

"Who knows? Maybe the poacher was hunting something else. It's gun season for fox."

"Yeah."

We were silent for a few minutes. "Quinn?" she asked as she pulled into the driveway and stopped the car.

"Hmm." I was suddenly completely and utterly exhausted.

She turned in her seat to face me. "You really scared me today. While you were sleeping, I was thinking that maybe hunting isn't the best idea for you right now. I'm not trying to talk you out of doing it forever. Though, if you decide you're done with it, that would be okay with me," she added laughing. "But maybe for at least the time being, you're better off not venturing out into the wilderness with a bunch of weapons strapped to you. After today, I'm scared you're really going to hurt yourself."

Or someone else. She didn't say it, but she didn't have to. I'd already thought of it.

I had a pretty decent idea of what had happened. The gunshots had been a trigger, one that made perfect sense. One second, I had a firm grip on reality, and the next, I was lost somewhere in the past, unsure if I was in Indiana or Afghanistan. Kind of like when I was sleepwalking.

"I agree. I won't go out there again."

She sighed in relief. "Let's get you to bed. Are you sure you don't want to sleep in the house? You can have my room and I'll sleep on the couch." She looked hopeful.

"There's no way I'm taking your bed. What kind of knight in shining armor takes the damsel's bed?"

"Umm. One who is in distress?"

An irrational piece of my bruised psyche bristled. I didn't like her thinking of me as being in distress. I should be taking care of her, not the other way around.

I opened the car door and hoisted myself out of it. I hobbled my way over to the steps with Willow right on my tail. The boot banged against every step until I made it to the landing and pushed my door open. I thumped my way across the room and sat down on my bed with a huff.

Willow's eyes were wide. "I don't understand why you're mad at me. What did I say?"

"Nothing but the truth."

"It was a joke. I don't really think you're in distress."

"You'd be right if you did."

"Quinn," she said wringing her hands. "Please don't push me away. I can feel you closing down on me. Please don't. I only want to help you."

My rage flared again. I knew it wasn't fair, but I couldn't stop myself. "Don't you get it? I don't want you to help me, and I don't want to be another one of your projects to make you feel good about yourself. Just another one of Willow's charity cases."

She backed slowly toward the door, clutching her stomach. "It's not like that. It's not like that at all." She doubled over. "I have to go. You're hurting me, Quinn."

I squeezed my eyes shut and listened to the door slam behind her. She had every right to be angry with me. It had been unfair and undeserved. I wasn't even sure where the anger had come from. One second, I was fine. The next, I was a raging lunatic. I threw myself back on the bed. However mad she was at me, I was madder at myself.

Unbelievably, sleep came right away. I dreamed of gunshots and running through the woods. I dreamed of does with wet noses and Willow.

Mostly, I dreamed of Willow.

Twelve

Willow

"ORDER UP." RYAN RANG THE bell and slid a plate through the window.

I stomped my way to the back of the restaurant. Stomping had pretty much been my only mode of transportation all day. I didn't have to worry about anyone else's emotions playing with my mind. My own were causing enough havoc.

"Geez, Willow. You're running off the customers."

"I am not."

"No, you really are." I looked at him sideways and glared. "Here," he said, sliding an order ticket at me. "Maybe this will help."

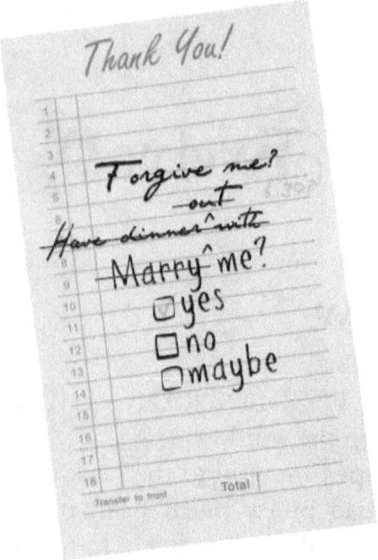

"I take it this isn't our thing anymore. I always knew somebody would steal you away eventually, and he even took my note, too."

I read it again and the floodgates opened ... again. Silent tears streamed down my face.

"Oh, for crying out loud, Willow. Go talk to him. Clearly, he wants to talk to you."

"I'm working," I sobbed.

"Les and I can handle the place for thirty minutes. Walk your sad ass across the yard and talk to him. Fuck him while you're at it. It will do you both wonders."

"Ryan!" *If only it were that easy.* For the first time, I'd began to understand why Quinn was so hesitant to take our relationship to the next level. Aside from the fact that we'd only been seeing each other for a couple of weeks, he hadn't been exaggerating when he'd said his head was a mess. And he couldn't possibly comprehend exactly what dragging me into his problems meant. If he wasn't ready for a relationship, we would both suffer. And I would suffer enough for the both of us.

"I vote you don't do that," Les said, bringing me out of my own head and back to the dilemma at hand. "Save yourself, pretty woman. Save yourself for me."

I rolled my eyes and pointed at the plate still sitting under the warmer. "Will you please deliver this to Clive Hansen at table six?"

Les' come-ons hadn't let up during his two days working at the diner. To the contrary, they were getting more and more bold. If he kept it up, I was going to start worrying about his safety. Quinn would pound him into the ground if he heard some of the garbage that came out of his mouth.

If he still wants you. If I still wanted him.

Did I?

I'd known what I was getting into. The rainbow surrounding him was an emotional billboard. I couldn't really claim to be surprised he'd exploded last night. It had been a long time coming. I just hadn't expected him to direct it at me.

"Come on, Willow. Cut the guy some slack," Ryan said. "You know how it works. You lash out at those you love the most."

"He doesn't love me."

"How could he not?"

"You're crazy."

"And you're stubborn. Go see him."

"Fine." I reached around behind my back and untied my apron. I threw it through the window at Ryan and swooped up the note.

"You'll need this," he said, tossing a pen at me.

I paused momentarily to consider the pen I held in one hand and the note I held in the other and decided I already knew my answer. I checked the box for the third time and slid out the back door so no one could distract me. It would only take one person asking for something for me to lose my nerve under the guise of being distracted.

I crossed the yard, making a beeline for the garage, and ran up the steps. I knocked on the door and waited. Nothing. One more time and still nothing.

I made the trip down the stairs. His truck was sitting in its usual spot, but it wasn't as if he could drive it with the boot on his foot. I ran across the yard and threw the back door open. I was nearly to the front door, thinking he might be relaxing on the front porch, when I heard banging coming from the second floor.

He was on a ladder, installing a ceiling fan in the only finished bedroom.

"What are you doing?" My voice echoed my incredulousness. "You shouldn't be on a ladder. You're going to kill yourself."

He grunted a response, and my gaze fell on his injured left foot. "Where's your boot?"

"Somewhere in the garage," he said with a shrug.

"You have to wear it for six weeks."

"It doesn't hurt today."

I walked a circle around the ladder, eyeballing his tennis shoes. "What do you mean, it doesn't hurt?"

"When I woke up this morning, I tested it out. It felt fine, so I took off the boot. Weird, I know, but

I'm certainly not complaining. I can get a lot more done without that thing on my foot."

"But that's not possible. I saw the X-ray. You had a hairline fracture right there." I walked closer and pointed at his foot. "Seriously, I saw it."

He shrugged as if it was no big deal. "I must have really unphotogenic bones because this has been happening my whole life. I can't tell how many times I've been misdiagnosed." As if it finally hit him I was actually there, he turned bashful on me. "Umm, Willow—"

"I have something for you," I interrupted. I thrust the note at him.

He took it and smiled while climbing down the ladder. "Yes?"

"Yes."

He folded the note and then pulled out his wallet and stuffed it inside. "I don't deserve it," he said, looking at me with downcast eyes.

"Of course you do."

He scrubbed his hand down his face in apparent frustration. The effect was to scrub the room of its color, shading everything gray. "But I was so mean to you and it wasn't even the truth. It's not that I don't want your help. It's that I don't want to *need* your help."

"I imagine it's a new concept for you—needing help—but Quinn, you are not just another charity case. You are helping me just as much as I am helping you." I raised my arms up and turned in a slow circle. "Look at what you've done for me, and I haven't paid you a dime."

"And I wouldn't take your money if you tried. This is good therapy."

"But is it your only therapy?"

I reached for his arm. "Even though you've done this for me and I owe you more than I could ever repay, *my* need to help you has nothing to do with this room. I wanted you to stay in the house with me last night because I need you close to me. Even when you're too much for me, I need you close. When I lose you in a fog of despair, I need to feel the moment you emerge on the other side.

"I want to know what makes your heart ache, Quinn. I want you to tell me about every bruise and crack. I want you to name your demons so I can be beside you when you slay them. I want to *be* your therapy, Quinn."

His arms came around me, and he pulled me against him, his grip so tight I could barely breathe. "Come away with me. Let's go to Louisville today like we planned. It will be good for us to escape for a little while."

"Are you sure you're well enough?"

He shifted on his feet as if testing them out. "Barely any pain at all."

"And your head?"

"Perfectly fine."

"I have to finish my shift."

Somehow, his arms managed to squeeze me even tighter. "But that means I'll have to let you go."

"I'll come back. I promise."

He pulled away slightly, tipped my chin up, and brushed his lips against mine. His kiss was apologetic and hopeful. "If you must, but hurry back."

I skipped my way back across the yard, much lighter on my feet than I had been a few minutes before. "Get everything all patched up?" Ryan asked when I came in through the back door.

"Yes," I said, grabbing the coffee pot to make the rounds. The thank you I sent him was a non-verbal one garnering me a nod and a knowing look.

I bounced through the diner filling cups to their brims because it was how I felt—filled to the brim. While I'd done most of the talking, he'd said what I needed to hear. I knew he regretted the things he'd said as surely as I knew the forgiveness pouring out of my heart.

Someday soon, I hoped my confessions would mean something too.

I approached Old Man Hansen with an unusually bright smile, even for me.

He held his hand over the cup to stop me from filling it. "Well, you're certainly in a better mood now. I assume the boy has something to do with all of these ups and downs." He scooted his chair back to get up.

I smiled sweetly, not about to let a grouchy old man—even one who might have been in love with Janice at one time—dampen my new good mood. I'd earned it. "Relationships are rarely easy, Mr. Hansen."

He grabbed the cane he'd propped against the wall. "Especially if they're harder than they need to be. If you'd read the books, it would help your friend in the back, too." He grumbled a few more unintelligible words and then muttered his goodbye.

"He's a weird, grouchy old man," Ryan said when I got to the back again. "Don't go getting any ideas."

"I feel like he's trying to tell me something. He keeps talking about books and you. Maybe we could have a real conversation if there weren't other people around."

"Or maybe he would slice you up into Willow stew."

"Sick. I know you don't believe that anyway. You're the one who made hash browns for his dog."

"I'm not impervious to human—or inhuman—suffering, Willow. His dog was getting ready to die, and for some reason, he let me know it. That dog loved my hash browns, by the way." Ryan slid another plate under the warmer. "Speaking of human and inhuman suffering, are you and Romeo still leaving town this afternoon?"

"Yes."

He gave me a sly smile. "Good. Enjoy yourself."

I AWOKE WITH A START and sat straight up on the seat of Quinn's truck. I looked out the window at the surrounding skyline. "Wait. Where are we?"

He laughed from behind the wheel. "Your hair is going every which way. Did you have a nice nap?"

I flipped the visor down and found the mirror to be cracked. Doing my best, I smoothed my hair back into place. "I did. I guess I needed it, huh? How long did I sleep?"

"Long enough to surprise you. Did you sleep at all last night?"

I shook my head sheepishly. "No, not much."

He gripped the wheel a little tighter and grimaced. "That's my fault, and I'm sorry." He was still beating himself up over the night before. There was enough azure melancholy and guilt in the car to wash us both away.

"Stop. We're all good now." I squinted out the window, wanting to change the subject before his bad mood worsened and made me ill. I'd downed as much tea as I could before we'd left. On the road with Quinn was not the time to get sick. There was no refuge to be found in his truck. "Are we in Cincinnati?"

"Yep."

"Did I really sleep all the way through Louisville?"

"You fell asleep not long before we went through there."

"And you thought you'd keep driving until I woke up?" I asked. He'd taken us twice as far as we needed to go.

"Nope. I couldn't believe my luck when you fell asleep. It couldn't have worked out more perfectly."

I gazed out the window longingly. "But the store I like is in Louisville."

"Lowes?" he asked with a chuckle. "Cincinnati has a few of those as well."

"Oh, really? That's good," I said, nestling back into the seat. A spring poked me in the back and I remembered why I'd slumped over in the first place. Quinn's truck was a heap, but since we were shopping for some big items, it hadn't made sense to bring my little car.

"You don't get out of Woodland Creek much, do you?" A playful smirk pulled at the corner of his mouth.

"Not really. Never have much of a reason to."

"You know there's an entire world out there. Look, just today you've been in three states."

"Right, but I missed one of them," I said, yawning. "I can't believe I slept the whole trip. I'm sorry I'm such bad company."

"I like watching you sleep."

"That's so romantic and creepy."

Quinn laughed as he exited the highway, taking us right into the heart of downtown.

"So what are we doing in Cincinnati?"

"We're almost there. Don't ruin the surprise."

We rode in silence. With each passing block, Quinn's level of excitement rose, tinting the truck a tangerine color that gave me the warm fuzzies. After a few more turns, he pulled up outside an old brick building with something of a theater-style entry. The sign inset into the brick façade boasted quite auspiciously that the building was some sort of museum.

"A museum?" I asked, thoroughly confused.

"I decided we need toilets, faucets, and culture. This place has it all."

"And a valet," I said as my door opened.

"Ma'am," the tight-faced valet said. "Checking in?"

"Quinn?" I turned to ask him, but he was already outside the car. "I'm not sure what we're doing. You'll have to ask the man in charge," I answered as I hopped out of the truck and let the valet shut the door behind me.

Quinn and the valet spoke in hushed tones to each other while I stood patiently waiting on the sidewalk by the front door. Finally, the valet nodded and took the keys from Quinn. As he walked around it, he sized up the truck and found it obviously lacking. "Feel free to front park it," Quinn said with a smirk.

"You're terrible," I said as we walked inside.

"Did you see the way that jackass was looking at my truck?"

"He doesn't know you've had it since high school."

"Actually, I think he does and that's the problem."

"Forget him," I said, looking around. The outside of the building had all of the adornments of a historic landmark, but the inside was completely new and modern. A cluster of couches and chairs sat in a big open area to the left of the large heavy front doors.

"Why don't you sit while I go take care of something?" Quinn walked away from me without even a hint of a limp. The fact he'd gone from relegated to wearing a boot for six weeks to walking again perfectly within less than twenty-four hours was some kind of miracle.

He disappeared around a corner, and I did as instructed, taking a seat on a white leather sofa. It was tufted and sleek, and I suddenly felt as unsophisticated as our mode of transportation. I looked down at my jeans and wondered again why we were here. There was a restaurant to my right, but I was sure they had a dress code. A woman in a mink stole and the skinniest high heels I'd ever seen clipped her way out of the restaurant and past me, confirming those suspicions. The Metro made Pond & Duck look like Burger King.

"We're all set. Ready?" Quinn asked, sneaking up behind me.

"Ready for what?" I asked. "If you were planning on having dinner here, I'm afraid we're underdressed."

He smiled a simple, reassuring smile. "We can talk about it later. Come with me." He held his hand out to help me up, and we walked hand-in-hand to the elevators. The tiles around the elevator doors were an intricate mosaic of light blues, pinks, and lavenders—all of my favorite Quinn colors. The good colors. Unfortunately, they didn't reflect Quinn's mood. Not exactly anyway. He was a rainbow of conflict as he shifted his weight from one foot to the other. Jumpy and nervous, yellow mixed in with the good colors. I squeezed his hand, thinking how completely odd it was that I'd come to accept this as a new form of normal. He was spectacularly beautiful and sexy as sin in my eyes. I pitied those who didn't see him in living color as I did.

The doors opened, and we stepped inside. The ride to the sixth floor took no time at all, and when the doors opened again, I finally realized why the valet had asked if we were checking in. It was possible the museum had a museum in it somewhere, but it was also a hotel.

I let go of Quinn's hand and whipped around so I was standing in front of him, blocking his path. "We can't stay the night." His face fell, gutting me. My voice was a whisper. "The diner, Quinn." I'd never regretted the decision I'd made to keep the diner running after Janice had died—never before that moment. But it tied me down, taking away alternatives I'd never considered before. I was suddenly tired. So, so tired.

"Ryan and Les have it covered." He smirked.

"Les? He's worked there two days. Only one of which was he an actual employee."

"I think, between the two of them, they can figure it out."

"Or burn it down." I looked longingly down the hall. "Which one is ours?"

"Number 610. Do you want to see it before you decide?"

"Can we?"

"Come on." He grinned wide and then pulled me down the hall. After scanning the key, he propped the door open and stepped aside so I could pass.

A bounty of white assaulted me. The bed linens were white, the couch was white, even the bathroom was floor to ceiling white. Only the carpet, a few accent pieces, and a hopeful Quinn added color to the room. It was a blank canvas, waiting for his color to fill it.

"Well?"

"It's beautiful." My eyes fell again on the double beds.

"I'm a restless sleeper," he said as if it was explanation enough.

It wasn't.

Two beds was one too many in my opinion, but the fact that he was willing to sleep in the same building with me was progress. And they looked soft and clean and heavenly. I could use a night away. A morning when I could actually sleep in would be a dream come true. Would my body even allow me such a luxury after years and years of getting up before four? Wouldn't I like to find out? Surely, Ryan and Les couldn't run the diner into the ground in one day.

It would also keep us away from Woodland Creek for most of the weekend, which was a good thing. Halloween weekend marked the end of the month-long celebration in the old part of Woodland Creek. It wasn't something Quinn would be welcome at even if I could tell him about it. The guest list was exclusive to only those with magic running through their blood.

A knock at the door startled me. Quinn walked past me to open it. The valet from downstairs stepped inside with two bags in his hand. "Where would you like these?" he asked.

Quinn arched an eyebrow at me in question.

"Right there is fine. Thank you." A grin spread across my face.

Quinn shoved a few dollars toward him and quickly ushered him out.

"You packed a bag for me?" I asked.

"Nah. Ryan called Vanessa over to help. She packed your bag for me," he said, shocking me. I was almost as flabbergasted Vanessa had helped him as I was that we were here in the first place. It wasn't as if she and I were good friends. Maybe I hadn't given her a fair chance, though. "I certainly wouldn't have had any idea what to pack. Besides, I figured I shouldn't be digging through your panties before I've been in them."

I snorted. "That *would* seem like some sort of breach of privacy. Where did you hide them?" I asked, pointing to the bags.

"They were in the bed of the truck. Good thing it didn't rain or we'd be wearing wet clothes tomorrow."

The fact Quinn pulled off this grand gesture suddenly overwhelmed me, and I pounced on him. We fell back together on one of the beds, and it was a little like falling into a cloud. "This is amazing, Quinn. I can't believe you did all of this for me." He rolled over and propped himself up over me, causing my heart to dance in my chest. We were alone in a hotel room, a hundred miles away from all of our worries and fears. I desperately hoped they hadn't chased after us and would find us.

"I figured I owed you a big-time apology," he said, watching my mouth as he always did when he was contemplating kissing me. His fingers threaded through mine, pinning my hands to the bed. If I could peel my eyes away from his, I knew I'd find the white bedding purple with desire.

"It was forgotten hours ago," I promised, willing him to stop talking and act on what we both clearly wanted.

"Not by me. I hate that I hurt you. This is exactly what I feared would happen." His voice was deep and rough. He closed his eyes as if the memory of it haunted him.

"You don't *want* to hurt me and that's enough for me." My heart pounded in my chest. "You can kiss me now, Quinn."

His lips brushed against mine with a reverence reflecting my own devotion to him. Our tongues danced—tasting, devouring, and begging for more. Kissing Quinn was like standing in the midst of a raging thunderstorm. Desire rolled around us like dark, dangerous thunderclouds threatening to pour down upon us at any moment. Need sparked all around us, causing the ball of yearning in my stomach to catch fire. My hands clutched at him. My fingers dug into his skin even through his shirt. If he didn't take me soon, I was going to be the one who detonated.

He rolled away, sitting up on the edge of the bed, leaving me ruffled and befuddled. "We better get ready."

"Ready for what?" I reluctantly rolled to the other side of the bed and sat with my back to him while I got my bearings. *I am ready!* I wanted to scream. Why wasn't he ready? Why was it so easy for him to push me away?

"We're going out. We have things to check off our list."

I sighed and stood. I grabbed my bag and threw it on the now empty bed with a force reflective of my frustration. I looked up to find him watching me with a thoughtful expression. Not much got by him.

I turned my back to him and dug through my bag to see what Vanessa had packed for me. "What's the dress code for tonight?" I asked, pulling out the black dress from the night before. I couldn't really blame Vanessa. She didn't know what I'd worn the night before, and it was probably all she'd been able to find in my closet, which was filled mostly with clothes suitable for food slinging. "Vanessa packed the dress I wore last night." I could hear the irritation in my voice.

His arms came around my waist and pulled me against him. He might have pushed me away, but I could feel through his jeans he hadn't necessarily wanted to. His lips brushed against my neck, and I melted into him again. "I wouldn't worry about it. I doubt there's much overlap between the crowd downstairs and the crowd last night."

"You're the only one I care about, and you've already seen me in it." I looked sadly at the dress as I dropped it on the bed.

"And I can't wait to see you in it again," he said, moving against me. "Don't think this is easy, Willow. Denying myself is the hardest thing I've ever done. Can't you feel how much I want you?" His voice was husky. His breath was warm on my skin but created goosebumps in its wake. "I want you more than I've ever wanted anything. But what if I'm not good for you? I showed my true colors last night."

I shook my head. The only thing his colors had shown me was he was conflicted and angry and equally as remorseful. "They were just words. I wasn't in any real danger."

"Words can inflict as much damage as a hand, Willow."

"Quinn—"

He cut me off. "Sometimes, I feel so out of control. I don't know where I am or what I'm saying. Sometimes, I don't even know who or what I am anymore." His arms tightened around me. "There's a monster living inside of me, Willow. I can feel him fighting for control, making me do things I don't understand. I don't want you to be another casualty on my hands."

I turned in his arms and wrapped my own around him. I laid my head on his chest, listening to his heartbeat. "I'm not afraid of you, Quinn Dearborn. I'm afraid *for* you. You are a good man with a pure heart. I know this, but this guilt you carry on your shoulders is going to eat you alive. I don't know what you've been through. I can't even possibly imagine or understand it, but whatever happened, you need to talk about it." I closed my eyes, as my breathing seemed to synchronize with his. "Talk to me. You aren't alone."

He sucked in a ragged breath. "Okay. But not tonight. This trip is supposed to be relaxing and fun, so let's pretend for one night I'm not messed up and you're not affected by it."

I looked at him with a question lingering on my lips and a confession on its heel.

"What?" he continued. "You seem to be able to read me like a book. I must wear my emotions all over my face. Maybe I shouldn't have shaved my beard so I could remain a mystery to you for a little longer."

His laugh warmed the room around us and made me slip my confession back into the little pocket of my soul where I kept it hidden. "There's plenty about you I haven't figured out," I said. He was a riddle I couldn't solve. A puzzle with too many lost pieces.

He smiled down at me. "It's probably better that way. Let's just enjoy tonight. We'll worry about the rest tomorrow."

"Sounds like a plan."

He pulled away from me. "Let's go then. Work before play."

Quinn

WILLOW'S PERFECT LIPS PULLED AT the corners as I pulled into the parking lot. "This is the errand we had to run before dinner?" Her laugh was brighter than the blue and white Lowe's sign glowing on the top of the building.

"I thought this was your idea of a perfect night in Cincinnati. Is it not?" I tried to look wounded.

"No, it's exactly what I expected on this trip, so it is perfect."

"Well, you have a spa appointment in the morning, so I wanted to go ahead and knock some of this out tonight."

"Spa appointment? What are you talking about?"

"There's a spa in the hotel. I made you an appointment for a massage. They're also going to paint your nails. Fingers and toes."

"You're spoiling me, Quinn. You're going to turn me into a monster."

I could tell she regretted the words as soon as they left her lips. I didn't ever want her to feel as if she was walking around on eggshells with me, though. "You work too hard," I said, hoping she wouldn't turn it into a thing. "You deserve to be pampered. And I'm still groveling."

"If this is your kind of groveling, then go ahead and slip up from time to time. I can handle it."

"Easily done. We have to hurry, though," I said reaching for the door handle. "We have dinner reservations back at the hotel at nine."

She was still grinning from ear to ear when we entered Lowe's. We headed straight for the bathroom fixtures. I stood back and let her make magic as she picked out sinks, faucets, and toilets. I gave my opinion only when asked. After all, it was her house and her would-be bed and breakfast.

We loaded up a huge rolling cart with everything she picked. The manager had agreed to store it for us overnight if we paid before we left. That way we wouldn't have to take it back to the hotel; though irritating the valet guy might have been worth the hassle.

After about an hour of perusing through tiles and cabinetry, we headed for the lumber department. She didn't know what I was looking for, so I pushed the cart ahead of her. Lumber was stacked clear to the ceiling. Just as I realized we would need to get help to get what I needed, a small forklift came wheeling around the corner. Perfect timing.

I pushed our cart over to the side. "Let's wait here for him to unload and then we'll get him to help us."

"What are you working on now?" she asked.

"Some shelves in the upstairs hall closet." The house had very little storage. She would need somewhere to put extra linens and those little complimentary bottles of shampoo and conditioner I imagined would be in all of the bathrooms. "You'll need—"

A crash, followed by a familiar rat-a-tat, sent me flying into Willow. I threw myself on top of her, shoving her to the ground. She landed with an oomph I felt more than heard as the gunfire continued over our heads. I covered her body with my own, keeping us as flat as possible. The enemy couldn't have her. They'd taken too much from me already.

After only a few seconds, the gunfire subsided, and it was only then I realized Willow was gasping underneath me. "Nooo," I heard myself yell. I rolled off her to check for injuries. There was no blood, but I ripped open her shirt to look for the shot that would rob her from me.

She slapped my hands away. "Quinn! What are you doing?" Her voice was strangled, her eyes wild. "Stop!" She yanked her shirt closed.

She's okay. I ran my hands through my hair, clawing at my scalp mercilessly. The sound of gunfire continued to echo through my mind. Starting at my feet, a tremble rolled through my body. I felt like I was on fire, I was so hot.

Her hands were on my face. "Quinn. Come back to me. Quinn," she whispered, her voice filled with the desperation I felt. "It's okay. I'm okay."

She's okay. She's not hurt. I stared into her wide, unblinking eyes.

"I'm okay."

She's okay.

I blinked at her, trying to figure out why she was there and thanking God above that she wasn't hurt.

"Can you stand up?" she asked. "How's your ankle?"

I looked down at my ankle and the events of the past few days assaulted me. Willow and me at dinner. My confession about my condition. The deer blind. Willow and me at the hospital. Driving home afterward. The awful things I'd said to her. Waking up in the forest behind the house again. Discovering the boot was gone but my foot was better. Watching her sleep in the car. Wishing for that kind of peace.

You'll never sleep like that again. Not with your condition, I told myself.

Your condition. The agony of the truth barreled into me. It had been another episode. Just another episode. I looked around to discover quite a few people gathered at the end of the aisle. They watched me curiously. They looked at Willow with pity.

The employee from the forklift spoke first. "Ma'am, are you okay? Are you hurt?"

Had I hurt her? She was holding her shirt shut. Her arms wrapped around herself. I knew instinctively I'd done that.

I tugged at my hair and she grimaced, bending at the waist in half. She held out her hand to the Lowe's employee. "I'm fine. I promise."

"Would you like to call the police?"

"No, he's with me. He didn't hurt me."

"Are you sure? You don't look well."

I listened to their exchange, feeling sicker and sicker by the second. I'd done this. Confused a pile of falling wood with enemy gunfire. Confused an aisle in Lowe's with an ambush in enemy territory. Humiliated her.

"I'm fine. He's my boyfriend. He didn't hurt me. He was protecting me."

I turned and ran, her words echoing through my head over and over. *He's my boyfriend. He didn't hurt me. He's my boyfriend. He didn't hurt me. He's my boyfriend.*

I dodged the crowd at the end of the aisle and continued until I was standing beside my truck. I opened the door, climbed inside, and gripped the wheel. I wanted to run away, to spare us both any further humiliation, but I couldn't leave her after what I'd done to her. The least I could do was get her home safely. I tried to talk myself down using the techniques the Army doctor had taught me. I counted down from one hundred but couldn't match my breathing to the numbers rushing from my mouth.

"Quinn. I'm here." She tapped on the window, warning me before she even opened the truck door. She was so scared of me that she was afraid to get in. I'd fucked everything up again. I rolled my forehead back and forth against the steering wheel.

The door opened, and she slid inside.

"Aren't you afraid to get in here with me?"

"Why would I be?" she asked. Her voice was barely more than a whisper.

"Because I hurt you. I threw you to the ground and ripped your shirt." Even saying the words caused my heart to ache. She would never trust me again. Never want to be around me.

"You did not." I squeezed my eyes shut. "Quinn, you didn't hurt me. You were protecting me. I completely understand what happened, and it's fine."

I groaned. "I ripped your shirt. I humiliated you in front of all those people."

"For days, I've been hoping you'd rip my shirt off. This wasn't really what I had in mind," she said with a hint of amusement. "But I'll take you any way I can get you."

She spoke her last words with such force that I turned to look at her only to wish I hadn't. Her body language didn't match the conviction of her words. She'd thrown her arm across her lap, and she was nearly doubled in half again. "Are you sick again?"

"It will pass. I just need a few minutes."

She was positively green. "I'm taking you to the hospital." I raised my hips off the truck seat so I could dig through my pockets for my keys.

"No," she groaned. "You can't."

"Why not?" I said, turning the ignition. The truck sputtered back to life, but Willow grabbed my arm before I could put it into drive.

"We aren't going to the hospital, Quinn. They can't help me there."

"What do you mean 'they can't help you'?" A myriad of bad scenarios skated through my mind. One seemed to ring louder than the others did. Willow was sick a lot, but despite my pleas, she'd refused to go to the doctor, putting me off with one excuse after another. Now, she was flat out refusing to let me help her. It could only mean one thing. "You already know what's making you sick."

"I've wanted to tell you, but I didn't know how."

Oh, my God, no! I can't lose anyone else. I can't do it. It was as if someone had their hands around my throat. "Are you dying?" I choked out.

"No." The warble of her answer did little to reassure me.

"You are, aren't you? And you've been afraid to tell me." I gestured wildly to the store and her and myself. "Why are we doing this then?"

"I'm not dying," she said, gasping and clawing at the dashboard. "It's you. Just you. If you would settle down for a minute, I'd be fine."

I stilled immediately, staring at her for a moment while our conversation at Pond & Duck replayed in my mind. *I have an extremely sensitive stomach. Being around people can be very difficult for me,* she'd said. *It's you. Just you.*

"I make you sick?"

"It's not what you think. Let it go, Quinn," she pleaded.

"But I do, right? I make you sick? You said it depends on what's going on around you, but what I think you meant is, it depends on if *I'm* around you." Even as the words rolled off my tongue, I didn't understand them. How could one person make her ill?

She leaned back in the seat, seeming to resign herself to something. "You're confused. I understand, but if you'll calm down, I'll explain."

I turned off the truck again and took several deep, measured breaths. Willow remained silent while she waited for me to do as she'd asked. When she put her hand over mine, I felt infinitely better. When my breathing was more regular, she spoke. "Not everyone in Woodland Creek is what they seem. It is a town full of people with special abilities." She turned toward me, looking much more like her normal self. "I'm one of those special people, Quinn."

Of course, she was special. Her special had been giving me a reason to get up every day.

"Do you know what an empath is?"

I shook my head at a loss for words.

"An empath is someone who is affected by other people's energies. Some empaths are weak receptors. They may only have a vague feeling of positive versus negative. They may not even know who the source of the energy is. Other empaths, like me, are strong receptors and can pinpoint every emotion the people around them are having when they're having it. In my case, I feel other people's emotions as my own."

I ran my hands over the steering wheel. "So you're like a mind reader?"

"No," she said adamantly. "I don't know what you're thinking. I only have extra insight into *what* you're feeling, not the thoughts and motivations behind it."

"You feel what I feel? When I'm feeling it?" It was complete and utter nonsense. I'd always known Willow was a different kind of soul, but I'd never considered she was insane.

She leaned her head back against the seat and closed her eyes. "If you're angry, I'm angry, too. If you're grieving, I do, too. When you think about the past, I'm right there walking beside you. I don't know what happened while you were in Afghanistan, but I feel your losses as if they are my own."

"What am I feeling right now?" My words were short and punctuated, directed at Willow just like the enemy gunfire I'd thought I'd heard in the store.

"Confused. Disbelieving. Angry."

"Well, that's easy. You're spouting nonsense at me. Of course, I'm confused and disbelieving. What are you feeling?"

A tear rolled down her cheek, but she didn't open her eyes. "Confused. Disbelieving. Sad."

"Because that's what I'm feeling?" I asked, already reaching for the door handle.

"No, because I know I just lost you."

I was out of the truck and running, listening only to the sound of my boots pounding the pavement and ignoring the nagging voice in my head.

Running was the only thing that would help. It was the only way I could make sense of the world around me. Cincinnati sidewalks were a poor substitute for the woods behind Willow's house, but I ran with little regard for my surroundings. Commercial turned to residential, and I realized I'd been running for a long time, likely more than an hour. Purposely or not, I'd put miles between myself and Willow.

I still didn't know how I felt about what she'd told me. *Maybe I should ask her*, I thought bitterly.

I immediately hated myself for even thinking it. Willow had never done or said anything to hurt me. In fact, she'd only tried to help me. Even though every fiber of my being wanted to reject her explanation for her illness, certain things made more sense now. As ludicrous and unbelievable as it seemed, it explained how she always knew how to deal with me. She seemed to know me better than my only family did. She knew when to push me and when to back off and leave me be. Or did she give me time alone when I needed it because she also needed the time to recover herself? Were the broken pieces of my soul cutting her too?

She is fine and well when you are happy.

I thought about all of the time we'd spent working on the house together, laughing at stupid jokes and making out when we should have been working.

When you take a turn for the worse, she does too.

'I can feel you closing down on me,' she'd said in my apartment the night before. Afterward, she'd doubled over in pain, clutching her stomach as I lobbed vile, spiteful words at her that came not from anything she'd done but from the hate growing inside of me.

'You're hurting me, Quinn,' she'd cried.

I turned around and began running back toward the store with all of our best moments running through my head faster than my feet could carry me.

Willow's eyes begging me to kiss her the first night.

Her thighs clenching around me when I'd finally kissed her in the kitchen two days later. I'd known then it was my last first kiss.

Willow dancing around the coffee table and raising the hem of her shirt teasingly after the Clue game.

The feel of her skin under my mouth as I brushed kisses across her stomach.

The shudder that ran up her spine as I did it.

One great moment after another flashed through my mind. It was only when I reached the empty truck that I realized I still held the keys in my hand. I'd left her alone in an unfamiliar city with no way to get back to the hotel or, worse, home if it was what she wanted. I started the engine of the truck once again on a mission to apologize, something I seemed to spend a lot of time doing.

Fourteen

Willow

THE CAB RIDE TO THE hotel had been a dark moment for me, something I rarely had on my own. I ignored the cab driver's glances in the rearview mirror and pushed away the sympathy the Plexiglas barrier separating us couldn't keep out. I stared out at the window as we passed unfamiliar streets and I slipped further and further from Quinn.

Begging the front desk clerk for a key to our room wasn't fun. I'd explained that my boyfriend had the only key, and we'd lost each other in the Halloween festivities downtown. Calling Quinn my boyfriend to the Lowe's employee felt like the truth. To the hotel clerk, it was as much a lie as my false explanation of where I'd lost him.

I didn't know what he was to me, or if he'd ever let me be anything to him.

In our room, I curled in the chair by the window and watch the clock tick away the minutes. Our nine o'clock dinner reservation came and went, and I turned my gaze to the distant river, knowing he was somewhere out there, trying to unravel the future I'd imagined for us.

I'd confessed what I was—at least partially—and his revulsion took root in my heart. If he couldn't handle even that part of me, there was no way he could handle the rest. I knew from my time with him that grief was a way of life for him. But now, I grieved for him instead of with him because, in my heart, I knew he was unreachable.

It wasn't the first time I'd told a man about the curse I lived with, and it wasn't the first time I'd been shunned afterward. I didn't blame Quinn though. The truth uncovered weeks of lies. He would feel violated and betrayed—how could he not—and that was only if he believed me, which was doubtful. Unless you grew up shrouded in magic the way I had, it was nearly impossible to believe in it. To accept me for what I truly was, a man had to believe in the intangible, place an unquantifiable amount of trust in the unknown, and have faith I would never betray his trust. Most men didn't have it in them. My desire for a normal boy from the normal side of the tracks had taught me that.

Tim had been the first to teach me the lesson. His mind hadn't been broad enough to understand that reality is often more than what the human eye can see. I'd opened up, explained why I always seemed to know things he would never tell me, and his response had been incredulous doubt. He'd walked away and then spread awful rumors about me around town. He'd painted me as a crazy and a weirdo, and every time he came into my diner, I was reminded there was some truth to it.

Now, Quinn would do the same if he came around me at all.

I wasn't worried he would hurt me as Tim had. Whether he knew it or not, I knew his heart as well as my own. For a moment, I'd held it in my hands.

A rustling noise pulled my gaze away from the window. My eyes fell on the door as a slip of a paper slid beneath it. I leaped from the chair and bound across the room, remorse urging me forward.

I swiped the note from the floor. Nothing been added. It still read, 'Forgive me.' The yes box was still marked from earlier that morning. The check was written in pen—not because I hadn't been able to find a pencil, but because my answer would always be the same.

I threw open the door and my future stood in front of me with a tentative and contrite half smile on his face. He didn't need to speak. The apology was written all over his heart, and it enveloped mine.

He stepped into the room, bathing it in deep purples and warm, vibrant reds. It reflected everything I felt, making it impossible to discern where his feelings stopped and mine began. He cupped my face in his hands, his emerald eyes full of longing and sincerity. He brushed my cheeks with his thumbs and blanched at the tears he found there.

"So this is what it feels like to feel someone else's pain as your own." It wasn't a question. It was a statement. An acknowledgment of acceptance. He believed me. He accepted me. He'd hurt me but had hurt himself more in the process. He empathized with *me*.

All of my curses and disabilities were forgotten. All of his flaws and afflictions be damned. He was unpredictable, damaged, and volatile. I was overly sensitive and hexed. We were a match made in either heaven or hell, but I wanted him regardless.

My fingers burned to touch him. My heart ached to welcome him back. I wanted to feel him under my fingers and over my body and kiss our mistakes away.

In seeming agreement, he slid a hand around my head, threading his fingers through my hair, forcing me to look him in the eyes until his mouth covered mine. Our tongues tangled with one another, speaking silent promises that nestled into my soul and made a home there.

I was only vaguely aware of the hotel door slamming shut as we moved further into the room. Our hands everywhere all at once, we were pulling at clothing that seemed to disintegrate into thin air. I ran my fingers up his bare chest, marveling at every ridge and ripple. He was beautiful and perfect, and I kissed the small scars peppered across his chest. To him, the scars were probably merely another reminder of the war he'd fought and the battles he'd lost, but to me, they epitomized all of his best qualities. Brave, resilient, and strong.

He pushed me backward onto the bed with a wry smile, and I propped myself on my elbows while I watched him pull off his jeans. His boxers followed, and he stood gloriously naked in front of me, knowingly and willingly this time and without an ounce of the humiliation I'd sensed before.

I sucked in a breath, my eyes wide, and my heart rattling in my chest.

He'd been magnificent in the yard with only the light of the strobing thunderclouds behind him, but it was nothing compared to the sight of him naked, bold, and bright in a room he filled with streams of Dearborn colors.

"Your turn." His voice was deep, rough, and intoxicating as he leaned over me. He trailed kisses across my bared stomach as he hooked his thumbs into the sides of my panties. He pulled them down my legs, moving away from me as he did so, leaving only the heat of his gaze to warm me. "You are the most beautiful thing I've ever seen, Willow."

I smiled as his mouth reversed where his eyes had been, first planting small kisses up the inside of my thigh and then exploring everything he'd been unable or unwilling to accept until this night. I fell backward, unable to support myself any longer, and weaved my fingers through his hair as his mouth paid reverence to my body.

So many feelings. So many sensations.

Moments like this were rare. The only thing clouding my mind and coloring my feelings was Quinn's adoration.

A hiss escaped my lips as he found *the* spot.

I uttered intelligible words, begging for more of him, all of him.

Quinn's hands, rough from the weeks of working on my house, pushed my thighs up so I spread wide and bare as he climbed higher over me. "So worth the wait," he mumbled into my neck.

Those words alone were nearly enough to send me over the edge, but I held on, not wanting to let go until he did. I reached down and wrapped my fingers around him. I guided him to where I needed him and then held my breath as he slid inside.

I was filled to the hilt with him as well as some emotion I knew better than to try to label.

He paused, waiting for me to adjust to the moment, and when he moved again, my breath hitched. His pace was slow and purposeful as he looked into my eyes. There was no question in them now. He knew how he felt about me and how to show it even if he couldn't speak it.

His fingers left blazing trails across my skin while mine dug into his back.

I quaked beneath his touch.

He found *that* spot again, and more incoherent pleas rolled out of my mouth.

He responded, quickening the rhythm he'd set until we both, nose-to-nose, gasped in unison. I rocked against him and the world came alive as he bathed me in his color. A shudder ran the length of me and I laid silent, reveling in the feeling of him all around me.

When I finally opened my eyes, he was watching me tentatively. "What do you feel now?" he asked, his breathing still ragged.

I brushed my fingertips up and down his arms. "Content. Satisfied. Deliriously happy."

He chuckled, and it filled my heart with warmth. "I didn't ask how *I* felt. I asked how *you* felt."

He collapsed around me, pulling me against him and wrapping his arms around me. Somehow, it felt as if he was everywhere at once, touching every piece of me.

I was probably still smiling as I drifted off to sleep.

I AWOKE TO FIND THE bed empty and the room dark. When my call for him went unanswered, I pulled myself begrudgingly from the bed. I rummaged through my bag for a pair of yoga pants and a t-shirt, somehow knowing he hadn't gone far.

I stumbled through the hotel lobby with bare feet and groggy eyes, using my intuition to find him. He sat alone at the end of a long hall in the exhibit area of the hotel. His fingers lightly tapped on the edge of the bench. He was lost in thought, absorbing the pieces hanging on the walls around him.

I cleared my throat so as not to sneak up on him or startle him. When he smiled in return, I took it as an invitation and took the last few steps to sit down beside him.

"Were you having trouble sleeping?"

"Not like usual, no. I slept really well, but then I was wide-awake. I didn't want to disturb you. The sign out front for this exhibit caught my attention earlier this afternoon. I wanted to come check it out."

It had caught my attention too. "It's lovely," I said, gazing at the bronze sculpture of the mounted doe head that had held Quinn's attention before I'd approached. She was dainty and sleek in comparison to the magnificent hammered copper buck hanging beside her. My eyes naturally drifted to the male, but Quinn's were riveted on the female.

He was quiet for a moment and I waited.

Finally, he took a deep breath as if he needed it for what he would say next. "How do you do it?"

"What?"

"If you feel everything I feel, then how can you stand to be around me? Why would you want to be in such an ugly place?"

I slipped my hand into his and threaded my fingers through his fingers. I thought of how it felt to finally sleep next to him, our legs intertwined and his chest expanding against my cheek. "I want to know you, Quinn. All of you. The grief I sometimes feel when I sit next to you is because of the road you've walked. You'll have to walk it again if you want to move forward, but you won't walk it alone."

I rubbed my thumb against his wrist. "Besides, there is no part of you that is ugly. I think you're beautiful inside and out. Every scar. Every flaw." I tore my eyes away from his face and looked again at the exhibits. "You're just as beautiful as everything in this museum."

He was quiet for a few minutes.

"There was this deer in the forest the other day," he finally said. "She was so beautiful. Her coat was glossier than I'd ever seen on a deer in our area. When I came out of my PTSD episode, she was lying smack-dab against me as if she was trying to keep me warm or keep me company. She looked at me with these big brown eyes, and it was almost as if she was speaking to me, telling me to stay calm because it would be okay. When the guys got close, she let out a bleat and then ran away. I swear she was telling them where I was."

I squeezed his hand. "Maybe she was. Animals are very intuitive, you know. She probably knew you were in trouble."

He shook his head as if still in disbelief. "Maybe so, but I've never known a wild animal, especially a deer, to act like that." His eyes swept the walls, roaming from one mount to another. "I can't shoot them anymore. There's no way. She doesn't realize it, but she risked her life by being there. Will, this is going to sound crazy, but I almost want to find her and thank her. Give her a carrot or something. I don't know."

I giggled. "I'm sure she would appreciate it. What deer doesn't enjoy a carrot?" I rubbed my thumb against his hand and then squeezed it. "Quinn?"

"Yeah, babe?"

"Will you take me back to bed?"

He stood, scooping me into his arms at the same time. "You'll never have to ask me twice again."
He carried me, nestled in his arms, back to our room where we rocked each other back to sleep.

Fifteen

Willow

QUINN WAS ON THE MOVE again. I rolled over and watched him walk naked toward the open doorway of my bedroom. Shoulders back, head up, his body was a wonderland of angles and curves I was still getting to know.

He'd stayed with me both nights since we'd returned from Cincinnati. The first night, I woke up and he was already gone, but this time, I'd caught him in the act. I definitely preferred to see him coming rather than going though he was a vision from any angle.

I patted the bed to get his attention. "Where are you going?" I whispered. When he didn't answer, I assumed he was sleepwalking.

I'd always heard you shouldn't wake a sleepwalker, so I decided to follow him instead. Truthfully, after watching him come back naked from the woods the week before, I was a little curious to see where he went in his sleep. I didn't like him being out there by himself.

I pulled on the sweatshirt thrown across the end of my bed and a pair of yoga pants while walking down the hall. Quinn walked through the house as if

214

he knew exactly where he was going and let himself out the back door. I purposely kept my distance, waiting until he was halfway across the lawn before I followed so I wouldn't spook him.

His pace was a leisurely stroll until he hit the tree line and then he took off at a sprint. I shot across the yard after him but came to a sudden halt when the air around him turned iridescent. It shimmered and quaked, and in a flash of a second, Quinn was no longer a man but the most glorious animal I'd ever laid eyes on. While I stood silently as a field mouse behind him, he snorted and tossed his head. He stamped on the ground and then took off, leaping over the creek in a stunning display of grace. He zigzagged through the trees as magic I'd never sensed from him glittered around him.

Quinn was two-natured and beautiful and my heart capsized from the sheer amount of adoration it held.

But a darker cloud of realization was fast on its heels. I didn't need to count the tines on his head to know he was the eighteen-point monster the town was clamoring to kill. His rack was more than impressive, reminding me of the stories I'd been told about another buck who'd roamed our woods many years before. Just as everyone in town referred to Quinn as The Monster, the one before him had been known as The Legend. Was it possible Quinn came from the same bloodline? His white tail disappeared into the denser part of the forest while fear kept my feet rooted to the ground.

Dread filled my chest.

That massive set of antlers had been a death sentence for the one before him. It had turned otherwise cordial hunters into fierce competitors. They tracked him and baited him. They shared stories of sightings, even going so far as to devote a small article in the Sunday paper to him every week but tucking away the best information into their own pockets. They all wanted him, but no one suspected The Legend was a Woodland Creek citizen and that losing him would also mean losing the new doctor who'd moved to town not too long before.

To both sides of the community, it had all seemed like harmless fun. The hunters took to their tree stands, but the deer shifters considered themselves too smart to ever be caught in the crosshairs of a rifle. That confidence had cost them. They'd underestimated the tenacity of the hunters and their desire for the grand trophy upon The Legend's head.

He'd fallen on a November morning, not unlike the current one. The hunter who brought him down had tracked him for miles before losing him in the woods. He'd told the story many times, and no one doubted his story since The Legend was never seen again.

I squinted, trying to catch sight of Quinn through the trees. He wasn't safe in shifted form just as The Legend hadn't been safe. We were in the middle of deer season, and while it was unlikely that there were any hunters out at this time of night, any reported sighting of Quinn would only fuel the fire.

I ran to the tree line, knowing it was futile. I'd hesitated too long, and he'd disappeared into the trees—just as the doctor had disappeared so many years ago. Wrapping my arms around myself, I paced along the tree line. The chill of magic was still in the air, begging me to ask myself some hard questions. Why, when I'd told Quinn about the special natures of the citizens of Woodland Creek, had he looked at me with such disbelief? Why hadn't he told me the truth about himself then? Surely, he knew I could accept he was different too.

And why had he seemed to have such a hard time accepting what I'd told him? As far as I knew, I was the only empath in Woodland Creek, but many two-natureds had special powers in addition to their ability to shift. As a two-natured, he would know that. Learning about my special abilities shouldn't have been such a shock to him; yet, it clearly had been.

I continued to pace, kicking through the brush as I tried to piece together the puzzle that was Quinn Dearborn. I laughed at the clue that had been right in front of my face all along. Like Ryan's last name of Balere, Quinn's name hinted at his heritage. Then again, the name belonged to his mother, and to my knowledge, she wasn't two-natured.

My foot kicked something and I brushed the leaves away with my foot to discover Quinn's boot. Another piece of the puzzle fell into place, filling a gaping hole that had been nagging at me. One day, Quinn's ankle had been broken. The next, it was well enough to walk on and climb ladders. By the evening, he hadn't had a limp at all.

Of course.

It was a known fact that shifters were rapid healers. Even in human form, they healed faster than average humans did. In shifted form, it was downright miraculous. If Quinn had shifted during the night before our Cincinnati trip, his ankle could have easily healed by morning.

I chided myself for not figuring it out then, and racked my brain trying to remember exactly what he'd said about it. Had he given me any hints? I was sure he hadn't. He'd looked as confused as I'd felt when he'd said he'd tried standing on it that morning and discovered it was better. He'd said he'd been misdiagnosed all of his life. He seemed to accept that answer, but why had I?

I'd been stupid. Blinded by my infatuation with him and my desire to have a relationship with someone who hadn't been touched by the magic of Woodland Creek. The signs had been right in front of me.

I marched myself back to bed and stripped my clothes off so he wouldn't know I'd followed him. In a few hours, it would be time for me to get dressed again and open the diner. I hoped Quinn would rejoin me before then because I had a confrontation in mind.

I tossed and turned with no real hope I would fall sleep. My mind was all over the place, wanting to accuse Quinn of lying to me but knowing I had no right.

When he crept back into the room more than two hours later, he walked, not with the straight back and proud shoulders he'd had when he left, but as a man with a guilty conscience. I squeezed my eyes shut and saw streams of weary browns and cautionary yellows. The combination was acidic; eating holes through what I'd decided was the truth only moments before.

An anomaly among otherwise proud creatures, he slid into bed, still smelling of cedars and crisp Indiana air. He settled beneath the thick down blanket, and his heavy heart instantly defused my anger.

"Where did you go?" I whispered.

He froze and then let out a long, frustrated breath. Regret and confusion filled the space between us. "I assume there's no point in lying to you. You'll see right through it." There wasn't a hint of annoyance in his voice, only resignation, proving he was close to accepting the intrusive nature of my abilities.

"Only if it gives you a guilty conscience." I slid closer and slipped my leg over his, curling into his side. His arm came around me, pulling me against him. "Would it give you a guilty conscience?"

"Lying to you? Yes." His conviction hung heavy in the air around us. "And why would I after everything we've been through?"

"Does it feel like too much sometimes? I worry it's too much with everything else you're dealing with." We hadn't been together for very long, but nothing had come easy for us.

"What do you think?" He was testing my abilities.

"I think you know you can handle it," I answered honestly.

"I know I can handle you." As if to prove it, he slid his palm up my bare thigh. The pads of his fingers grazed along the curve of my backside. I closed my eyes reveling in his touch and the adoration of it.

"And I can handle the truth, Quinn. I can accept anything you tell me. Where were you tonight?"

He was quiet for a few long seconds before he spoke. "Would you believe me if I said I'm not sure?"

"Yes," I answered because I knew both were true. I ran a hand up his chest and found his skin to be warm under my touch. Another clue I'd missed. The doctor at the hospital had said his temperature was high, and I'd assumed he had a fever, possibly the beginnings of pneumonia since he'd been found out in the cold snow. Now, I knew he always ran warm, which was the normal thing for a shifter. "Were you sleepwalking again?"

His hands stilled. "I must have been. I don't remember leaving." I could feel his confusion as he racked his brain trying to remember. "This happens a lot. Most nights since I've come back home if you want the truth. I have many nightmares. War stuff I can't get out of my head. The Army shrink said they are PTSD flashbacks trying to escape my subconscious."

I kissed his shoulder to let him know I was listening but remained quiet in hopes he would finally open up to me in the quiet blackness of my room.

"In most of the nightmares, I'm running away from something. Sometimes, I'm trying to find something." He paused, melancholy and momentarily lost. "Sometimes, I'm looking for someone. But either way, I'm always running. I think that's why I get up in the night. To search for what I lost back there."

I squeezed my eyes shut, overcome by the pain living inside of him. I laid my head on his chest to be closer to it, hoping that my touch would relieve his discomfort as his did mine. He pulled me in tighter, nestling me against him, and I listened to his heartbeat slow.

"I run. And run and run and run. And then when I wake up, I don't know where I am or where I've been. It used to take me hours to find my way back home, but I'm gradually becoming more familiar with the land around here."

"Maybe you find comfort out there. I do. When I need to shut off the world around me because it becomes too much, that's where I go too. When you wake up, do you remember any of it?" I asked, wondering specifically about tonight.

"Some of it. I can remember my feet hitting the ground, but my head is all screwed up. It's as if my feet know I'm in Indiana and know where to lead me, but my head still thinks I'm in Afghanistan. It feels like my instincts are fighting against my memories if that makes any sense.

"It's not until I'm fully awake again that I even realize what's happening. And then I find myself naked in the middle of nowhere—sometimes standing in the pouring rain—and I have to find my way home."

"Naked? Every time?"

"It's the damnedest thing, Willow. No matter what I wear to bed, I always wake up naked. I've tried wearing layers of clothes to bed, but more times than not, I wake up naked. Sometimes, my clothes are in a pile on the floor in my room, but usually, I never see them again. I must have left half a closet in the woods before I finally gave up and started sleeping this way."

I held my breath while I processed what he'd just told me. Was it actually possible Quinn had no idea he was no longer in human form when he was running? Was it possible he didn't know he was shifting? I was no psychologist, but I'd been Googling

PTSD since he had told me he had it. From what I'd read, it seemed likely that PTSD was to blame for his nightmares. But was it also possible the PTSD was somehow masking the truth of who he was so he didn't even know he was a shifter? It seemed impossible. He should have started shifting when he was around sixteen or seventeen, before he'd gone away to the war.

"When did this start happening?" I asked.

"The nightmares?"

"No, the sleepwalking."

"Almost immediately after I got back to Woodland Creek."

"Did you have the nightmares before that?"

"Well, yeah. Those started after …" His voice trailed off, and I closed my eyes to see the stream of undulating cobalt coloring his broken heart. My heart split open for him. He couldn't even say it aloud. He'd never get past the nightmares until he could at least name the cause for them. It was something for us to work on after we figured out his other issue—an issue I now believed he didn't even know he had.

"But you didn't sleepwalk before you came back to Woodland Creek? And you never woke up naked before that?" I didn't like the feeling that questioning him gave me, as if I was putting him through the wringer, but we needed answers.

"Not that I can remember. I've thought about leaving again. I feel cursed in this place. I thought if I ran away, I could maybe outrun all of this madness."

The thought of him leaving town was almost more than I could bear. "I don't think it would help, Quinn, but why haven't you tried?"

"You." His fingers, which had been tracing light circles on my back, paused. He tapped me twice. "Just you. I was all set to leave. I didn't have a clue where I'd go, but I knew I needed to get away from here. I was planning to leave after I met the guys that first time at the diner. My bags were already packed, but seeing you again gave me a reason to stay."

"Really?" I asked, craning my head to look at him. His hands came around my waist, and he pulled me over on top of him so I was straddling him. I searched for his eyes in the darkness as his hands slipped down over the curve of my backside again.

"I'd rather face my demons than leave you. I don't even know what they are, but I'd rather face them than not have you in my life. I think a part of me always knew, if I came back to Woodland Creek, it would come down to this."

"Come down to what?" I asked, running my hands up his chest. My touch was light until I reached the slope of his shoulders where I reversed directions and raked my fingernails back down again.

He groaned and shifted beneath me, realigning us in a most perfect way. "Fighting tooth and nail to hang onto my sanity so I could hold on to you."

I glanced at the clock and then leaned over so we were nearly nose-to-nose. "Trust me when I say this, Quinn. You're not mad. And if you are, it's exactly my kind of madness." I brushed my nose against his nose and the tips of my nipples rubbed lightly against the dusting of hair on his chest, sending a spark straight to the throb between my legs. "And I want and need every part of you I've seen. I'm yours to keep."

He arched his hips, rubbing his hard length against my warm center. "I don't deserve you, but I feel like we were made for each other. I think you were the force drawing me back to Woodland Creek. I just didn't realize it at the time."

It was a wonderful thought even though I knew it wasn't the case. "Enough talking for now. I need to get ready for work soon." I ran my tongue along his bottom lip, begging him to use his for something else now.

"And you want me to give you something to think about while you're there?" he asked, nibbling on my upper lip.

"Mmmhmm."

He rubbed his thumb in sweet slow circles over the spot sure to set me on fire and devoured my mouth in a kiss that nearly stripped me of my own sanity.

I wanted to be mad together.

FOUR HOURS LATER, QUINN WAS still the only thing on my mind.

It could have been because of all the things he'd given me to think about that morning, but the more likely reason was my human disco ball was sitting at the counter, throwing Christmas-themed strobes all over the diner while he ate his breakfast. Les might be the target for the evergreen-colored daggers, but I was claiming the lusty red ones all for myself.

"If you want me to stay out of your heads, then you both need to stop thinking so much," Ryan growled at me through the window.

I grinned guiltily even though his complaint served as a reminder I still hadn't told Quinn about Ryan's special talents. He was not going to like it when he found out that nothing was off-limits when we were both around. Between the two of us, neither his thoughts nor feelings were safe.

"No way, Will. That's my secret to tell."

I rolled my eyes at him. "Oh, please. Like you haven't told Vanessa all of my secrets. Hang on tight or that high horse you're on is going to buck you off."

"That's different," he said under his breath. "She's a two-natured, too."

I arched an eyebrow at him. *So is he.*

His eyes went wide. "What?"

You know the monster buck everyone is talking about? I shot a glance over my shoulder at Quinn and then waggled my eyebrows at Ryan.

"What the fuck. Are you kidding me?"

I cocked my head and gave him a quick mental rundown of what I'd learned that morning. *I wouldn't believe it if I hadn't seen it with my own eyes*, I finished.

"So do you really think he doesn't know?" he asked.

I'm positive he doesn't.

"Well, this has to be the most messed-up thing I've ever heard." Ryan leaned forward so his round face filled the whole window. "I haven't picked up a shifter vibe from him, which is a first for me."

Me either. I don't get anything non-human off him at all.

"So how are you going to tell him?"

I shot another look over my shoulder at Quinn, who was finishing the last of his chocolate pie. *I don't know. He's fragile.*

It was Ryan's turn to roll his eyes. "Fragile? He's a six-foot-four, two-hundred-and-twenty-five-pound trained assassin. And apparently he has a killer rack." He paused to laugh at his own joke, but the smile fell from his face when he saw I wasn't in the laughing mood. "Seriously, though, Willow. The sooner he finds out, the better. You've heard people talking about him. He's not safe out there. Shit. He's even hunted himself."

I nodded slowly as tears pricked at the corners of my eyes. I couldn't bear to think of what could happen to him if he was in the wrong place at the wrong time. Luckily, it seemed he only went out in the middle of the night so while there were other things to worry about in the woods, I wasn't as concerned about hunters.

"What about his parents?" Ryan asked.

Maybe. But why did they keep this from him all of these years?

Ryan's forehead wrinkled in thought. "By the way, how did you manage to keep it from me all morning?" he asked.

"I had other things on my mind, I guess."

He snorted. "I'll say you did. Speaking of, you had better get back to lover boy. He just caught Les looking at your ass, and I think he's about to take his head off."

I whirled around to find Quinn had turned the entire counter area into an inferno of crimson rage. "How's my favorite customer?" I asked gliding over to him. I picked up the coffee pot and topped off his cup.

He tore his eyes away from Les to meet mine. "Better now that you're here. What are you and Ryan cooking up?"

"Nothing. Wedding stuff." I hated lying to him but didn't have much other choice. I slid a second piece of pie in front of him to make up for it. "So what do you have planned for today?"

He shot a warning glare in Les' direction. "Looks like I'm sitting here all day."

"For the pie or so you can stalk Les?"

"I'm not stalking Les. He's stalking you."

I laughed. Having a man get crazy jealous over me was a new thing for me. I could see where it could be annoying if he took it too far, but so far, it seemed pretty harmless. "If it weren't for him, I wouldn't be able to hang out talking to you," I said, swirling my finger in the air and then pointing at him. "Besides, I've let him know where my interest lies."

"And where would that be?" My favorite lopsided smirk made an appearance.

"After the way I rocked your world this morning, I can't believe you have to even ask."

A retching sound came from the kitchen, causing Quinn to break into a full grin. "That guy has ears like a bat."

"Among other things."

Quinn's eyebrows shot up and his expression turned wary. "Do I even want to know?"

"No, but sharing is caring so I'll fill you in this evening over dinner and a bottle of wine. That should give you sufficient time to prepare yourself."

"And stew," he grumbled before shoving another forkful of pie in his mouth.

"Hey, Quinn," I said leaning forward on my elbows. There was no graceful segue into this conversation, so I jumped in with both feet. "You've told me about your mom, but I've never heard you mention your dad. Is he around here?"

"My dad?" he asked surprised.

"Yeah, I was thinking about Ryan and his problems with his family and Vanessa's family, and I realized I don't even know your parents."

His eyes softened. "You want to get to know my parents?"

I could feel a blush creep up my face. "Well, yeah. I mean, no rush or anything. But ... yeah ... eventually, I would like to get to know your parents."

"I can take you over to meet my mom, but my dad's not around here. I've never met him and don't want to." He said it matter-of-factly, without a trace of emotion, as if he'd had years to practice and perfect the line.

"I'm sorry, Quinn." Though the subject didn't seem to bother him, I still felt a pang of regret for bringing it up, especially under false pretenses.

Quinn shrugged. "No worries. He was a visiting adjunct professor at the college who was only in town for a year. When he found out my mom was pregnant, he disappeared. He wasn't interested in knowing me, so I've always felt the same way. It's always been just the two of us. My mom did her best."

"Well, I'd love to meet her," I said, leaning across the counter and kissing him on the cheek, "because I think she did a fine job."

"I'll see if I can set up a dinner for the three of us. She's been harassing me to meet you, too."

Hearing that made me very happy, though I had a feeling she was going to meet me before Quinn would get the chance to introduce us. I had a few questions for her.

I pushed off the counter again. "I would really like that. So seriously, what are you going to do today? As much as I'd like for you to, you can't hang out here all day. You're too distracting."

He smiled. "Well, let's see. I have a bathtub and a toilet to install, and I need to go pick up some paint, but it can wait until tomorrow."

I nodded at the window. "You better do it today. They're predicting snow this afternoon."

He groaned. "Already?"

"Tonight or tomorrow."

"Why do you look so excited about it?"

"Because I can't wait. There's something so romantic about the first snow," I said wistfully. "Cuddling on the couch with a blanket in front of the fire. A glass of wine. You. Maybe a game of strip Clue."

He laughed. "Well, you certainly know how to sell it. I better get going then. I guess I have more to do today than I thought." He abruptly stood up and started digging through his pockets.

"No way, buck-a-roo." I walked the length of the counter and rounded the end to meet him on the other side. "Your money's no good here anymore. My pie is free."

"But only for me, right? Nobody else gets the free pie." He hooked an arm around my waist and pulled me against him. "I will not share the pie." His voice was husky next to my ear, his breath warm on my skin.

I wrapped both arms around his waist and pressed my nose into his neck. Even freshly showered, I had to admit I loved his woodsy, musky scent more than a little. "Quinn Dearborn, are you saying you'd like to be my boyfriend?"

"Well, you see. There's this girl, and I kind of have eyes only for her." I looked up and found his emerald eyes sparkling with amusement. "Turns out she has the best pie. I cannot get enough of her pie."

I slapped him on the chest. "You are trouble. Get out of here before something bad happens."

He kissed me with gusto. As if we were alone in my kitchen and not in in a diner full of people. When he pulled away, he smacked me lightly on the ass and winked. "Admit it. You love me just a little," he said as he walked away.

I watched him walk out the door and then grabbed the coffee pot from the counter so I'd have a reason to run to the window. As I refilled a cup, I watched him walk across the yard to the house. He stood tall and proud again, shoulders back and head up.

You have no idea, Quinn Dearborn. No idea.

A gruff, archaic voice interrupted my thoughts. "Ain't love grand?"

"Mr. Hansen," I said, nodding to the owner of the cup I'd absentmindedly filled. "How was your breakfast this morning?"

"Funny. I don't know since I haven't gotten it yet."

I stared at him aghast. "Give me two minutes, Mr. Hansen."

I ran to the window. "Where's Clive's plate?"

"Right here," Ryan said, shoving it at me. "I know I'm breaking your rules and all, but I thought you should know Quinn's buddies are all headed back out to the Reyburn land again this afternoon. Some stupid 'first snow' nonsense. Apparently, it's a tradition or something to kill something on the first day of winter."

I grabbed the plate but dropped it on the ledge again when it burned my hand. I reached for a towel. "But it's not the first day of winter." Ryan shrugged. "Besides, he won't go out there again."

"Are you sure about that?"

"Later," I said, picking up the plate using the towel as a potholder. "We'll talk about it later. Hansen's pissed."

I set the plate down gently, careful not to dump it in his lap, so I didn't have to buy him another meal. "I'm so sorry, Mr. Hansen."

He narrowed his eyes at me. "Since you apparently don't work anymore anyway, why don't you have a seat? We need to talk."

I looked around quickly, but the diner looked to be in pretty good shape. Les was making his rounds with the coffee pot again. I gestured to let him know I was going to sit down. He nodded before getting on with the business of making the customers happy. Quinn could object all he wanted about Les, but he wasn't going anywhere. He was a hustler and good for business.

Clive was talking almost before I had my butt in the seat. "I thought after our last talk I'd given you enough hints to send you scurrying, but I guess you're not as quick as Janice gave you for."

231

"Honestly, I thought about coming to see you, sir, but Ryan warned me off."

"Such a scaredy cat, that one. If he'd grow a pair, he could straighten his own life out."

"Frankly, if this was the way you were going to treat me, I'm glad I didn't." I looked away impatiently. "I don't mean to be disrespectful, but what is it you want to talk about? I have a lot on my mind."

"I see things are getting hot and heavy with you and the Dearborn boy."

"That's it? You want to talk to me about my relationship with Quinn?" I'd just sat down, but I'd already had enough of the mangy old coot. I wasn't going to talk about my love life with an old man who looked to be about a million years old. I started to stand, but a bony hand on my arm stopped me. Instinct caused me to recoil in my chair.

"I'm sorry. I shouldn't have said that. Jealousy can be a bitter pill to swallow." He pointed toward my house. "I had that once, too—what you and the Dearborn boy have—only, in my case, it wasn't the figment of someone else's imagination. It was real and pure and true. And someone stole it from me."

The fact that this scraggly old man had found someone to love him was proof of miracles in and of itself. It gave me hope for my own future.

His laugh sounded about as brittle as he looked. "I was young once too, you know. Oh, about a million years ago."

"Not you, too," I said, placing my fingertips on my temples and groaning.

"Here and there as I wish. I can block what I don't want to hear."

Great.

"Sometimes. But it can be a real nuisance, too. But you completely understand, don't you?"

"Yes."

"You can thank Janice for that. Things would be so different if she hadn't liked to stick her nose where it didn't belong."

"What was your relationship with her? It doesn't seem like you liked her very much yet you were here every day, even when she was running the place."

Clive steepled his fingers and leaned in as if he was getting ready to let me in on a big secret. "Not many people know this, but Janice was my half-sister. We had different fathers, and we were raised separately. Our mother was, shall I say, free-spirited before being free-spirited was cool."

My cheeks flared with heat. "I thought maybe you were lovers."

He leaned back in his chairs with obvious distaste on his face. "Heavens, no."

"I'm sorry. She never mentioned she had a brother." It suddenly occurred to me that the old man probably had as much claim to the house as I did and might be why he was hanging around even after she was gone. "And I'm sorry for your loss."

"Nonsense," he said, reading my mind again. "What would I want with this place? She wanted you to have it, and it's yours. Besides, I really like your bed and breakfast idea. Janice wouldn't have been in the poor house if she'd thought of it herself."

"Mr. Hansen, I won't allow you to talk about her like that," I said, my voice adamant. I wasn't going to let this man—half-brother or not—disrespect my friend in the business she'd built.

"You're sweet, Willow. I like you. Like her, your heart is in the right place, but you're gullible. And you don't know everything there was to know about Janice."

"I know everything I need to know." I looked at him defiantly, though something deep within me niggled my subconscious.

"How about this? Let me tell you my story. Maybe it will affect the story you'll have to tell someday. When I'm done, you can decide whether I have the right to hold a grudge against my sister."

All doubts aside, I really didn't want to hear about how Janice had wronged this half-brother who she'd never talked about. I was worried about Quinn, and I needed to spend my energies thinking about his problems.

"I may have the answer you're looking for if you listen closely," he said addressing my thoughts.

I sent him a warning glare. "Fine, old man. You talk and I'll listen, but I'm going to tell you what I tell Ryan. Stay out of my head."

"Fair enough. It's a deal."

I sat quietly in my chair for almost an entire hour as he told me about the beautiful raven-haired fox who'd stolen his heart. According to Clive, she'd been so lovely she'd had more suitors than she'd known what to do with.

"Now, I wasn't the most handsome of the lot and I wasn't of her kind, but I had things to offer her," he explained. "I had a decent job. I was using my powers for good, working at the apothecary back then. I bought a house in Old Town. I knew there were other men courting her, but what was happening between Clara and me wasn't just special. It was extraordinary. I never doubted her and what we would become."

He shredded a paper napkin as he talked, tearing it into tiny bits. They fluttered chaotically to the tabletop. "Then Janice heard around town about the other gentlemen callers. I don't know if my dear sister doubted Clara or me ... doesn't matter ... her intentions were good, but she was young and inexperienced," he rambled. "She didn't understand her own abilities and their limitations, let alone the karmic ramifications of testing free will."

"A love potion?" I asked. I knew Janice had dabbled in that a bit.

"Even after her own husband died and right up until her death, she was an incurable romantic. But there's a difference between love spells cast to find love and love spells cast to force love. To give me an edge over my competition, Janice put a spell on Clara that amplified her feelings for me and squashed any she might have had for the others. She attempted to force what I believed would have ultimately happened on its own if given time. A seed of love already planted. It needed water, not fertilizer, to grow into something wonderful." With two only semi-cooperative arthritic hands, Clive brushed the napkin pieces into a mound, which he then artfully arranged into the shape of a heart.

"What happened?" I asked completely enthralled with his story.

"Janice learned at all of our expense that one should never attempt to force two people together. Even with the best of intentions, misused magic can have horrific consequences." He looked out the window toward my house and then up to a window on the second floor where I knew Quinn was working. "Negative energies affect people differently. Some people are able to handle it better than others are. Clara was not. It drove her to madness."

His grief rendered us both speechless for a few moments. Finally, he pulled his eyes away from my house and stared at the paper heart he'd built. "Just as Janice had directed her to, my love chose me over the others." With a shaky hand, he traced a finger over the heart.

"She chose me, but she didn't choose *us*. All I have left of her is the note she wrote right before she threw herself from the cliff out at Fool's Gold Hill." He leaned forward, and with a single puff of breath, blew the paper heart. Tiny bits of napkin scattered across the table's surface. Some slipped off the table. A few fell into my lap. The heart destroyed, and mine ached for his.

"I'm so sorry, Mr. Hansen."

"The sad truth of it is I think she would've chosen me on her own if left alone, but I'll never know for sure." He leaned back in his chair and looked me directly in the eyes. "I'd like to say Janice learned her lesson, but I know better than that. Her intentions were always good—never ever doubt it— but her execution was off at times."

"Mr. Hansen, thank you for sharing your story with me, but what does this have to with me?"

"One should never try to change someone else's destiny. If you want to understand your friend, you need to read the books."

The books.

It was the third time Clive had mentioned the books. "What books, Mr. Hansen?"

He huffed as if I should already have figured it out on my own. "Janice's diaries. She kept notes. All of the women in my family did. They're somewhere in that old house. Find them and go back to 1962. You can read about Clara on your own. Twenty years later, you'll find Quinn Dearborn's name. Eons before that is the Balere-Birdwell feud. It's all in the books. Knowledge is more powerful than magic, my dear, sweet Willow."

"I have to go," I said, jumping from my chair.

He nodded with a sad, satisfied smile on his face. "I thought you might. Godspeed, my dear."

I ran into the kitchen, tossing my apron into the basket. "Ryan? Can you and Les handle lunch without me?"

"Sure. Why?"

"Were you not listening to my conversation with Old Man Hansen?"

"Not much. The old geezer doesn't let me in most of the time. I hate conversations where I only get one side of the story."

I rolled my eyes. "That's how the rest of the world lives, and we seem to manage. Listen, I have to go. The answer to Quinn's problems is in Janice's old diaries in the basement."

"Go," he said pointing at the back door. "I'll let Les know."

I flew across the yard with a singular purpose, barely even registering the heavy clouds looming over Woodland Creek. I slipped into the house through the back door and listened for Quinn. Music and banging drifted down the stairs. I didn't want him to know I was in the house. As quietly as possible, I tiptoed down the hall, avoiding the squeaky boards, and opened the door to the basement. I didn't plan to reemerge again until I knew why Quinn was in Janice's books.

Sixteen

Quinn

THE GATE WAS CLOSED WHEN I got there, but it didn't necessarily mean I was alone. Tim kept it locked whether he was there or not to keep out trespassers and poachers. I parked my truck by the fence and hoisted a leg over the gate. Technically, I was a trespasser too since I hadn't replied to any of the text messages flying around all afternoon.

Hunting during the first snowfall was a silly tradition of no real strategic merit. It wasn't as if the white stuff made it more likely to get a deer, but it was something we'd done all through high school. I knew now it was a tradition they'd kept up all of these years. I wouldn't tell the guys this, but Willow's idea for the evening sounded better than hanging out in the brutal cold by myself.

I stepped carefully over the land, mindful not to make any noise that might scare off an animal. The idea that I would actually find her was a ridiculous one. Even if I spotted a doe, there would be no way really to know if it was mine. There were literally thousands of doe in Craft County. As fun as it was to imagine her walking right up to me again, it was unrealistic. As gentle and docile as they looked, deer were just like any other wild animal—unpredictable and easily spooked.

When I made it to the blind, I eyed it warily. Climbing inside wasn't appealing, but neither was freezing my nuts off outside. The cold front had come in earlier that afternoon, and even with the protection of the trees, the wind was wickedly frigid. I climbed the ladder, hoping my dismount would be a little more graceful than last time and spare me a trip to the hospital.

After I had settled inside, I patted the pocket of my jacket to make sure I hadn't forgotten the carrots in the truck. I'd wanted the big kind with the fluffy greenery on top because nothing said thank you like fluffy greenery, but all I'd found in Willow's fridge was a bag of baby carrots.

I unzipped my jacket a little so I could pull out my binoculars. I wasn't sure how long I'd give her to make an appearance, but I had some time to kill since it was Willow's late night at school. A part of me wanted to see my little savior again, and another part of me hoped she was far, far away. With the guys coming out later, I didn't want her hanging around. She wasn't their target, but if any of them had bagged a buck the weekend before, they'd be limited to taking a doe. If she showed at all, she was going to have to dine and dash.

I put the binoculars to my face and prepared myself for a long wait.

Willow

THE WATER HEATER CLICKED ON and I nearly jumped out of my skin. The basement was definitely spookier when you were reading someone's private diary of spells.

As tempting as it was to find the book from 1962 and read Janice's version of Clive's story, it would have to wait. Quinn was my only priority as I skimmed through the entries.

Luckily, Clive had given me a clue as to where I should start. Twenty years after Clara's death would have been 1982, but since Quinn wasn't even born until 1983, I started there. I was well into the month of August when I found something promising.

August 19, 1983

Margaret Dearborn visited today. Lovely young lady in a bit of a pickle. The girl looks as if she might burst. What to do? What to do? She seems like a sweet thing, and she's had such a rough go of it. Her story was compelling, but I should speak with Clive first.

After she had left, I had another visitor. Seems the Reyburns are in need of some quick cash. Since I sure would hate for him not to be able to pay his bill at the country club, I obliged him.

Footbath for Money:
    Ingredients:
    ~Black Cohosh Root
    ~Cup of boiling water
    ~Small bottle
    Directions: Soak the root in the cup of boiling water for fifteen minutes. Strain the water and throw away the root. Put the liquid in the bottle for six days and leave it

alone. On the sixth day, rub the liquid all over the soles of your feet. Be alert to intuition until money comes your way.

I found it interesting that Tim's father had come to Janice because of money problems. I would bet my own measly bank account that Tim, who'd never seemed to want for anything, had no idea his father had stooped so low as to use witchcraft to pay the bills.

More interesting than the Reyburn's financial problems was Margaret. It seemed safe to assume the pickle she was in was Quinn. I read on to find out, and three days later, the Dearborn name was mentioned again, but only in passing.

August 22, 1983

The moon is full and the crazies were at the market today. If banishing spells weren't off-limits, I would still be following the bastard who stole my parking spot just so I could watch him do U-turns to get away from me.

Speaking of my conscience, I talked with Clive today. He disapproves of my plan to help the Dearborn girl. Back to the drawing board.

The entry hadn't provided me with much information, but I had to smile at Janice's twisted sense of humor. I missed it terribly. If she'd still been around to guide me through this mess with Quinn, she would have made me see things from her unique perspective.

Five more days had passed before Quinn's mother had paid her another visit.

August 27, 1983

Margaret came back again today. I think her water may have broken while sitting in my kitchen. That or the dishwasher is leaking again.

She is already feeling the labor pains, and she suffers all by herself. She is giving her child her name rather than his father's because she doesn't want the town to know the father's true identity. The irony of it is not lost on me. He will carry the name of Dearborn to protect him from the fact that deer born may be exactly what he is.

I'm torn. But who better to decide what is right for the child than his mother? Russell Buckley's death was felt by both the two-natured and human communities. He was a great leader and a talented healer. Anyone would be proud to call him their father, but she only dated him a few months before she became pregnant and his would be some big shoes to fill. Margaret doesn't want her baby to grow up in The Legend's shadow when he may not even inherit the gene. She wants him to live a quiet, happy life, no different from her. I can hardly blame her.

Nevertheless, the situation causes me to worry. I will have to make Clive understand. He knows as well as anyone what it's like to lose the love of your life. There's a fifty-percent chance all of this worry is for nothing anyway. If the child doesn't inherit the gene, any magic will be non-magic.

I told her to return if she can keep the child's true identity a secret for six years.

PS. — It should be noted for future reference that Gus Reyburn is allergic to Cohosh. Hospital bills offset windfalls. Oy vey.

My knuckles were white from tightly gripping the book. I'd suspected Quinn might be from the same bloodline as The Legend, but it had never occurred to me that he was his son. I tossed the book aside and hunted through the stack for the book from 1989. I flipped pages until I reached the end of August.

August 30, 1989

What a beautiful boy Quinn Dearborn is. Such a happy child too. Makes me think that Art's and my decision not to have a child of our own may have been a mistake. What I wouldn't give for a daughter. If I weren't opposed to conjuring, I'd conjure up a little brunette with big chocolate eyes ... but I digress ...

Margaret Dearborn has upheld her end of our deal, and so I made good on mine. It is too soon to tell whether the boy has inherited the gene, but the protective cloaking spell should mask any two-natured qualities he may have. No shifter will be able to sense him as long as he is of healthy mind. If he can withstand the pull of the ley lines and leave Woodland Creek behind, we may never know what he could be.

While I may not agree with her, I know she only has her child's best interest at heart, and I think I may have found a way to offset the effects of the cloaking spell in a way that will please Clive. For three years, I have researched a protection spell that will make him more susceptible to any non-shifter magic and powers. So while the shifters may not sense him, his true destiny may find a way no matter what that may be.

Cloaking Spell:
Ingredients:
~an open mind
Directions: Chant three times through:

He's a mere human can't you see?
For so long as he believes.
His energies are plain Jane gray
For there is no other way.

Protection Spell:
Ingredients:
~an open mind
Directions: Chant three times through:
A human may be all you see,
A human may all he be.
But in his presence your powers grow
Until he decides it isn't so.
Note: The spell will naturally expire when and if
his two-natured abilities bloom and he accepts himself for
who he is.

Finally, I had my explanation. Quinn was under two spells, but the cloaking spell masked them both so he projected only human characteristics. The reason Ryan and I had never sensed he was a shifter was because the cloaking spell prevented it, but she'd attempted to counteract it with the second spell. The second spell was why Ryan and I both felt Quinn was a screamer. Ryan heard his thoughts louder, and I felt his emotions stronger. It was the cause of what I'd come to affectionately refer to as the Dearborn Effect. I was sick and saw colors when he felt strongly about something because the spell amplified his emotions. Janice had wanted to make sure that someone like me wouldn't miss someone like Quinn.

I sifted through piles of journals again to find the one for 2001. The recipe book from the same year was still upstairs hidden in the cabinet where I'd thrown it to keep Quinn's prying eyes out of it. But I wanted more than just the recipe for Willow's Tea. I wanted to know the story behind it.

When I found the book, I flipped it open to the entry that also included the tea, and then I backed up a week before that. I skipped briefly down the pages until I found my name on October 3rd.

October 3, 2001

I watch the way Willow stares at the boy and the way he laughs at her jokes, and I regret everything I've done in my life. I see in them what Clive saw in Clara: a future. I will not resort to magic to make sure they find their way together for I know in my heart now that some things are destined. For these two, it's only a matter of time.

That doesn't mean I can't in good conscience give them a little push, but I shall do it the old-fashioned way with my wallet and some elbow grease. Margaret told me the other day that Quinn is having trouble in math. My Willow is a whiz at math, so I have arranged for her to tutor him.

I can't think of a better investment than in Willow.

My heart swelled. Not only had Janice encouraged me to take the tutoring job, but she'd also created it. She'd invested in me as I'd invested in her. She'd known before anyone that Quinn would make me happy.

I flipped to the next page.

October 5, 2001

Ghastly deeds. Quinn's protection spell is making my Willow ill. I have done this, and I must find a way to fix it.

October 6, 2001

All is right with the world again.

Willow's Tea:
  Ingredients:
  ~ Chamomile
  ~Ginger
  ~Cinnamon Bark
  Directions: Brew a pot of water. Mix all ingredients together and pour them into a coffee filter. Tie the coffee filter shut with thread and make sure it's tight. Put the tea bag into a metal bowl and pour boiling water over it. Allow to steep for 6 minutes. Stir and say:
  As I stir, three times three,
  All who drink this magic tea,
  Shall feel well and whole,
  For serenity lies within this bowl.

I hopped up from my spot on the basement floor and took the stairs two at a time with the three books under my arm.

The house was oddly dark and quiet. It was only as I pulled my keys off the hook by the door and peered out the window that I realized how much time had passed while I was in the basement. A blanket of snow now covered the ground, and the sun, wherever it was behind the thick blanket of clouds, was setting, turning the world a magical and iridescent silver.

Quinn's truck was gone. My guess was he'd tried to get to the paint store before it closed. By tomorrow, the snow would likely be too thick to be passable. If I knew Quinn, he would have the dinner and wine waiting and be ready for the game of strip Clue when I returned. I just hoped he was still fully dressed because my hope was I wouldn't return alone.

I grabbed my heaviest coat from the hall tree on my way to the front door. In the car, I gripped the icy cold steering wheel and reversed down the driveway. I would never agree with Margaret Dearborn's decision to hide his true nature from him. She'd done more than deny him his father. She'd denied him his destiny and attempted to change fate; something I now knew could end disastrously. If things continued down the path we were on, the same karmic forces that had stolen Clara from Clive might steal her son from the both of us. I couldn't bear to think about that outcome, but luckily, I didn't have to. The wrong could be righted before it was too late.

I didn't know how Margaret would feel about my plan, but I had to give her the opportunity to step up and do the right thing. Like Janice, I didn't doubt her protective motherly intentions. She hadn't done this to hurt him, and I was going to give her the opportunity to help him. One way or another, Quinn would find out tonight who and what he truly was.

The road to New Town was slick and my wheels spun before finally gaining traction. When I got to the main intersection, a traffic accident and police barricade blocked the road to New Town forcing me to turn left instead of right. I would have to take the long way along the back of the convent and cemetery. I was nearly to the turn off when a truck parked along the fence line caught my eye. Even with a sheet of snow over it, I knew it belonged to Quinn. The old rusty tailgate and faded red paint were a dead giveaway. I pulled onto the gravel drive leading into the Reyburn property and considered my options.

Ryan's warning earlier in the day played through my head.

Quinn's buddies are all headed back out to the Reyburn land again this afternoon. Some stupid 'first snow' nonsense. Apparently, it's a tradition or something to kill something on the first day of winter.

The snow was here, and no doubt, they were now up to mischief, but I didn't understand why Quinn would be here too. He'd been sincere in the museum when he'd sworn off hunting any more deer. What had brought him out here when he knew the men would be hunting?

Panic gripped me and had me shrugging off my coat. Quinn was here to find the little doe that had rescued him. My heart twisted and thumped as it filled with dread. I closed my eyes and listened to the wind.

Magic surrounded the property.

Either Quinn had shifted or he was not alone.

Or worse—both.

Seventeen

Quinn

AS WAS OFTEN THE CASE, I'd fallen asleep and awoke on the run again. But this time, it felt different. I wasn't running from something. I was running to something. *Or someone.*

A thin layer of ice covered the snow and crunched with every footfall. The wind had died down and the sun had set while I'd slept, but the air still hung heavy over Woodland Creek. More snow would fall overnight. This, the first snow, marked the beginning of months and months and inches upon inches of dismal cold. I welcomed it though I couldn't tell you exactly why.

Always on a mission, my feet traveled fast over the frozen surface. They'd run on more treacherous terrain than this. The mountains of Afghanistan had prepared me well for my current task. No heavy boots. No weapons. No packs. I'd never felt lighter on my feet. A branch slapped me in the face, and I barely felt it.

I am free.

There'd been a time when running was the only way to quiet the noise following me day after dreaded day. It couldn't always find me out here. It was a sweet relief after enduring the awful, clanging, never-ending racket that came with the memories. They wouldn't let me go. I was bound to them as I was bound to the people in them. For a long time, running had been my only real relief, and sometimes, even that didn't work. Luckily, I'd found an even better therapy.

I am not alone.

Willow was my new quiet. She'd crept silently into my life and was rearranging the way I looked at everything, including myself. This morning, I'd handed her a piece of my broken, battered soul and told her about the nightmares and the midnight runs and the embarrassing reality of waking up lost and naked every morning. She hadn't even flinched. As she always did, she accepted my truths and apologies and pulled me forward. She'd taken the offered piece of my broken soul and tucked it away for safekeeping. There was more where it had come from, but it wouldn't be long before she held them all.

I was in love with her.

It had been inevitable. She was as perfect as I was bruised. She was as pure as I was soiled. She was my perfect counterpoint, and I was in love with her. I would try harder to be whole again because she deserved that, but there was freedom in knowing that the broken pieces were as valuable to her as the whole would be. She hadn't told me as much, but I already knew she was in love with me too. Knowing it and knowing I could and would tell her about this run when I got home filled me with happiness.

I leaped over a stream and found my footing. It would be a skating rink soon, making it harder to find water. Something instinctual told me it was something that should concern me, but it didn't tonight. Nothing concerned me as I neared the spot where I'd seen the doe last.

She is here.

Somehow, I could feel her presence ahead of me. I burst through the last line of trees and into the clearing with more gusto than warranted. My feet pounded across the ground until I slid to a stop by the big cedar tree where I'd laid covered in leaves just days ago.

Big brown eyes peered at me curiously from across the way.

Just as I remembered, she was the most beautiful creature I'd ever seen. Dainty but still somehow powerful. Graceful and lithe. Long, thin legs looked as if they might snap under the weight of her, but I knew they were stronger than they appeared. I longed to watch *her* run.

Large, pert ears stood tall on her head, not missing a thing. She blinked at me and then cocked her head as if to size me up. *I knew you'd come back,* she seemed to say.

'Of course,' I wanted to tell her. 'I came to thank you.'

I wondered how close she would let me get today. I took a tentative step, and she watched me.

She seemed to blink her submission. *Go ahead. Come closer.*

It was delusional to think she was actually speaking to me. Obviously, no audible words were exchanged, but in my head, I could hear her as clearly as if her thoughts were my own. It was almost as if there was a direct line between her soul and mine. Some thread that tethered our hearts and gave me access to her thoughts. *Is it okay?*

We can't stay. It's not safe here.

I took a few slow steps in her direction and waited. She followed my lead and then stopped. We repeated this dance until less than a few feet separated us. I held perfectly still as she circled around me, suddenly seeming unsure. She craned her long neck as if listening to something behind me.

Shhhhh. Her fear was tangible. Her big brown eyes blinked in warning. Yet, I couldn't comprehend the danger even as it struck.

The arrow pierced flesh with a thud that shouldn't have sounded so hollow for the damage it was causing. It sliced easily through her chest and protruded awkwardly. Instantly, she was gone, bolting away from her attacker and away from me.

I followed because I had no other choice. The invisible line tethering us pulled me along behind her as she ran. What I hoped were her words echoed in my head. *Come closer. Come closer.*

'I am coming,' I wanted to call to her. 'I will help you somehow. Take you somewhere. I will take care of you.'

"Damn it. I think I got the wrong one." The voice was a familiar one, and I didn't have to rack my brain long to place it.

Tim had shot my beautiful doe. I hated him for it, though I would've done the same thing only a week before.

She jumped the fence line not a minute too soon, and I winced at the pain in my chest when she landed. I ran behind her as we quickly put needed distance between Tim and us. As we ran north through the western part of the cemetery, I pondered how I could make good on my promises. Where do you take an injured deer? Were there veterinarians, possibly large animal doctors, who would be willing to help her? Would she even allow me to touch her? I didn't know how to save a wild animal. She wasn't a bunny I could put in a box and take home to nurse back to health. She was beautiful but wild.

And possibly mortally wounded.

I followed her through the outskirts of the cemetery, losing sight of her from time to time as she wove in and out of trees. She crossed the road near where I'd parked my truck, and I wanted to yell at her to wait because it was the best chance for her survival. But there was no way for me to communicate that and no chance of her listening anyway.

Flashing lights marked the scene of an accident to the west, but she didn't get close to it. We ran for what felt like miles, parallel to the major roads but just far enough away from them to remain unseen. I was vaguely aware after all of my late night and early morning runs of where we were, and I questioned why an injured animal would head directly into town rather than away from it.

Even when I couldn't see her, the pain in my chest never abated, letting me know instinctually she was there, ahead of me, and that her heart still beat in her chest. The same instinct drove me forward as we headed north, but it brought me to a sudden stop before we reached the creek, which marked a familiar property line.

My doe stood on its banks, unable to make the final leap over it. The house loomed dark and empty behind her.

Not like this.

I wasn't sure which one of us had thought it. It was ludicrous to think it was her, anyway. I wouldn't be surprised if our entire conversation had been only in my mind. Or if she didn't exist at all and was merely the creation of my fragmented mind.

Those beautiful, soul-searching eyes blinked at me. *I'm as real as you are. Help me, Quinn.*

Before I could get to her, her knees buckled. She wobbled and then fell to the ground, rolling on her side so that the arrow pointed up at the milky gray sky. Her chest rose and fell with every labored breath. I listened for her voice but heard nothing more.

A familiar whomp, whomp, whomp intruded on our moment. I closed my eyes and wished it away. It grew louder and I imagined it was the sound of her heartbeat, assuring me she was going to be okay. I had myself nearly convinced when it became harsher, turning into something that didn't belong here.

As I had so many times before, I looked up to find the bird in the sky and was surprised to find it was sleek and white with the name of a hospital printed on the side. It flew low, on a mission too, and within seconds, it disappeared over the treetops. The sound of the rotating blades faded but left in its wake the debris of my life. All of the noise I'd successfully evaded had found me again.

I pushed and shoved against it, trying to rid my head of it all. I had to keep it together. The doe was dying in front of me. Our roles had reversed, and I was her only hope. I stared at her, trying to come back to the here and now, all the while knowing the better parts of me were still lost on a continent thousands of miles away.

She let out a bleat that sounded like a plea, and it

triggered something in me—a survival instinct I thought I'd never find again—and snapped me out of the fog the helicopter had dropped over me. In its place, the brittle evening air sparkled and shimmered off the reflection of the snow, promising me that, together, we'd survive this night.

The air around the doe suddenly glittered and shook, and I dropped to the ground beside her as she disappeared before my very eyes. In her place lay Willow, naked and bleeding. The arrow stuck out of her chest now rather than the animal.

My heart thumped out a beat of shock even louder than the bird's blades had been. *It's an episode,* I told myself. *A fucking episode and you've finally lost it.* I squeezed my eyes shut and tried to clear my head.

"Quinn." It was Willow's voice though it sounded smaller somehow.

I opened my eyes again to find nothing had changed. Willow was as beautiful and lovely and naked. Blood streamed down her torso, and the end of the arrow pointed horrifically at me. All at the same time, I wanted to worship her and cover her and heal her.

"Please, Quinn," she pleaded hoarsely. "There's something wrong."

Something's wrong? I shook my head, and it suddenly felt so heavy. *Everything is wrong.*

"Please, Quinn!" she said again, more desperate this time. Tears welled in her eyes, and she coughed a ragged cough. "I need you to change. I can't hear your thoughts like this."

Change? Hear my thoughts? I shook my head again, more vehemently this time, not knowing how to respond even if I could.

"Look at yourself," she begged.

I looked down at my broad chest and my legs folded beneath me. Four legs were where two should be. Hooves in the place of feet. Short rust-colored fur instead of skin. It was preposterous.

"You are magnificent," she whispered.

There was no me, as far as I could see.

I needed to run away from the abomination around me. I stood up and counted each time a leg straightened to support me. Four in all. It was a complete annihilation of everything I knew to be true. What was I? A monster? Would that make my sweet Willow one too?

I stamped my feet on the ground and took off running. I hit a nearby tree hard enough I bounced backward. I winced and moaned as the crack echoed through the forest. Neither of the sounds was familiar. The crack wasn't brittle enough to be a tree. The moan was a noise I'd only heard when the animals I'd shot hadn't died right away.

"You have to accept it, Quinn. I can't handle this right now." Her voice was as labored as her breath.

Accept it? What was she asking me to accept? That I was a monster? I looked at the tree, now marked by my disbelief, and my eyes drifted to the ground. A broken stick lay near the base of the tree. It was too pale and too smooth to be a part of the tree. But how was it possible it was a part of me?

I turned again to Willow. I could see the pain in her eyes but somehow she managed to smile. "If you want to be human again, just wish for it," she said. "The change is uncomfortable at first, but it doesn't hurt exactly." Each word came out slower than the next. Her breath hitched, and her beautiful features twisted on her face. I wanted to tell her to stop talking, but I sensed there was no way to do so.

Wish it.

Please let me be normal again.

I wasn't even sure anymore who I was praying to, but I barely had time to think it before it was happening.

Exactly as it had when Willow had changed places with the doe, the air warbled and warped around me. Glittering and shining, it came alive at the same time my body did. An electrical current zipped through me, making my skin—or what should've been skin—crawl and my bones ache. But when I looked down again, it was just me—the same man I saw when I got out of the shower in the morning, the same man who snuck in with the dawn almost every day. Except, in addition to being naked, I was covered in blood.

Instinctively, I reached up and touched my head. The proof of the wound was slippery between my fingers, but the blood wasn't enough to cause me worry. More likely, the blood sprayed across my chest belonged to Willow.

She gasped, and it was the wake-up call I needed. I crouched beside her. "I'm taking you to the hospital."

"No time." Each breath left her body on a wheeze.

"They won't be able to help her." I jumped at the garbled voice behind me and my head whipped in its direction. I recognized the old man as one who ate breakfast at the diner nearly every morning. As he glanced back and forth between Willow and me, I was suddenly and awkwardly aware we were naked. The desire to cover her body with my own was overwhelming, and I was sure I would've if it wouldn't hurt her more.

"Trust me. I've seen it all before." His expression was concerned and knowing. "I'm a doctor of your kind."

My kind. I no longer knew what my kind was.

"Can you get her into the house for me?" he asked.

"Yes, of course," I stammered. I studied her for a second, strategizing the best way to move her without bumping the arrow or jostling her more than necessary, and then I scooped her up in my arms.

"Something's wrong, Clive," she groaned. "I didn't shift on my own."

"It's probably a reaction to something. Maybe the arrowhead is dipped in silver," he said, following along behind me. "Curious."

She nodded and then her head listed to the side, coming to rest against my shoulder.

"Silver is poison to the two-natured," he said as if he knew I was light-years behind the two of them. "It will cause an involuntary reaction and force them to shift when they don't want to."

The two-natured. Was that what she was? And me?

"What do you think?" he asked, holding the door open for us.

I walked through the house with Willow in my arms and Clive hobbling steadily along behind me. As I laid her on her bed, I realized, whatever she was, I'd already accepted it. Maybe it was because she'd already confided in me about her empath abilities. Or maybe because I'd watched her change from a deer to a woman right before my eyes. There'd always been something magical about her.

"And you, too."

It was the second time the old man had seemed to answer a question he'd plucked right out of my mind.

"Yes, I'm clairvoyant and telepathic, too, when it suits me," he said, doing it again.

"So you *know* what I'm thinking?" I pulled a blanket up over her as much as I could while still avoiding her wound.

"Much like Willow can read your emotions. Don't hold a grudge, though. It's why I'm here," he said setting a black bag on the bed I hadn't noticed before that moment. It was the type of doctor's bag used for house calls back when doctors still made those. "I fell asleep while watching *Wheel of Fortune* and had a dream she'd been shot with a silver arrow. You appeared to be in distress as well."

I added this to the ever-growing list of impossibilities I now knew were true.

As he pulled out a stethoscope, I brushed her hair away from her face. Her eyes were closed, and she looked so peaceful it scared me. "Then you can tell me what she's thinking."

He held up a finger while he listened to her heart. The room was deadly silent, and for the first time, I considered the possibility Willow wouldn't make it. The idea of life without her ripped my recently rejuvenated heart from my own chest.

After a few long seconds, he pulled the stethoscope from his ears and set it on the bed. "You should ask her yourself while I'm gone. Try to keep her awake."

"You're leaving?" I asked, bowing up to the tiny

man as if he wasn't fifty years older and a hundred pounds lighter than I was. Only over my dead body would he be leaving this house. I'd already placed all of my faith in him and wasted precious time.

"No, no, son. I need to gather some stuff from around the house. Do you know if Janice's *things* are still here?"

"The basement," Willow whispered. Clive scurried off, and she smiled a weak smile. "Strange little bird, isn't he?

"Not the weirdest thing I've seen tonight."

"Quinn? Get dressed, okay? Just in case."

"In case of what? I think Clive only has eyes for you." I winked at her.

Her lips pulled into a thin smile. "Just do it. If I don't make it, then you'll have to call people."

There was no response to that. I crossed to the dresser and dug through the drawer she'd given me only because she'd asked me. I'd do my damnedest to move heaven and earth if she asked me. Without paying attention, I pulled out the first thing my hand touched and slipped on a pair of athletic shorts and returned to her side. I got down on my knees and leaned against the side of the bed. Reaching for her hand, I closed my eyes ready to make every bargain I could to have some more time with her.

I'd give up thousands of days alone for only one more day with her.

"Don't be so sad, my love. You're clouding up my happy."

"I'm sorry …" The words caught in my throat. It was the closest either one of us had ever come to any sort of proclamation. My heart was suddenly too full to contain it all. I had to tell her. *Just in case.*

"I love you, Willow," I blurted. It was so ineloquent. So completely insufficient, considering how I truly felt. I wanted the first time I said it to be under different circumstances. Those three little words should be a promise for the future, not a goodbye.

"I know," she whispered. A smile pulled at her lips. "And I love you, too. Honestly, I'm so happy."

There was an arrow sticking out of her chest, she could barely speak, and some strange voodoo doctor was wandering around her house. "How can you possibly be happy?"

"I'm just so glad I got to see it." Her eyelids fluttered closed as if she was imagining it. Whatever *it* was.

"What?" I stroked her hand.

"You realizing what you are." She intertwined her fingers with mine. "You are so magnificent. There is no other word. Magnificent. I wish you could see you through my eyes."

"I am a freak. A monster."

"Then I am too."

"No." She was anything but a monster. "I'm so sorry. You wouldn't have been out there if it weren't for me. I know you were out there because I was looking for you."

"So you can accept me for what I am and love me anyway?" she asked, blinking at me. Her coppery eyes searched mine, begging me to say yes.

The eyes were the common thread.

Willow's eyes and those of the doe who had curled up beside me in the cold were the same. They held the same amount of love and showered me with the same amount of reverence. I could see it now.

"No matter what." I nearly choked on the words.

"But you can't accept you are the same? That we were made for each other?"

I brought her hand to my mouth and kissed the back of it. It was so much easier to accept whatever Willow was than it was to accept the truth about myself.

"Two perfect counterparts," she continued. "Two souls destined to find our way back to each other." She coughed again and winced.

"You need to stop talking now, Willow. There will be a lot of time to talk later." I hoped I wasn't making promises I couldn't keep.

"But I have so much to tell you. Your dad—" Another cough tore through her body, and she cried out in pain.

I was on my knees, ready to beg and plead. "No more. Only one thing matters right now." With our hands still entwined, I leaned over and brushed a kiss across her lips, careful not to touch her anywhere else. "I don't know what I am, but I accept us … whatever that means. I want more time with you, and I'll take it anyway I can get it."

"Good enough." Her breath was faint against my lips. Too faint.

"I'll help you through this, and then you'll help me get through whatever's next. Deal?"

She smiled. It was weak but determined. "Deal. We have to prove to Clive that this is real. Isn't that right, Clive?"

"That's right," Clive said from behind me. His voice was wrangled and his eyes moist, and I wondered how long he'd been standing there. He crooked a skinny finger at me. "Come here, Mr.

Dearborn."

We stepped away from Willow though I never took my eyes off her. "What's the plan? By my estimate, the arrow is embedded a couple of inches into her chest."

"At least that much. The plan is you're going to pull it out. The quicker, the better because it's going to be painful and—"

"No," I interrupted. I knew enough about wounds to know what he was suggesting would only make her injuries worse. She needed surgery. Anesthesia. A sterile environment. We had none of those and apparently no means to get them. "Ripping it out will cause too much damage."

"No choice. We have to get the silver out of her system. It's killing her."

"How long?"

"Minutes, not hours."

I swallowed my fear. "And if she bleeds out?"

"She won't. As soon as you get it out, I'll spread this on the wound." He held up a small bowl. "It's a tincture of Burdock, Echinacea, ipecac, milk thistle, and yellow dock. It will reverse the effects of the silver and slow the bleeding. You be ready to apply pressure to it, and when she's ready, we'll take her outside. She'll need to shift as soon as she's able."

"Is that wise?" I'd felt what it did to my own body. Whatever was involved in the rearrangement of our molecules to make such a thing possible couldn't be good for her in her current state.

Clive patted me on the arm and smiled. "You have a lot to learn, my boy. As soon as she shifts, the wound will start healing. She'll be walking around on two legs by morning." He smiled. "If that's what you

264

prefer."

"I'd feel better if you stay with her," he continued. "It looks like you could use a little time to heal yourself." He nodded to the open wound on my head. "That's a nasty cut you have there."

"I think I broke something."

"I saw, but when you shift again, your antler will be as good as new. Now, let's get your teacher fixed up so she can show you what you're made of."

Clive handed me a towel and then moved around to where I'd been standing next to Willow. "You better get on the other side of her."

Silently, I crawled across her big bed, cognizant that every move probably hurt her. Her eyes were closed again, and her breathing shallow.

"On the count of three," Clive said.

"No," she said. "No warning."

Her face was so serene and peaceful. Doing anything to disturb it required me to give myself a pep talk. Don't twist it. That will hurt more. Pull straight up. Hard enough to get it out on the first pull. I met Clive's eyes and, in agreement, he nodded.

One, two, three.

Willow's back arched off the bed and she gasped and sputtered obscenities of the sort I'd never heard come from her mouth. I tossed the arrow away and reached for her shoulders to help keep her still for Clive. She struggled against us with more strength than I thought her tiny frame possessed. But within seconds, the wound was covered with the salve. With both hands, I held the towel pressed firmly over it as Willow's rigid body gradually succumbed to the healing tincture. Slowly, the fear and agony drained from her face, and she sank into the bed. Her breathing deepened.

I didn't dare move, not even when Willow's gray cat jumped up on the bed and slunk to the head of the bed. I growled at him as he curled around the top of her head. He hissed and matched my expression. Neither of us was leaving.

"That damn cat," Clive said looking fondly at the animal. "Reminds me of Janice. Annoyingly stubborn and fiercely protective."

"He makes Willow happy," I conceded. "She has a soft spot for annoyingly stubborn and fiercely protective creatures." Clive put the bowl on the bedside table and took a few steps toward the hall. "I'm going to disappear for a bit."

After everything I'd seen and heard, I couldn't help but wonder if he meant it literally.

He chuckled. "No. I thought I'd give you some time together. You can remove the pressure in about five minutes and add more of the tincture. I'll be back."

Gaston and I held vigil over her as Willow fell into a deep sleep.

I waited twice as long as Clive had suggested and then peeked at the wound. It was raw and angry, but the salve seemed to be doing its job because the bleeding had all but stopped. I applied more of the medicine and then stretched out beside her, taking her hand in mine and muttering promises I knew she couldn't hear.

Eighteen

Quinn

"I THINK SHE'S READY," CLIVE said, nudging me awake. "Be careful. You're kind of … all tangled up there." He shook his finger at me, but his expression was more amusement than disapproval.

"Oh," I said, trying to peel myself off Willow without disturbing her too much. With one leg thrown over hers and an arm draped across her waist, I was worse than the cat still curled around her head. "I'm so sorry. I guess I was completely knocked out."

Her lips turned up into a sweet smile. "That's a good problem to have." It was something that only seemed to happen when I slept beside her. Another good problem to have.

"Do you think you can walk?" Clive asked. "I let you sleep for a while. You both looked like you needed it. But I think you better get a move on now." According to the clock on the bedside table, more than half the night was gone.

"Yes, I think so." Her voice was steady, and her breathing unlabored. She'd made a lot of progress in a short amount of time. Clive's tincture had obviously done its job well.

"I can carry her," I said, not because she needed

me to, but because I wanted to. I swung my feet to the floor and scratched my head.

"Get her to the trees," he said with a knowing smile. "Then let her do the rest."

My hand hit the tender spot, and I immediately looked at Willow to see if she'd felt it too.

She wrinkled her nose, and she looked around the room as if maybe she could see it in the air. "Nope. Just normal stuff."

Clive leaned over Willow and looked at the wound. "Nothing normal about the two of you, I'm afraid, but you both should heal just fine now."

"Thank you so much, Clive. What would we have done without you?"

Clive ducked his head. "It felt good to practice a little medicine. It's been a long time."

"Anything else we need to do for her?" I asked. It seemed impossible to me that after everything she went through and with the still open wound on her chest, he was giving her a clean bill of health and sending her on her way. Maybe it was their way, though.

Their way.

Our way.

"I would just suggest the two of you stay off the Reyburn land and maybe any other land where you think you might get shot at." He zipped up his little black bag. "At least until after Christmas. Maybe spend a little more time exploring Running Deer Park. Hell, it's named for you."

Willow grinned. "I try, but this one's been keeping me on my toes."

"I know he has. Proof that it does no good to fight destiny." He turned toward the door. "I'll hang around to make sure you two get off okay, and then I'll let myself out the front."

"Clive?" Willow asked. "Would you want all of Janice's things? The basement is full—well you saw it—and I need to find a good home for all of her stuff."

Clive slipped off into thought for a moment and then nodded. "I'll take everything but the books ... those are yours to keep. I have too many bad memories wrapped up in them. I prefer to remember the good ones."

"I understand. I'll keep them safe for you in case you ever change your mind. We can bring you the rest in a few days."

Janice's things. Books full of bad memories. I stared dumbly at the two of them with no idea of what they were talking about.

Clive had been right. I had so much to learn.

"Ready?" she asked.

"I think so."

The smile on Willow's face was worth it all. I didn't have to have her empath abilities to know she was truly excited about the prospect of going out there with me. Her eyes lit up with the promise of many midnight runs to come. "Let's go then," she said, trying to sit up.

"Whoa there, tiger," I said, scooping her up into my arms, careful to leave the sheet draped over the top of her. After all, Clive was watching, too. If she thought I was going to be okay with her running around naked in front of men ... even old ones ... she had some things to learn, too.

Clive snorted. "You'll get used to it. I bet half the town has seen her naked."

"Now, that is not true," she protested. "I'm very discreet. I'm a shifter, not an exhibitionist. But I'm glad to see *everyone* is back to their old selves."

Clive's wrinkly old face stretched into a grin. "Some things never change, no matter what I've seen of ya."

"All right. That's enough, you two. We're burning moonlight."

I carried her through the house and out the back door. Leaving Clive behind, we crossed the lawn. "How do you feel?" I asked.

"I'll be okay. The bigger question is how do *you* feel?"

I didn't see how my emotional health was more important than her physical one, but Willow was always more concerned about me than she was herself. "Don't you know?"

She answered with a sly grin. "Maybe, but I'd rather hear about it from you."

I swallowed my pride, and it went down surprisingly well. "Well, I'm nervous. Anxious. Scared. Am I making you sick?"

She shook her head, and her soft brown hair brushed against my shoulder. "I'm pretty sure the spell is broken."

"Spell?" I stopped at the creek. "You ready to stand?"

"Yes." Gingerly, I set her on her feet but didn't let go until I was sure she could support herself. The sheet slipped to the ground, and she stood there, naked and unashamed. "Let's do this," she said. "My feet are freezing."

I hadn't even noticed until she said something, but mine were, too. "What about my shorts?"

"Do you like them?"

"Well, yeah, I guess so."

"Then drop 'em." She waggled her eyebrows at me. "Seriously. If you don't, they'll be torn to shreds."

I ran my thumbs along the waistband, suddenly shy.

"I've seen you naked, Quinn. Inside the house and out here. Trust me, there's nothing for you to be ashamed of."

She was the one who shouldn't be ashamed. Her pale skin glowed in the pale moonlight, brighter than the snow. Small but perfect breasts pointed at me in the cold night air. My eyes drank her in. From head to toe, I worshiped her, my eyes lingering on places I'd only begun to explore.

"Oh, there'll be plenty of time for that too when we get back."

"Change with me and I'll tell you everything."

Just wish for it.

I didn't know if there were special words I was supposed to say or if an intention was enough. I took a deep breath and went for it. *Make me a deer again.* Unseen forces within me shifted and twisted, but I kept my eyes on Willow, marveling instead on what the change did to her. Through the haze of the glimmering air around us, I watched her two legs become four. A rich, sandy brown coat replaced her creamy skin and curved down to a snow white underbelly. Her nose was big and black and round, possibly the least dainty thing on her. A pair of pert little ears sat high on her head. But her eyes—

–they were the same.

She blinked at me. *We can talk like this now.*

I looked down and realized I'd been so

271

mesmerized by her that I hadn't even noticed my own discomfort as my body had morphed into something I still didn't recognize. *So we can read each other's minds? Like Clive?*

Not exactly. I can hear what you want me to hear and vice versa. It's much like talking only we don't need to. If you don't want me to know, I won't, but you have to be careful. Not everyone has filters.

Some people can hear everything.

Ryan can hear everything all of the time. She somehow appeared apologetic. Or maybe I could pick up on her emotions like she could mine when we were walking around on two legs. *I've been meaning to tell you that.*

I stamped my feet. *Ryan is a mind reader, too. Good lord, I bet I've given him some good material to relay to you.*

I don't play games. If I won your heart unfairly, it wouldn't really be mine. I've asked Ryan to stay out of our heads. She took a few steps to try out her own legs. *Though sometimes he breaks my rules and sometimes I have to be okay with it. His heart is usually in the right place.*

She took a few more steps in my direction and nuzzled my neck with her nose. *I wouldn't have known you were going out to Tim's land if he hadn't told me.*

I wish he hadn't. You wouldn't have been shot.

But it would have been you, and you wouldn't have known what to do or even that the arrowhead was poison. You probably would have died, Quinn. Alone. Without ever learning the truth. Things happen for a reason.

And sometimes they happen for no good reason. I would've taken the shot for you even if was my last heartbeat.

I know you would've.

Ahhhhhh. I didn't think I said that out loud.

She nudged me again. *See. I told you. You have to be careful. Learn to filter. Right now, you're like an open book.*

Let's walk for a bit. She took a few steps and then turned back to look at me. *Right after we get over the creek.* Several fast strides and a leap later, she'd cleared it. I followed right on her heels, making it a good two feet farther than she had before sinking into the snow.

Very nice. You're so much bigger than I am. I won't be able to keep up when you really get going.

I'm in no rush. Even as I said it, my legs twitched. I wouldn't leave her behind, but something innate in me made me need to fly through the trees. It would have to wait, though. She needed to heal, and I needed information.

I let her lead. Something told me it wouldn't always be the case.

What do you want to know first? I didn't know if she was reading my mind or not. I didn't have the telepathy thing down.

I don't even know where to start.

We walked a few paces in silence before she spoke. *Have you ever heard of The Legend?*

Of course.

He had died before either of us was born, but supposedly, he was massive. Every hunter in three counties was trying to get him between their crosshairs.

Tim's uncle claims to have been the one who took him down though he never could prove it.

So I've heard, but my point is that I would imagine it was a lot like now. It seems everyone is looking for the big buck you guys call The Monster. Do you realize the first sighting of The Monster was about a month after you came back to town?

I suddenly realized where she was going with this. *Are you saying I'm The Monster?*

That's exactly what I'm saying. I'm sure of it, in fact. I

273

know you can't see yourself the way I can. But you're huge. You tower over me. As far as I can tell, you usually go out at night, and people have only spotted The Monster at night. And of course, there's the rack. That is one phenomenal rack. She turned to look at me, and if a deer could look coy, she did.

I think I'm supposed to say that to you, not the other way around. So you're saying I've been hunting myself?

Isn't it ironic? The Monster is safest when you, a trained sniper, is looking for him. But Quinn, it was early in the evening when I found you today. Did you fall asleep while you were waiting for me?

I think so.

I have a theory. I know you have nightmares a lot and you sleepwalk. I've seen you do it a few times. I followed you this morning.

You did?

Yes. You walked out the back door, down to the creek, and then you shifted and took off. I was too shocked to follow. By the time I pulled myself together, you were gone. Honestly, I never guessed you were one of us. Normally, we can sense our own kind. But neither Ryan nor I picked up any kind of two-natured vibe from you. So when you shifted in front of me this morning, I was completely shocked. Ecstatic but shocked.

No one was more shocked by these revelations than I was. *But you didn't say anything when I came in this morning. We talked about my nightmares.*

Honestly, I didn't know how to tell you. You should've started shifting when you were about sixteen, but I could tell this morning when you came back home and we talked about your nightmares that you had no idea you were even doing it. I wanted to do some research before I talked to you about it.

So I've been doing this for half of my life and I didn't even know it? There was no way.

No, I don't think so. I think you're a late bloomer. It's been sitting dormant in your system, waiting to be triggered. I think either the PTSD triggers it or the ley lines triggered it when you came back to town.

Ley lines?

They cross and run through Running Deer State Forest and act like a magnet drawing creatures and other magical beings like us.

Ley lines. Magical beings. None of this seemed real. *So you think they're to blame for … this.*

Well no, I think they triggered the shifter in you, but they aren't to blame for it. That's your parents' doing, and I was actually on my way to your mother's tonight when I saw your truck out at Tim's and stopped. As soon as I got out of my car, I could feel the presence of a shifter nearby. So apparently, I can sense you in this form but not your human form.

I just … I don't know. I stopped to try to look at my reflection in an iced-over creek, but there was too much snow on the top of it. She snorted a real deer snort and then I heard a giggle in my head.

You can shift at home so you can look at yourself if you want, but you had better not tear up my house.

I laughed. *With my magnificent rack?*

She ducked her head. *Exactly. Look, your mother should have told you all of this years ago. It's your heritage and your story, and she withheld it from you. I was going over there to confront her. One of us was going to tell you the truth tonight, and I wanted to give her the opportunity to make it right.*

Is my mom one of you too?

One of us, Quinn. Us. No, she's not.

So then my dad was?

He was. She pressed her big black nose into my neck, and I felt her need to be closer to me. *I spent the afternoon doing some research, and I know who your father was. He wasn't who your mom said he was. His name was Russell Buckley, and he was a well-respected doctor who moved to town a few years before you were born. By the humans in town, he was known as The Legend.*

My chest suddenly felt heavy. My head sagged to the ground. *Tim's uncle shot my dad and killed him?* I asked.

He was hit by a silver arrow like I was today. Apparently, those stupid silver arrows are a fancy-pants Reyburn thing.

I knew it to be true. They had them custom made and each one was actually imprinted with the Reyburn 'R.' Once upon a time, I'd thought it was cool. *Do they know about us and want to kill us? Is this some crazy vendetta?*

We don't think so. After your dad had died, there was some discussion about that, but ultimately it was decided that it was just a horrible accident. Still, my family wasn't pleased when I briefly dated Tim.

I bristled and stamped the ground a few more times.

Your dad ran, she continued. *It's instinct when you've been hit, and he ran for miles. He made it almost to the park before the poison in his system forced him to change back to his human form. The herd sent out a search party for him, but it was more than a day before they found him, and it was too late.*

She stuck her head under my neck and nudged my head up again. *So can you imagine what it was like to be your mom at the time? She was young and crazy in love with your dad. Apparently, no one even knew they were dating when he died, leaving her alone and pregnant. I think she protected you the only way she knew how.*

By not telling me who my father was? I snorted out a

puff of air in anger.

According to Janice's diary, Janice was the only person she told. Since your mom's not a shifter, there was only a fifty percent chance you'd inherit the gene and continue the bloodline. I guess she couldn't bear the idea of you following in the footsteps of your dad, so she took matters into her own hands. It was wrong, but I don't blame her.

What do you mean?

Janice wasn't one of us either, but she was well versed in magic.

I couldn't help myself. I snorted and then could practically feel the eye-roll coming from Willow.

You saw what Clive did for me tonight. He's Janice's half-brother. All the 'stuff' I was talking about him taking is her wizardry stuff down in the basement. I've been hanging onto it all this time because I didn't know what to do with it. He saved my life, and who knows, maybe Janice saved yours. I don't know what would have happened if you'd shifted the first time while you were away. There would've been no one there to explain what was happening to you.

Willow had sufficiently returned me to my place of little knowledge. *I'm sorry. So what exactly did Janice do for me?*

At your mom's request, she put you under a cloaking spell. It hid you from us, making it so we couldn't sense your second nature.

How'd you figure all of this out? As crazy as it all sounded, I believed her.

Clive has been giving me some hints, but I didn't pick up on them. After watching you shift this morning, though, I had a little chat with him, and he led me to Janice's diaries. It's all in there. You can read it for yourself if you want to.

I shook my big heavy head. *I think I'll take your word for it.*

There's something else. A few weeks ago, Clive called my love for you contrived.

Rage flared through me. He'd saved her life, and for that, I would be eternally grateful, but there was nothing contrived about the way we felt about each other.

Easy there, tiger. She nudged me again with the side of her head, and my anger instantly dissipated.

Do you know any of those?

She giggled again. *A few. You know a bear.*

Who?

Ryan.

That's fitting. He looks a little bear-like.

I know, right?

Vanessa?

She's a woodpecker.

Oh. So there's no problem with interspecies dating?

In their case, yes, but not generally. Love is love. Get it any way you can seems to be the general consensus. But Vanessa and Ryan's families have always been at each other's throats. After I get you taken care of, I need to work on their problem next. Clive also hinted that the answer to their problems is in the books, but you're my only concern right now.

I'd kind of like to kiss you right now.

She giggled. *I'd kind of like to kiss you, too. Let's head back. I'm feeling much better.*

Roll over, I commanded her.

She cocked her head at me and then immediately did as I asked.

You're a born leader, Quinn. Don't abuse it.

I didn't have the first clue what she was talking about. *I only wanted to see your wound. Ohhhh.* Unbelievably, it was almost completely healed. The skin was pink but closed. *It looks really good.*

We are quick healers, even in human form, but especially in animal form. That should have been my first clue you were one of us. She rolled back over and hopped up on her spindly little legs. I brushed the snow off her back with my muzzle. *Your ankle healed overnight. It was also the first night I saw you come out of the woods naked. I should've known then you were a shifter, but you were embarrassed as you ran across the yard and that's not a normal shifter trait, so it threw me for a loop. Then you said you'd been misdiagnosed your whole life. I don't think you were ever misdiagnosed, Quinn. I think you just healed faster than the average person did.*

So my ankle was broken.

I think so. I think you had a PTSD nightmare that night, sleepwalked, shifted, and healed. I found your boot in the woods. Where did you wake up?

I thought for a minute. *I don't know. Somewhere out by the high school.*

Long walk home when you're naked.

Yeah. It happens a lot.

We started walking toward the house. *Wait*, I said. *You said there was something else. Something to do with contrived love.* My anger flared again though to a smaller degree this time.

Clive and Janice have a sordid history. I'll tell you about it sometime, but he didn't always agree with her use of magic and the cloaking spell she put on you was one of those times. He felt like she was trying to alter fate, which is a no-no. They do operate by some ethical standards. So to counterbalance the cloaking spell—and keep Clive happy—she put you under a protection spell to make you more susceptible to all other kinds of magic. It's why you're so much louder in Ryan's head than anyone else in the diner is. It's why I can feel your emotions so much stronger than I feel anyone else's. I call it the Dearborn

Effect because no one has ever made me sick the way you do.

Ahhhhh. As I'd always feared, I was not good for her.

You are good for me, Quinn. But it drew you to me and made you more susceptible to my empath abilities. In Clive's eyes, it made our relationship a false one.

Like a love spell?

Kind of.

But you said the spell is broken.

Yes. It broke when you accepted who and what you are. I used to see rainbows around you. Different colors for every emotion. I haven't since we woke up. I'm going to miss it, honestly. You were the most beautiful chaos I've ever seen. Sadness laced her voice.

Are you actually worried about what Clive said?

You won't be drawn to me now. Not like you were.

Nothing's changed, Willow. When I woke up wrapped around you, it wasn't because some magic spell drew me to you, it was because I feel safe when I'm with you. When you were standing out in the snow in all your gorgeous naked glory, if you hadn't had a hole in your chest that needed healing, I would have aborted this mission and carried you back to bed. When we're standing here on far too many legs than possible and all I want to do is touch you, it's not because I'm drawn to you. It's because I love you.

I love you, too.

You're calling in sick today.

Aren't you bossy?

You did say it's in my nature.

I did, didn't I?

What are we going to do with our sick day?

We're going to spend the entire day making our own magic.

Keep up, she said as she bolted toward the house.

I chased after her, still happy to let her lead. In the course of one night, my life had become something else entirely. I was a shifter. A descendent of a legendary man who'd been withheld from me my whole life. A foreigner in a new world I still didn't understand.

But as we ran for the house with all of the magic stripped away, all I could think about was Willow. My heart raced, but not because of my legs pumping beneath me.

It was all because of her. Everything I was and everything I would become was because of her.

Epilogue

Willow

I CLOSED THE DOOR BEHIND the last of the guests, turned, and leaned against it, content and happy. My eyes traveled up the stairs. Quinn had actually pulled it off. In only seven weeks, he'd turned my dilapidated old house into a stunning historical landmark. Well, a historical landmark with some flair since a different crazy theme decorated each of the four bedrooms upstairs.

The Arabian Nights room was his favorite. The floating magic carpet bed hanging from the ceiling was amazing, but the one time we'd tried it out had made me a little seasick. I preferred the Enchanted Forest room instead.

Quinn had turned each post on the four-poster bed into a tree and hung a canopy of leaves over the top. He'd even allowed Les into the house to paint a mural on the walls. It was so incredibly relaxing that I sometimes went in there to unwind when the people at the diner or school became too much for me. To be honest, I was a little sad I was going to have to share with my guests when we opened after the first of the year.

"Thank you so much for everything, Willow,"

Vanessa said, stepping into the entryway. The heavy wool coat she wore over her wedding dress hung open. She'd developed a tiny little baby bump over the last few weeks. I was pretty sure she'd picked that particular dress because the empire waist accented it. They were proud of their baby, and it turned out many other people were happy about it too, even if they didn't know why.

"You're so welcome. It was a really pretty wedding."

"The most beautiful Christmas wedding ever," she said. "Really. It means so much to me that you did this for Ryan."

I stepped forward and put my arms around her. "For you, too. It's been fun planning it with you. I know you and Ryan and little bear are going to be very happy."

She squeezed me a little harder and whispered in my ear, "He could turn out a woodpecker, you know. And wouldn't that just chap his hide?"

"Nah," Ryan said, stepping up behind Vanessa. "My hide is fine with whatever *she* turns out to be." He wrapped his arms around us both, squishing Vanessa between us. "Look, Willow. We made a pecker sandwich."

Vanessa squirmed between us. "I swear. Maybe I had better hope for a girl. I don't think I can handle two infant boys in the house."

A plate shattered in the kitchen causing us to jump apart. "You want a rundown on what just happened in there?" Ryan asked.

I glared a warning at him. "Stay out of his head, Ryan. I'm serious."

"If you insist, but I think you're going to like

what's going on in his head tonight. It's got your big bad Army boy shaking like a leaf and breaking dishes."

"I think he's more pissed off than anything. He finally had it out with his mom this morning over all of the secrets she kept from him. We haven't had a chance to talk about it, though. I've barely seen him today." I suspected Quinn had been avoiding me all day, and I didn't like it.

I broke my own rule and directed a pointed look at Ryan. He'd probably picked up on all of the anxious thoughts dancing through my head. Knowing him, he'd been listening to Quinn's and my thoughts all day. But if he had, he gave nothing away. His expression remained stoic.

"Hmm. Took him long enough. I would have thought he would have done that right away," he said vaguely.

I shrugged. "Quinn does things on his own timeline."

"That he does," Ryan said, shaking his head. "He certainly does."

"He's been spending a lot of time with John and Bryson," I said, ignoring his bad attitude. "I think they've been good therapy." One was a preacher and the other a counselor. I encouraged him to spend as much time as possible with them. Even though Tim had no idea he'd shot me, Quinn preferred not to hang out with him now.

"You're good therapy," Vanessa chimed in. "For all of us. Look at what you did for our families."

"Speaking of, we need to get going," Ryan said, wrapping an arm around Vanessa's waist and pulling her toward the door. "You know you and Quinn are welcome to come tonight. Woodpeckers and deer and bears. Oh, my. Think of the fun we'll have."

"No," I said, laughing. "This is a special time for your families. You don't need any outsiders there."

"It wouldn't be happening if it weren't for you," Vanessa said. "Who would have guessed all of these years of fighting were because of a spell? It's like one hundred and fifty years of madness, over what? A little unrequited love?"

"If your great-grandmother had just given it up to my great-grandfather, then all of this could've been avoided. Why any woodpecker wouldn't want to hook up with a big manly bear like me is truly one of Woodland Creek's greatest mysteries."

"It truly is," Vanessa said, rolling her eyes before looking at me. "I'm just glad it's over, and we have you to thank for it."

I smiled at the two of them. How they were able to put up with each other was Woodland Creek's greatest mystery of all. "I swear I didn't do anything. You guys did it when you made this little pecker bear." I reached over and patted her tiny round tummy.

"If I'd known the little bastard was going to fix everything, I would've knocked her up years ago."

Vanessa shoved him away from her and stuck her hand in his face. She pointed to the gold band on her finger. "Ryan Balere, don't you ever refer to my child as a bastard again. My little pecker bear is a bastard no more."

A pan crashing in the kitchen cut my laugh short. It clanged like a cymbal on the ceramic floor and visions of cracked tiles danced in my head. "I really should go help him. I need my dishes and pans. My livelihood kind of depends on it."

"Are you sure you're going to be okay while we're gone next week?" Ryan asked, reaching for the door.

"We'll be fine. Quinn is quite the cook. I'd starve if it weren't for him. Besides, we both know you're going to leave me soon anyway."

He ducked his head as he stepped out onto the porch. "I do really like the volunteer firefighting thing. It's kind of nice, using my special skills for the greater good rather than to eavesdrop on people."

Vanessa and I both nodded. There was no arguing with that. Just the week before, he'd help rescue an elderly woman from a house fire because he'd 'heard' her cries for help when no one else could. "You'll be an asset to them. I always knew you wouldn't want to be my chef forever."

"It's going to take some time to get certified, so you've got me a while longer. Besides, when you open your dinner theater, you're going to need someone with more culinary expertise than I have anyway."

I cupped my hand around my mouth and whispered, "I'm thinking about sending Quinn to culinary school. Do you think he'll be game for that?"

Ryan bellowed out a big grizzly laugh. "Yeah, I'd like to be here when you suggest that."

"Ryan, say goodbye," Vanessa said, tugging on his hand. "We're going to be late for our own wedding."

"Second wedding. See ya in a week, Willow."

I stood at the door and listened to them bicker all the way to the car.

"Woman, just because we are already married does not mean you can start bossing me around," he said before he slammed her door shut.

I was still grinning when I walked into the kitchen. Quinn stood at the sink with a towel thrown over his shoulder as he washed dirty plates. He took one look at me, standing in the doorway with stars in my eyes, and shook his head. "No, no, no. Don't get any ideas. This will not become a regular thing."

"But you look so good standing in my kitchen in Janice's apron. Say the word and we can make it a full-time thing."

"Nope. You know the deal. I'll cook it. But someone else has to clean it. This is a one-time exception because it's a special occasion."

"It is, isn't it?" I sounded a little too dreamy, but I couldn't help myself. I walked over to him and wrapped my arms around his waist. I laid my head against his back and listened for the beat of his slightly overzealous shifter heart. "As weird and frustrating as those two are, they really are perfect for each other."

"Kind of like another couple I know," he said, turning toward me. He held up his bubble-covered hands and kissed me softly on the mouth. "You look tired."

"I am. It was an emotional day. For *everyone*."

"I thought you might be overwhelmed. I made you a cup of tea. Why don't you sit at the table and drink it while I finish up."

"Oh, no," I said with an adamant shake of my head. "I've had enough tea to last me a lifetime."

His face fell a little. "Was it that bad? Putting up with me?"

I slipped my hands up his chest and around his neck. "I'd drink it every day for the rest of my life if I had to. You're worth a little nasty taste in my mouth."

He brushed his lips across mine again and then deepened the kiss. A familiar zing of electricity shot through my body, and I cursed the stack of dirty dishes when he pulled away.

"Well, you taste delicious." His eyes sparkled mischievously in the fluorescent lighting of the kitchen and I picked up a light red hue in the air around us. "Seriously, you look beat. Have just one more cup. For old time's sake. I even warmed it up for you. It's in the microwave."

I backed away from him, narrowing my eyes as he turned back to the dishes in the sink. "Quinn Dearborn, what are you up to? You've been acting odd all day."

He chuckled. "I'm probably the one who needs the tea."

"I think so." I turned toward the microwave nestled so perfectly in the spot he'd built for it. "God, I seriously love this hole," I said as I popped open the door. "Even if I have to stand on my tiptoes to see inside."

I reached in and blindly grabbed the mug by the handle. "Did you cook this? It doesn't even feel warm." I pulled it closer to the opening and smiled at the writing across the front of a mug I'd never seen before. "You bought me a 'HIS' mug. I love it." I pulled the mug to my mouth and was surprised to find it was empty, except for the folded note he'd hid inside.

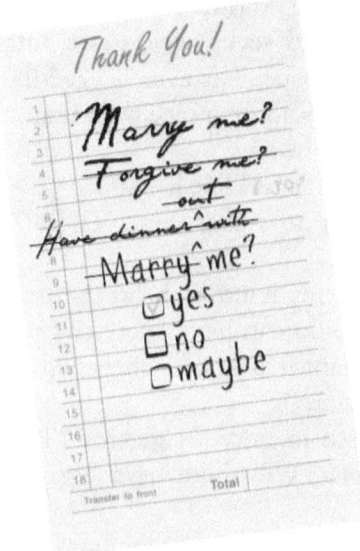

My hands shook so hard I nearly dropped it. "Quinn?" I turned and nearly fell over him.

He was bent on one knee, bearing his soul and the most beautiful emerald ring I'd ever seen. It was dark and gorgeous. The exact shade as his eyes. But even as pretty as it was, it was nothing compared to the bright red hue filling the room.

The color of love. His. Mine. It was everywhere. So overwhelming, it had no choice but to spill out of us.

"Willow Ryker," he began, in a confident tone meant to hide the jitters I felt coming from him. "Will you marry me?"

I laughed. My heart pounded like it wanted to jump right out of my chest and find a home in his. A nest of butterflies fluttered around my stomach. "Quinn," I whispered. "We've known each other seven weeks."

"When you know, you know. Besides, I think fifteen years and seven weeks is a sufficient amount of time, don't you?" His eyes begged me to say yes.

"Yeah," I said my voice wavering.

It was too soon.

But it didn't feel like it.

I wanted to marry him. There was nothing I wanted more.

He took my hand and slid the ring partially onto my finger. "You can have every day of the rest of my life if you want it. I know when and where. I have it all planned out. "

I erupted in nervous giggles. "I bet you do, my little strategist. Will there be a big white tent in the backyard?"

"Yep. And those heater things."

I narrowed my eyes at him. "Swans?"

He cocked his head and grinned. "Do we know any?"

"Maybe. But I want fifteen of them. One for every year I've waited for you."

"Sixteen then."

I stuck my lips out in a pout. "Why sixteen?"

"Because it will be sixteen before the next first snow rolls around again."

"We're getting married on the first snow!" I squealed.

His face erupted with a big happy grin. "Is that a yes?"

"Yes!" He slid the ring all the way onto my finger, and I leaped at him, knocking him backward onto the floor. I held the mug and note against my chest to protect them as we fell to the ground and then I smothered him with kisses.

His hands came around my head, pulling me to him until I didn't think I could get any closer. I pressed my body against him, wishing for nothing more than for him to engulf me and set me on fire. When we finally came up for air, I was so breathless and drunk on his love that I couldn't see straight.

"I have one condition," I panted.

He narrowed his eyes at me. "You already said yes."

"It's a tiny little thing." His eyebrow arched in question, and I stroked my finger along his jawline. "Grow the beard again for me."

He laughed so hard I almost bounced off him. "Seriously? I'm not furry enough for you?"

I couldn't really explain it—not to him—but there'd been something so primitive and masculine about the beard. "I want to feel it against my face." I smirked at him. "And maybe somewhere else."

"Do you know how crazy you make me when you talk like that?"

"I have an idea," I said pressing against him.

"And I have an idea, too, but first I need to show you something."

"Do we have to get up for it?"

"Yes," he said, laughing.

I crawled off him. "Are you sure? 'Cause I was sort strategizing a plan of my own while I had you on the floor."

He shook his head once. "I do love the way you think."

Before I could even stand up, he'd swooped me up into his arms, causing me to burst into another fit of giggles. "What are you doing? You can't do the threshold thing until you get me down the aisle."

"It's never too early for thresholds." He maneuvered us through the tight kitchen doorway. "Okay, can I trust you to close your eyes and keep them shut, or do I need to blindfold you?"

"Hmm, well, I don't know. They both sound interesting." I nuzzled into his chest and covered my eyes with my hand, drinking in the scent of Quinn. Breaking the protection spell had changed his scent, making him even more enticing. All my life I'd thought I wanted a normal boy from the 'right' side of town, one untouched by the magic of Woodland Creek. It turned out all I needed was Quinn. Just the scent of him set my senses on fire. "Okay, they are closed."

"Promise?"

"Promise."

I heard a door open and then I was being carried down steps. I hadn't been in the basement since we'd cleaned out Janice's stuff. I forced myself not to peek, but it was hard to resist.

Quinn didn't speak until his feet hit the basement floor. "Don't peek," he warned. "Or I'll have to take the ring away."

"You wouldn't!"

"I don't know. My mom had a hard time giving it up," he teased.

"Your mom?" It was hard not to peek at him after a comment like that, and my hand slipped off my eyes. With one look into his, I knew the visit with his mom had gone well. "Tell me everything, Quinn. Everything."

"Okay. Well, I was just giving you a hard time when I said she didn't want to give up the ring. She wants you to have it. My dad gave it to her after she told him she was pregnant with me."

I gasped. "An engagement ring?"

"More of a promise." He turned as if he was trying to maneuver us through another doorway. "But isn't that all an engagement is? And marriage, for that matter? A promise that I'll never look at another woman as I look at you. That I'll never stray. That I will do everything in my power to make every single day better than the one before. That I'll do things like *this* for no other reason than to see the smile on your face."

I split my fingers to peek through them at a room that was positively glowing. "What is this?" I whispered.

"Our room. Do you like it?"

Tears pooled at the corners of my eyes. "It's the most amazing thing I've ever seen."

He set me down on my feet so I could explore. Nothing other than a bed filled the middle of the room. It was so large it had to be custom. The bed coverings were a hundred different shades of green, and when I ran my hand across it, it was softer than any grass. A lit fireplace graced the wall closest to the foot of the bed.

But the very best part was the trees Quinn had somehow transplanted into the basement. They seemed to grow straight out of a seemingly unmarred floor, stretching to the ceiling where they fanned out, creating a canopy more natural and stunning than even the one upstairs. Through the bare branches, he'd strung Christmas lights creating, I thought, the most romantic place on the earth.

"It's gorgeous," I said, spinning in a circle. "I want to stay here forever."

"And it's just ours. No matter who comes and goes through our house, this space is ours and ours alone. This is where you can come to get away from everything and everyone. When it becomes too much, when the world wears you down, this is your refuge."

I sat down on the gargantuan bed and curled my finger at him. "No, Quinn. *You* are my refuge."

He stalked across the room with a glint in his eyes that I'd come to know well. His hands were immediately on my face in a move I'd also come to know so well.

"You love it," he said.

I nodded my head, pulling him closer until his lips just barely hovered over mine. "I love *you*."

They were only three little words, but they promised a lifetime of magic.

The End

ACKNOWLEDGEMENTS

This—thanking those that helped make Dearborn what it is today—is the easy and most important part (in order of who saw it first):

To my alpha readers, Vanessa Marie and Josie Bordeaux, who read this book one chapter at a time as it was being written and never once flinched when I said, "Oh I added in a new scene. Can you start over from the beginning?" Seriously. You two. When I think of you, I'm chest bumps and teary eyes. Our co-dependencies are everything. WTB, ladies.

To Jennifer Stevens, my queen bee beta reader, confidant, and friend. Thank you for being a walking encyclopedia and for talking me off a cliff when I nearly lost my vision on this one. Thank you for calling in your personal troops when I needed them. Thank you for entertaining me every single day.

To JM Miller and Brandy Rivers for your mad beta reading skills. Your thoughtful comments and constructive criticism were exactly what this book and I needed.

To Emily Avants, Lauren Battles, and Elizabeth Ward for pumping me up with your crazy excited text messages as you read and especially after you finished. You ladies are my rocks.

To JB Avants for doing an amazing turnaround on some speed editing. That first pass through is so important and I (and my beta readers) certainly appreciate it. Because of you, I've started my list of 'Just-Don't-Use-Them Words' and 'just' is one of them. When I finally stop talking like a valley girl, I'll have you to thank.

To Jennifer Munswami for putting up with me through multiple versions of this cover and repeated redesigns. Everyone knows the cover is almost as important as the words inside— some would say more so—and I appreciate your patience even when I didn't know what I wanted.

To Jenny Sims of Editing4Indies for your amazing work on this book. I'm so completely impressed with your skills and so happy to have found you. Thank you for making it bleed, and thank you for being so flexible when this book was three weeks late and twice as long as it was supposed to be. You were a trooper and I'll never forget it.

To Daniela Prima, for your ~~detail-oriented~~ OCD mind. You're at the end of this list because you were the last to get Dearborn in your hands, but you belong up there somewhere around the top. I know you poured over every single word, second-guessing, looking things up, double-checking, triple-checking, etc. You forgave me for my constant misuse of wrack and rack and shined my sentences without complaint. For all of that, I thank you. But, most of all, I thank you for being my friend.

To my family, for giving me up for hours and hours and hours. For eating a lot of pizza and grilled cheese sandwiches. For being supportive when you could just be annoyed. To my son, Dylan, for your love of paranormal and fantasy and for being my plotting partner.

Finally, to my repeat readers, who took a chance with this one. It's a little different than what I've written in the past, definitely an definitely an adventure for me. I took on this project to force myself to step outside my usual box, and I'm thankful that you are willing to come along. I hope you find that I've grown a little as a writer.

ABOUT THE AUTHOR

Jenni Moen lives in her hometown in Oklahoma with her husband and three crazy, exuberant kids who have the potential to burn the house down at any moment.

When she's not chauffeuring kids around town, performing her mom duties as a short order cook and maid, or vacuuming for her fastidious husband, she hammers away at her keyboard. Most of the time she's up to no good, but every now and then a new book is born.

Sign up for Jenni Moen's Newsletter and receive a FREE ebook of REMEMBERING JOY:

http://bit.ly/JMNewsletter

Want to chat? You can find almost always find Jenni in one of these places:

www.jennimoen.com
www.facebook.com/authorjennimoen
www.facebook.com/groups/twistedhearts/
www.twitter.com/jennimoen

OTHER WORK BY JENNI MOEN

REMEMBERING JOY
(The Joy Series Book 1)

Alexis doesn't believe in fairytales.
She knows first hand that life can turn on a dime – that
one stupid mistake can shatter dreams
and irrevocably shape the future.

Though her memory of that day is hazy,
She's spent the last ten years
trying to put it behind her and
focus on the future.

Adam is dark and brooding
and strangely charming. The film student
is the perfect distraction from the
mundane life she's created for herself.

Unfortunately, Adam's memory isn't hazy at all …
And what she doesn't remember, he can't forget.

OTHER WORK BY JENNI MOEN

FINDING JOY
(The Joy Series Book 2)

Love is patient.

It can happen when you least expect it,
where you least expect it,
with whom you least expect it.

Love is kind.

But love may not grow out of kindness.
It can happen with the person who hates you most
because love knows no bounds.

And it keeps no record of wrongs.
Love doesn't hold a grudge.
Love forgives.
Love forgets.

But when the healing of your heart
breaks the hearts of the ones you love,
it may seem impossible to …

Find Joy

OTHER WORK BY JENNI MOEN

WITH THE FATHER

I had a choice, and I chose wrong.

I thought I lost everything. But when the smoke finally cleared, I discovered I wasn't alone.

Father Sullivan was a force – a living and breathing force, a forbidden desire I couldn't resist. I didn't want to resist. But I wasn't the only one who wanted him, and by all accounts neither of us should have him.

For every action, there is a reaction. For every choice, a consequence.

If I hadn't chosen to live again, I would have never known what life could be like

With the Father